MONSTROCITY

OTHER BOOKS BY AUTHOR

AAAIIIEEE!!! THE BEST HORROR STORIES OF JEFFREY THOMAS

GODHEAD DYING DOWNWARDS

LETTERS FROM HADES

PUNKTOWN

TERROR INCOGNITA

MONSTROCITY

JEFFREY THOMAS

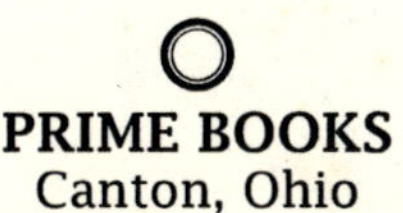

PRIME BOOKS
Canton, Ohio

MONSTROCITY

Published in the United States by **Prime Books, Inc.**
P.O. Box 36503, Canton, OH 44735
www.primebooks.net

Trade Paperback ISBN: 1-894815-62-9
Hardcover ISBN: 1-894815-61-0

DEDICATION

– For Joseph S. Pulver, Sr.

Cities are the abyss of the human species.
– Jean-Jacques Rousseau

PART ONE: GABRIELLE

It's all about time. Time and space.

2.8 thousandths of a second after I pull the trigger of the shotgun, the clump of pellets have just cleared the end of the barrel, still encased in their plastic cup. People don't think about the cup, because it breaks up shortly after it leaves the barrel. But I shouldn't get ahead of myself. The cup is ahead of the smoke, though, which mushrooms free of the muzzle at last after 3.5 thousandths of a second.

Let's jump forward in time a bit: 5.7 thousandths of a second after the hammer drops, the plastic cup breaks apart like I mentioned. 7 thousandths of a second, and the pellets fly on their own; they still hold the cup's shape for a while, haven't had a chance to disperse yet. These are small pellets, mind you, not the big double odd. Only nine pellets in double odd. But this will do.

I'm close to Mr. Dove, so we save some time there. The pellets don't disperse much before they cover the short distance. I've been reading about guns lately—I know some gun trivia now—but I don't know too much about killing people although this is not my first. Still, at this rate I figure it's under ten thousandths of a second between squeezing the pump-action's trigger and watching Mr. Dove's face ripple and flap and tatter in quick slow-motion, at the center of a big red mist like a summer lawn sprinkler with children jumping in and out of it. Burst water balloon.

He takes a step back. Catches himself, goes rigid as if he's tensed up waiting for a second hit. His head is riven jaggedly almost right down the center, and the left side (my left, his right) suddenly sort of drops down onto his shoulder. He takes another step back, as if wary of what I might do next. Not much blood touched his suit before, except for the settling red cloud, but now with him resting half his head on his own shoulder his expensive white shirt front goes crimson in a fast tide. His suit and tie are shiny black, luckily for him, so the blood doesn't show up as much or soak in. I've never owned a suit half that nice, and he's not even a human.

I contemplate—in another fraction of a second, though I think the shotgun thinks faster than I do—putting another concentration of pellets into him after all, but then Mr. Dove takes one decisive step toward me, reaches out with both his hands, gurgles sternly from the open top of his throat, and pitches forward. I dance back to avoid the splash. Lucky my new shoes are shiny black.

My heart is at full gallop, and I'm almost gagging from the nervousness, but not from the blood. I've lived my whole life in Punktown, after all—I've seen worse than this. But it was never me who did it, that's the thing. And now I've done it twice. He's not human, but people always have that politically correct dung drilled into their heads (pardon the expression) about humans and nonhumans and humanoids and the not remotely human being equal. I'm a murderer now. As of this moment, a serial killer. Things have been going so fast lately—and I don't just mean shotgun blasts.

I'm afraid to get caught—sometimes people report hearing gunfire, if they're trying to sleep or watch a favorite VT program—so I have to shake myself a little and I squat down over the body, the shotgun resting across my thighs. It has a pistol grip instead of a stock, so when I rise again I'll slip it back under my poncho-like rain slicker. It's dark purple, a current fad color, so I don't stand out, and it has a hood that I'm wearing pulled close around my face. I dart looks all around me, then tug at Mr. Dove's suit jacket. Rather than roll him over to get at the button, I rip the jacket open, then reach one hand under him, feeling for his lining pocket. His side, through his shirt, is too soft and warm; but it's like he's just sleeping, and solid cold would probably be worse. I'm hoping I don't get blood on my hand.

I close my fingers around the item I'm seeking. I'm a lethal pickpocket. I killed him for this tiny object. I'm a mugger. I'm trying to prevent the end of all civilization as humans think of it. I'm an assassin. I think I'm losing my mind, and I hope to finish this before I do.

Back on my feet. It isn't raining anymore but it's gray and raw. Shotgun under my slicker, the strap at the end of the pistol grip slung over my shoulder. The object I've stolen now stashed in my own pocket. I look down at Mr. Dove, lying on his halved face on the floor of a small octagonal courtyard with brick walls and a cobbled floor. We're in the oldest part of Paxton, which still bears traces of the vastly smaller Choom town that was here before the Earth people colonized this planet Oasis—like a few teeth that someone built a body around. A pretty enough part of Punktown, as this city is better known. Dove didn't expect me to kill him, especially not here.

Last look at my victim. His sundered head has no hair, and its flesh is an almost translucent gray, with squiggles of big black veins under it. His eyes are silver and lidless. He has no nose and his mouth is wide, almost as wide as a native Choom's, with slick black lips. He has lacy gills on either side of his neck, which are a slightly pinkish color. He's the best-dressed fish I've ever seen. His body should be on a bed of ice behind a glass counter.

I've killed two birds with one load of bird shot: I have the item, plus I killed one of the priests, though I think servant or even slave would be a better title for them. Cultist, crony, zombie. This one wasn't a human, but the first one was. The first one was harder. Especially because I loved her. I can't think about that now . . .

I could be caught. There are vigilante groups like the Ten Men to help fight back against Punktown's rampant crime. There are police; we call them forcers. And there are more priests out there . . .

I cross the courtyard. There's an old fountain in its center that doesn't spew anymore, but there's a stagnant pool of rain water in it, and trash floats on the surface. I pass close to the rim of its stone basin, and maybe a peripheral movement below the filmed water catches my eye, because I give a little spring forward and toss a look over my shoulder and I see this gray snake flash out of the pool, whipping at me but falling short, then it draws slithering back into the water and disappears, and it wasn't a snake but an arm, and I'm running now, out the other end of the courtyard. Mr. Dove didn't come to our little meeting alone after all.

* * *

In my flat, I have my wall-length vidtank on before I have my poncho off. It's unlikely that the murder of Mr. Dove will be on VT this quickly, not guaranteed that it will ever be reported on VT at all due to the sheer numbers of the murdered who compete for that brief stardom. I go to an all news channel, then to a subdirectory and choose *The Crime Report*. Sub-category: *Murders*. Then I pick today's date. Now, I take off my beaded slicker, drape it across the back of my sofa, rest the pump shotgun across the cushions. "Coffee," I say, and in the kitchenette I hear the coffee machine reply with a starting hiss/burble.

Today's report is dominated by a juicy story about two seven year old girls who killed a classmate they didn't like behind their school this afternoon during second recess (being too busy during first recess, apparently, swapping vidgame chips with other girls). They stuffed several power cells down this girl's throat to gag her and then cut her throat with a laser utility knife. I wonder where they got the idea to use the power cells, and I can't help wondering which size they used—CC or DD? I imagine the cylindrical shape and particular size of DD would work better in this application than the smaller and rectangular CC. In fact, there is a link that appears which offers to take me to an advertisement for InfiniT Power Cells, but I don't point my clicker at the link. I'm shown a close up of the dead girl's face. I can't imagine what might have made the other two girls want to kill her; she isn't a nonhuman, even has the same long, curly black hair both of them have, except that hers is matted to her face with blood. In the upper right corner of this blankly-gazing close up is a link to an ad for Guzman Hardware, makers of the utility knife with the laser blade. In a box in the upper left is a link to an interview with the killers. I fire my clicker at the miniature faces of the two girls, which then enlarge to fill most of the tank except for the ad banners and weather report ever scrolling across the bottom. The two girls seem composed, and speak in dull voices.

"What was it about Inez that you hated?" asks an off-screen voice, but there is a link offering to take me to a bio for reporter Paul Pope. I decline. One of the interchangeable girls replies.

"She stupid," this sullenly pretty, hard-eyed girl says with a little snap of a shrug.

"Yeah, she stupid," says the other seven year old. "Clothes be stupid. She like stupid games."

"She don't like *Sexbot* or *Bloodwhore*."

"Yeah, but she think she sexier than us. She no sexier than us—she ain't even like *Bloodwhore*."

"She ain't ever even sexed, but she think she sexier than us."

"She stupid."

There is the inevitable link to an article on the dangers of sex and violence in vidgames, and another link to an ad for *Bloodwhore 2: Slutty's Revenge*. There's a bio link for each of the girls; out of curiosity I click on one of them. It lists her birth date, favorite music (a whole column of links to the various artists), her favorite food, vidgames, VT programs and the name of her boyfriend. She has a cat named Slutty.

There is no news about the murder of Mr. Dove.

I remember the gray, boneless limb I saw come out of the fountain. Maybe they haven't found his body at all. Maybe something has taken care of that.

Gaby's murder was never on VT, either.

She was my first victim. And my lover.

But I think I've gotten ahead of myself again, here. I think I should talk about Gaby before I get back to the former Mr. Dove.

Click on the link to *My Past*. Sub-category: *Gabrielle*.

* * *

Gaby worked in a candle store on the second floor of the Canberra Mall, and she always smelled of their soft perfumes, as if her flesh absorbed the scents. Her skin was as white as wax.

I was shopping for my cousin Amy's birthday. My cousin has a thing for candles. I have a thing for flesh that looks like no blood runs beneath it. Gaby glowed in the dimness of the store, behind the counter as a pale luminescence. Her pallor was contrasted by her black hair—long, straight, parted in the center—and black garments. These consisted of shiny black gloves that ended half-way up her sensuous plump arms, a low cut dress with thin shoulder straps, and when I got close to the counter with my purchase I saw the skirt was short, and that she wore black nylons that ended at mid-thigh. Big ugly black boots. Her lips were heavy and purple. Her eyes were dark and narrow. Her figure was lush, full as an overripe fruit ready to spoil. She looked like she should be sprawled nude and languid on a divan for a painter of old. Up close, I saw what the low front of her black dress revealed: between plush breasts she had had her chest opened up, and a clear circular window gave one a view of her pulsing heart. This organ, like an animal viewed in an aquarium, had been embroidered with red neon-glowing thread which spelled out: MOM. Gaby had been very close with her mother. When you looked at Gaby upside-down, like when she lay sprawled on our bed naked and languid as if she posed for me, the tattoo on her heart read: WOW.

Her shiny black fingers brushed mine as I handed her my card. Her bruised-looking lips smiled at me slightly, without parting. "Hmm," she said, before bagging one of the larger candles, "this one looks about right for me."

I congratulated myself on how quickly I was able to join in her play. These skills are not second nature to me. I handed her a package of small tea lamp candles and said, "Here are some that are my size."

The purple smile inched a bit wider. She looked more directly at me. But I was disappointed that no further play followed. Had I gone too far? Misinterpreted her meaning? I mumbled a goodbye.

I was standing in line for a coffee on the first floor when I felt a hand in my jacket pocket. I spun, expecting a pickpocket, and nearly backhanded Gaby across the face with my bag full of candles. She took a precautionary step back and just smiled again. I felt in my pocket, not taking my eyes off her. Something slippery, like a slithering dry membrane. I realized it was a pair of silky panties. They felt black. I was right, of course.

I bought Gaby a coffee, and the first time we had sex that evening she wore nothing but those shiny black gloves that ended at her upper arms. Black fingers squeezed my own pale rear and she hooked her white legs over the back of mine. I tightly encircled her milky smooth back with both arms. Her pillowy belly and breasts were so soft beneath me that they were almost like flesh half turned to cloud. Her aureoles were very large but so light a pink that they looked more like a flush. When I took her from behind later that night, her smooth rear was spread large and inviting against my belly, a perfection of symmetry. Warm damp sounds of me moving inside her, like the sound of her heart.

She told me after, as she smoked an herb cigarette with black paper, that in the candle shop she had thought I was good looking in the almost homely way she liked. She hated the artificiality of surgical and genetically engineered beauty, and we were in harmony there. I don't think she really intended her chest–window as an attractive decoration (though some would find it so), but an ugliness to mar her too-pristine skin, a wound that could never heal. I kissed the window sometimes and she joked that she wanted me to pry out that lens and penetrate her there.

I was skinny (I prefer wiry) with short dark hair and a tired sort of face with a thin little mouth and a weak chin but my eyes can look mean enough when I'm serious, or crazy-wild enough when I'm excited, I guess, that muggers haven't jumped me more than a couple times. I suppose I should tell you now, better late than never, that my name is Christopher Ruby, because you'll hear Gabrielle-whom-I-called-Gaby refer to me as Topher. She had to be contrary, yang to the yin, never called me Chris.

I was twenty-nine and she was nineteen, but honestly I thought she was in her mid-twenties at least, maybe because of what Oscar Wilde said: "She looks like a woman with a past. Most pretty women do."

We had sex every day, at first. We both took a day off from work, once, because we didn't want to leave bed. She had no muscle tone, but no cellulite, and I still ache for her lovely indulged body, that I have pierced in love and pierced in murder.

In bed on that day we stayed home, one of her moist legs draped heavily over mine, Gabrielle said to me, "Topher, did you know that someone once told me that if you burn a candle in every corner of a room with eight corners, you can summon a devil?"

"That's nice," I said. I was using her purple lipstick to paint her nipples.

"Your room here has eight corners, I just realized."

I glanced around me. "The room is square."

"Der." She pointed to my bay window: two narrow windows on either side of a larger one. It looked down onto the side street on which my tenement house faced. My flat was on the second floor. "Count the corners in the bay window. That makes eight corners. Something about angles and corners makes it so you can conjure a demon."

"I've already conjured a demon," I said, rubbing her leg.

"If you do it right, the demon will obey your commands. My friend Maria said she got one to materialize for a few seconds. She's the one who told me."

"Isn't your friend Maria the one you said they found with her head cut off and missing?"

"They think that was a drug related thing."

"Isn't this like that dung where you have to walk downstairs backwards while looking in a hand mirror and when you get to the bottom you say something like, 'Show me a ghost', or something like that?"

Gaby propped herself up on one elbow with interest. "Did you ever do that?"

"No! It's an urban legend kind of thing. Something kids tell each other to scare themselves."

"Maria was very much into the supernatural, Topher, and the supernatural is just the natural that scientists haven't legitimized yet."

I connected both her nipples with a line of purple lipstick, in the center outlining the circular pane in her chest. I then connected up a line which ran down her torso and ended at the squint of her navel. From there, I traced a new line to the edge of her pubic hair, kicking off our blanket to do so. She went on talking like she only half noticed what I was doing.

"You know there are other dimensions—beings from a half-dozen other dimensions live right here in town. So we don't know how many dimensions there could be, right? So we don't know if ghosts are remnants of our energy that live on another plane, or if demons are actual creatures that exist in a dimension that ignorant people just call hell."

"Ghosts have been disproved."

"That's what they want you to think."

Sighing, I screwed the lipstick tube to poke up more of its phallic tip. It looked like a big gun cartridge in my hands. I began drawing an inverted triangle around her pubic triangle. "You can't compare heaven and hell with black holes and worm holes and . . . "

"Get your mind off my worm hole for a minute. Do you think I'm stupid, is that it? You can't wrap your little office boy mind around a new concept?"

I glared up at her. I didn't like it when the candle queen taunted me about working as a customer service rep for a netlink provider. After all, I spent as many days working from my home office in the next room as I did at the corporate office downtown. "It isn't a new concept, Gaby. It's an old, old concept. Like Ouija boards and rosary beads and holy books and all that dung."

"I tried a Ouija board once, with Maria," she said defiantly, her narrow eyes more narrowed. "It said to me FIND US. It said to Maria WE WANT YOU."

I didn't want to tell her that their own subconscious minds had directed the planchette. You can't reason with any denomination of zealot. I didn't want to make trouble; Gaby had a horrible temper and had already slapped my face one time for making a comment about a beautiful naked woman in a VT ad.

"So let's try it," I said, as I drew a line down her shoulder, to the inside of her elbow, along her wrist like a razor blade revealing the bloodless purple meat inside her. She absent-mindedly opened her hand so I could draw the line across her palm, ending it at the tip of her middle finger.

"All right. Let's," she said, still a bit icily.

I had no shortage of candles in my apartment these days; we often made love to nothing but the wavering glow of their light. I watched Gaby, still nude, squat to place a candle on the floor in each of the eight corners of my bedroom, the depressed bay window included. Gaby had let me finish decorating her with my geometric pattern. A line extended down both arms, now, and both legs, so that it looked like I'd charted the flow of her blood, or spirit. I had finished my composition by painting a last line with the crumbly lipstick down the center of her face, from the top of her broad forehead, down her long handsome nose, to the tip of her chin. She looked like some primitive tribal priestess. The voluptuous goddess of a fertility cult. I couldn't wait for this game with the candles to be over so I could make love to her looking that way.

Gaby took her cigarette lighter, and began circling around the room a second time, hunching down to light each candle on the glossy faux wooden floor. I hoped she didn't set fire to the curtains in the bay window, as I pulled my flannel bathrobe around me. Out of the warm nest of our bed, the big bedroom seemed chilly.

"Do you have to say some magic words?" I asked, trying not to sound too facetious, testing her temper.

"Yes, as a matter of fact. I took some of Maria's disks out of her apartment after she died, when her sister let me go through her music; one of them has this on it, I'm sure." Finished with the candles, she crossed the room to her pocketbook, dug in it for her palmcomp and a disk holder. In her voluminous handbag I glimpsed the small illegal handgun Gaby carried for protection; she had been raped a couple times. She found the items she sought, flicked the lid of the disk holder open and sat on the edge of the bed to thumb through the chips resting inside. "The red one," she said at last, plucking out an unlabeled disk and feeding it into the side of the small computer. While she activated it, I glanced again nervously at my curtains.

"You should look at this stuff yourself, some time, Topher—it may open your squinty little eyes," she said, while whisking through the contents of her dead pal's disk.

"Your candles are melting."

"Yeah. I was right. Here. It's a chant called 'Ascending Mode'. There's a banishing chant called 'Descending Mode'. To conjure and enslave the demon to do your bidding, you read the entire Ascending Mode . . . but if you just want to have a look at it, you read the first half of the chant, and then read the first half of the banishing chant to close the window again."

"Got it," I said solemnly, nodding.

All eight candles fluttered. Shadows rocked on the walls like the ghosts of all our love-making. Gaby got up and moved to the center of the room, where she cradled the palmcomp in both hands as if it were some moldering tome bound in human skin. She smiled up at me with her wry little sealed-lipped smile, gazed back at the small glowing screen that under-lit her features a faint blue, and began to recite the formula.

She either mutilated the chant, or it was supposed to sound like a person reciting backwards gibberish with their throat full of power cells and their neck cut. The palmcomp's screen reflected in her dark eyes. And when she was done—nothing happened.

She looked around us. I found myself doing the same. I even looked at the ceiling, as if I might really see a ghastly shadow writhing there across the plaster, or bony white arms reaching through it.

"I must have mispronounced it," she suggested.

"How could anyone pronounce it? Do you want me to try?" I offered lamely.

"Wait a second." She touched some keys on the device. "Maria recorded herself reading some of these passages . . . "

I edged closer to peek over Gabrielle's bare shoulder while she accessed the contents page of Maria's chip again. She had labeled the disk *Necronomicon*, I saw. She'd also stored some recipes on the disk, unless they were magic potions. Gaby went to a bookmark Maria had left, and opened it to a series of recordings of Maria reciting excerpts from this apparent spell book she had copied.

Gaby clicked on ASCENDING MODE, PART ONE and then Maria's face filled the screen. She had been pretty, but her eyebrows and hair had been shaved, and geometric patterns in glowing blue filament were embroidered into her scalp. They reminded me of my lipstick designs on Gaby.

It was eerie seeing Maria's disembodied head there, staring up at us. Was this where it had disappeared to? And then it began to speak.

The utterances sounded no less garbled, no less twisted coming out of her mouth. I had heard nonhuman colonists whose native languages were more legible-sounding.

When it was over, we both looked up again. Guttering firelight, undulating shadows ringed us and squirmed across our disheveled bed. Nothing.

"What was it supposed to look like?" I whispered.

"How the hell should I know? You, maybe. Maybe you're gone, and you're a devil instead."

"There's no tricking you, huh?"

"I better do the banishing mode anyway, just to close the portal. Just in case."

"Why not?" I said agreeably. I was glad to close up the whole experiment. Why contemplate the metaphysical when we were wasting good bed time?

Gaby found the appropriate recitation, DESCENDING MODE, PART ONE, and played it. I couldn't be sure, but it seemed just like the same recording of Maria as before, but simply played in reverse this time. When it was finished, Gaby shut off the palmcomp and padded over to her pocketbook to drop it in, without first removing the red disk.

"Oh well," I said, shedding my robe and ducking under the blanket. I patted the mattress beside me.

Gaby lit a cigarette from one of the candles before replacing it on the floor. She didn't extinguish them before joining me, and we made love in the ring of their flame, shadows rippling across Gaby's white skin with its priestess patterns.

* * *

When I awoke, several of the candles had gone out, the circle broken, and Gaby sat naked on the edge of the bed, her back toward me. I touched her, and her skin was cold.

Without turning around, she said softly, "I did the ascending mode twice. Once myself, and then Maria." She paused. "But I only played the descending mode once."

I wanted to sigh, but I was afraid to get her riled, so I suggested, "Play it again, then."

"It's too late."

She twisted around a bit to look over her shoulder at me. I saw my lipstick tattoos had been largely wiped away during sex and sleep. Her smudged forehead looked badly bruised. Her nipples looked blurred. And in the murky light, I could just barely make out her heart throbbing in her chest. Candle light reflected on the clear pane.

"Hey!" I said, sitting up in bed and taking her arm to turn her a little more toward me.

The red, neon-glowing tattoo on her heart had gone out. That cavity and that organ were dark now.

"What happened? Why'd it go out?"

Gaby looked down at her chest dreamily, as if she might be still half asleep. Was she on drugs? She knew I didn't approve of the drugs she took with her friends. Look where Maria's activities had got her.

"It just went out," she droned. "It isn't important."

"No? Well . . . hey . . . whatever. It's your mutilation."

Slapping barefoot across the room, I went to take a shower, calling out, "Coffee!" along the way.

When I got out of the shower, and poured myself a cup, I called out, "Gaby, you want some coffee?" But she didn't reply. And when I went from room to room, I didn't find her. Her clothes and her pocketbook were gone. All eight candles were now extinguished.

* * *

From work at the corporate office the next morning, I called the candle shop. A coworker of Gabrielle's named Ramona told me Gaby had called in sick. I thanked her and buzzed Gaby at home.

No answer.

As I gave up on the call, a strobe flash to my right drew my attention to my window, a narrow fortress-like strip; enough to say I had a window, but not enough to distract my attention from work for long. Lightning again flashed over the city, like a rush of glowing blood washing through a giant's veins. Rain pounded my pane, made the city ripple as though it were melting. Punktown was vast out there, even compressed in this limited frame. Towers seemed to disembowel the low-slung black clouds. Despite the storm, I saw fly-like helicars drifting between the looming structures. Lighted windows and holograph advertisements wavered like candle flames. A rumble of thunder, more felt in my body as a vibration than heard.

A call from one of our clients drew my attention back to my monitor. He looked unhappy. I tried to look pleasant. He couldn't access his own free netlink pages in our service's site-building station in order to update them. I told him the station wasn't down for updates; had he forgotten his password, perhaps? He snapped that he used a face recognition password feature, and he sure hadn't changed his fucking face. He was not the first abusive client to make me wish I could use a computer-generated face in place of my own, like a mask. I hated having to look pleasant, bland. Better yet, I wished I didn't have to work this job at all. He made me grateful for Gaby, who had entered my increasingly ant-like life to jolt a deeper rhythm to my heart. Even with her often volatile emotions, her weird interests. I'd rather be walking backwards downstairs reading incantations and staring into a hand mirror right now, I thought, than sitting in this cubicle staring at people who want to take their frustrations out on me. I'd rather be in bed, listening to the rain and thunder with Gaby.

And where was Gaby now?

* * *

I called her from home that night.

No answer.

I called the shop in the Canberra Mall again the next morning. Ramona seemed disgusted that Gaby had called in sick once again. I buzzed her apartment. No answer.

I considered zipping over there at lunch, but it was too far to be a zip. Instead, directly after work I took a tube from my office block to an old shunt station, and from there rode a sparking shunt line to the tenement row where she lived, practically in the shadow of the mall where she worked.

Was her door buzzer working? I had stabbed my finger into it three times already. At last, I pounded the panel with the heel of my fist. I started to yell her name, but choked it off when a disapproving or simply nosy neighbor poked his or her head out into the narrow, dusky hall. I couldn't tell if it were a human or an alien, for that matter: the bloated-faced being was apparently tremendously obese, and either a light blue from some light source within its apartment or wearing blue skin makeup. Perhaps that was its natural hue. The being had no hair or eyebrows, and when we locked eyes it slowly withdrew back into its apartment. When its door snicked shut I gave a funny little shudder, and turned to face Gaby standing in her doorway, studying me. I audibly gasped. It should have amused her greatly, but instead she looked tired and preoccupied.

"Yes?" she said.

"Can I come in?"

A few beats. She looked past me, down the hall where I had been gazing, and then with a lazy half-shrug slipped aside to grant me entrance.

"Where have you been?"

"Here. Just here."

"Well, why don't you return my calls? Are you angry at me for mocking you the other night?"

"I've been busy."

"Busy doing what?"

A few more silent beats. "Going into the net. Looking for more books like the ones Maria had on disk. I've been getting more interested."

"Well, I hope you don't lose your job over it."

"My job isn't important."

"Tell it to your landlord when you rent comes due."

"Did you just come over here to criticize me, Christopher?"

I didn't reply. I found myself dropping my eyes to her chest. She wore a too-large black sweater, black tights that nicely abstracted her curves, black Chinese slippers. If her heart tattoo had been fixed, her clothes didn't reveal it to me. After our last time together, she looked like a window that had been painted black.

"Do you want me to go?" I asked, craning my neck to peer past her into the next room. Her computer appeared to be on, judging from the odd low murmur I heard coming from there, and it made me curious about this new obsession of hers that was more important than her poor neglected boyfriend.

"I'd rather you did," she said. "I'll call you."

I flashed my eyes back to her. I hadn't really, really been serious about leaving. "What's with you, Gabe? Are you angry at me, or aren't you?"

"I will be," she said, but blandly, like a good customer service rep, "if you don't respect my need for some occasional privacy, Christopher." And with that, I saw her half-suppress a glance back at the next room. At her computer, and that murmuring.

"What is so bloody important about this dung, Gabe? Huh?" And with that, I stormed past her like a petulant child to see what she was so absorbed in on her computer.

"Christopher!" she snapped, like the old Gabrielle I knew, and I heard her start after me. "Wait! That's none of your business!"

I saw the monitor for several seconds before she eclipsed it with her black body and shut down the program. But what I'd seen had looked like a tangle of geometric figures; a spider web of curves and angles but without the obvious pattern of a spider's web. It had almost looked like a complex street map. The murmuring ended before I could tell if it had been music or muffled voices.

"Now I know all your secrets," I teased her in an unamused tone.

She turned to glare at me, still blocking the dead screen. "You're an empty-headed ass."

"Goodbye," I said neatly, and walked away.

She called after me, "If you were more open-minded, I'd share all this with you."

I stopped in my tracks, then half looked back at her. "Make a copy of that program for me, then. Let me take it home to look at. Then I'll tell you whether or not I think it's worth being open-minded about."

One, two, three beats of hesitation. Then: "No." Simply that.

"Come see me if you're ever so inclined. And you might want to go to work, too, someday, if you're ever so inclined." I opened her door, and repeated, "Bye."

I stepped out into the hall in slow motion, expecting her to call me back into the room. She always called me back—if testily—when I tried storming out after a fight. This time she didn't call me back.

I was in the hall again. Her door was closed between us again. For some reason I glanced at the door where that bloated blue face had peered out at me. The door was closed, but I almost felt eyes peeking at me through its surface.

* * *

Sometimes at work, for a change of scenery from the cafeteria, I took my break down in the parking garage in the sub-basement, where there was a row of snack machines along one clammy white-tiled wall. Other workers from other offices stood about like knots of people at a party, leaning against the walls or immense, tiled support columns. The parking area itself housed hovercars, helicars, and wheeled vehicles of every description, stacked one above the other above the other as if in bunk beds, to conserve space. I saw a car being carried along by a robot arm on a ceiling track, then being lowered and slipped into an available slot. People paid good money to reserve a spot. "Plot" might be a better word: the rows of cars were like metal caskets filed away in mausoleum drawers. Sliding right out for your convenient access. Public transportation suited my needs, and my salary.

I purchased a coffee from a machine that sounded like it was grinding up a donkey in order to make it. The black liquid was bitter. I imagined it was fluid siphoned out of the suspended vehicles, then directed via hoses into the back of the beverage machine. In fact, I heard a distant patter of fluid dripping from one of them, like water from a cavern roof. The bad coffee made me long for the coffee shops at the Canberra Mall.

Nearby, in front of a candy dispenser, two women who worked for another company in the building above us were complaining about the erratic behavior of their server; it had been opened up today and the brain had been found to be oddly swollen in its tank of nutrient solution. My own company also used a genetically engineered encephalon for its mainframe; I'd seen it a few times, convoluted grayish brain tissue looking green in its solution, appearing squashed in its rectangular, vertically-positioned four foot by two foot and six inch deep container, wires snaking out of the mass and wavering like plants in a bubbling aquarium. My brother once saw a badly wrecked truck which had been carrying a load of these big artificially-generated brains; he said they were seeping out the back of the truck, the green amniotic fluids running into the gutter. Anyway, I'd heard there was a virus going around, and these women were speculating that was what had caused their company's server to perform strangely.

There were pay phones near the snack machines. I went to one and punched up Gaby's home number. I didn't feel she'd be at the candle shop. I didn't even expect her to answer a call to her flat. But she did. The pay phone's vidscreen lit up, and at first I thought I had a wrong number.

"Yes?" said the stranger in the monitor. It was a woman with no hair. It was Gaby with no hair.

"What the hell did you do that for?" I cried. Peripherally, I saw the two white-bloused women glance over at me.

"Do what?"

"Your hair, your hair, damn it!"

"It was my hair," she said in a drab, nonchalant voice. More a dry truism than defensiveness.

"I loved your hair!"

I loved Gaby's voluptuous body as well, and her rounded, pretty face. But without the framing curtains of her deep, dark hair, her face looked too round. Too full. Almost as if the soft lower part of her face was wider than the bare top of her skull. I'd seen women who looked beautiful bald, or with just a layer of stubble, but it didn't seem to suit Gabrielle.

"Look," I went on, babbling heatedly, "you better buy yourself some acceleration cream and slather it on good, my dear, because your hair was beautiful and this look is not you."

"You act like you know me better than I do, Christopher."

"I know what I like, and I like hair. So grow back your hair." I tried to lower my voice so as not to seem like some domineering boyfriend to those two nearby women.

"You don't know me," she said. And then the new face of Gabrielle was gone.

"Jesus Jumping Christ," I muttered, whisking past the two women, embarrassed, returning to my favored spot closer to the coffee machine. "Crazy. Who needs this? Jeez," I said under my breath.

I wanted to cut it off with her. She certainly seemed to want to cut it off with me.

But more than that, I wanted my old Gaby back.

If she had parents I might appeal to them, but one time as we lay in bed she had told me that her mother had simply disappeared one day when Gabrielle was thirteen. Her father thought she'd been kidnaped and murdered. Gabrielle thought she might have run off with some other man. But Gabrielle told me that deceased friend Maria's theory had been that mom had become lost in the city somewhere, and couldn't find her way back to familiar streets. Trapped forever in the maze. It was ridiculous, of course. She could simply phone home. Stop a forcer to ask for assistance. Ask for directions. But Maria had insisted it happened; people vanished, seemingly into another city superimposed with this city, and couldn't cross back again, couldn't even communicate again with that former place. It sounded like more spiritual bunk to me. Or at least, like she was referring to an alternate dimension, instead of a literal labyrinth within the solid, material city itself.

Her father had thrown himself off the top of a seventy story building when Gabrielle was sixteen. He'd become alcoholic. For three years he'd sat up alone at night at the kitchen table, muttering to himself, weeping. He missed his wife, whether victim or betrayer. So he'd flung himself into the canyon of the city—flesh and anguish reduced to an anonymous blot like news ink—like a sacrifice tossed to a volcano god.

Late that afternoon I ran from my office building down the street through the rain to the nearest subway kiosk. Steam rose from a grille in the sidewalk near the kiosk, and I plunged through the vapors to duck into the underground.

This was a station for the orange line, which would take me back to my neighborhood. It was humid and damp as a laundromat and smelled like a gym. The wall and ceiling tiles alternated black and orange. People called it Halloween Station.

Soaked, I stood on the platform waiting for the tube. I didn't look over at the group of black youths to my right. You just didn't directly look at people unless you really had to. Just a glance might warrant a death sentence in the code book of some youth gangs. These boys wore shiny red jumpsuits, each one big enough to fit all his friends in, and on their heads each wore the latest style for black teen age gangers: a black fez with a tassel colored for their group. These ones had orange tassels. The orange line was their territory.

To my left, an obese woman was wrapped in a circus tent of a cloak, slick and dripping with rain, the hood pulled up around her face.

No one mentioned the dead man I saw down on the train bed, though they must have spotted him, too. Another suicide, like Gaby's dad? Someone pushed into the path of a rushing, hovering tube, maybe by that gang right beside me? (They were talking in reverse English, in the current manner of black youths and the many white kids who sought to emulate them.)

The clothes had been torn off his body. So had both legs, one arm, a few fingers on the remaining hand, and the head. The one-limbed torso itself was grimy, a bit scuffed, but fairly untouched, lending an especially unpleasant contrast to the raw points of disconnection. I flicked a look at the obese woman, to see if she were gazing down at the body, but the hood hid her features. Again, I didn't glance at the backwards-talking boys.

Identity obliterated. Once this man had been a beloved child. (A mother had teased a finger into that belly button to make him giggle.) Someone's brother. Maybe a husband. (A wife or girlfriend had kissed those nipples.) Maybe a child awaited his return this very moment. A sacrifice of meat tossed to the roaring subway god.

I thought of Gabrielle again. Bald. Her voice druggy. Transfigured.

A tube was coming; I could hear the distant sound like a hurricane blowing through the confining, arched and tiled tunnel.

I looked from the dark maw of the tunnel back to the torso. I hoped the body was far enough away from the actual path of the tube that I wouldn't have to bear witness to further obliteration.

When my eyes fell on the torso again, I saw a thin black arm pull itself into the neck stump and disappear. It had looked like the limb of an insect, but also like the fast arm and hand of a monkey. A skeleton monkey, the bones burned black.

It could be some vermin, I thought. Or a mutant that lived in the subway. But I couldn't imagine an entire animal or being secreted away inside that truncated corpse, so I had to attribute the glimpse to my imagination.

My tube pulled in. Advertisements flowed like colored fluid along its silver flanks. Gratefully, the abbreviated cadaver had previously tumbled out of the direct path of the hovertrain. Naturally I let the fez-wearing boys pile in before me.

The door slid shut behind me. Though the seats were mostly empty, I chose to stand and hold an overhead bar with a padded grip. I lurched a bit as the tube whooshed into motion once more, and as it pulled out of Halloween Station I looked out the row of windows at the platform where I'd been standing. The obese woman still lingered there. She hadn't boarded. And she might not have been a woman after all. Her skin, it seemed in the second that I saw her before utter blackness replaced my view, was a light blue in color.

* * *

If I wasn't so awkward with women, so nervous and shy about asking them for a date (it always seemed to me that she'd hear my offer as, "Do you think you and me could fuck some time?"), I'd be able to put

Gabrielle behind me. After all, I loved her, but was I really desperately in love with her? Well—was that even a realistic level of emotion to expect from any relationship? I'd only really felt that sort of desperate hunger for women who wouldn't go out with me at all. That kind of intensity is mostly longing, and you don't long for what you have.

Sitting at my computer at home, I idly watched the ad banner scrolling across the bottom of the screen. *Phixitol* promised to boost my self-confidence, to correct low self-esteem and better my self-image. But though I knew I was already nothing more than a chemical soup cooking on a burner of electrical discharges, like many people I had this fierce determination to work with the hand I'd been dealt, to jealously guard the random configuration of protoplasm and anxieties that was the only me I was familiar with. Loss of one's self is terror.

Didn't Gaby know that?

It's just the sex, I tried to tell myself. And her hair. Both are gone. Let her go.

Instead, I leaned forward and ran a netlink search on the book she had gotten from Maria, in an effort to better understand what had so obsessed her.

I misspelled it, but the computer interpreted my intent and brought up the proper name which I hadn't clearly remembered:

THE NECRONOMICON

Immediate information told me that the volume was a grimoire—a sorcerer's spell book—that had been written by an arab author, Abdul Alhazred, in Damascus (wherever that was on old Earth) in the 8th century. Original translations had been in Latin, Greek, and English. 800ish pages depending on its version.

Now, as to accessability; a notation came up that informed me the book was not available on the net for reading or transmission—unless someone (like Gaby) had it in a personal recording and was willing to send it. Hm. However much one thought that any information was available on the net, there was always some obscure or generally uninteresting little particle that managed to slip through the cracks, and hide away in the tangible world. Working as closely as I did with the net, I'd encountered this more than once. I'd found the experience to be extremely frustrating, mystifying, and oddly gratifying. Reassuring. But a nuisance to me, today.

All right, then to seek out a hard copy version. An actual book. Though there was no direct link to SELLERS: THE NECRONOMICON, there was a link to SELLERS: OCCULT BOOKS. I took it.

I weeded out the netlink only book sellers, cut the list down to physical bookstores located in Punktown (I could try nearby, larger, but vastly less interesting Miniosis later if need be). There were a good number of those that specialized in occult books. Names like DELIRIUM BOOKS. MINISTRY OF WHIMSY BOOKS. NECROPOLITAN BOOKS. MYTHOS BOOKS . . .

I randomly clicked a link for a store with a name that was intriguingly less dramatic.

DOVE BOOKS.

The name suggested books about crystals and channeling; it conjured visions of misty places and rainbows; I pictured long-haired naked men and women sitting around and holding hands and speaking in too-soft, too-friendly voices, with too many cats at home. But still, I went with my impulse and visited their home page.

A man appeared on the screen and swivelled in a chair to face me. "Hello!" he said amicably. "Welcome to Dove Books. I'm Mr. Dove. How might I help you?"

For a moment I thought the man addressed me personally, but then I realized it was an interactive recording. Mr. Dove had the aforementioned gray flesh cracked with black veins, silvery unblinking eyes, no nose and a drooping black-lipped mouth. Pinkish gills pulsed subtly at his neck. If he were an alien, he was one I hadn't seen or heard of before. I had the impression he might be a mutation or even genetically engineered (for an underwater colony?) instead. In any event, he waited for my reply.

"Um, hi," I said. "I'm looking for a book called *The Necronomicon.*"

The recorded Mr. Dove hesitated, as if pondering my request, or reluctant to answer it. At last he replied, "That's a rare book, and you would do better to see me in person about its acquisition. Dove Books is located at 14-B Morpha Street. Our hours are . . . "

"How about related books?" I asked impatiently.

Another hesitation. "I'm sorry—there are no related books."

"Similar books."

"I'm sorry—books similar to your request would also be categorized as rare. You should see me in person regarding this subject matter."

"Jesus Flying Christ," I hissed. I guess I wasn't going to find out in advance if a visit would be worth the effort. Then again, he hadn't outright said he didn't carry the book. "What's the address again, Mr. Fish?"

"Mr. Dove," he corrected me pleasantly—he'd make a great customer service rep. "Dove Books is located at 14-B Morpha Street. Our hours are . . . "

"Yeah, thanks," I said, clicking back to my desk page. 14-B, huh? The "B" meant that it was the street directly below Morpha Street. The underground portion of Punktown.

* * *

I was picking up Gabrielle's bad habits—I took the next day off from work. It was one of those days I'd been expected to be in the office, but I promised to do whatever work I could at home. I tried to look appropriately droopy and drawn when my boss saw me on her vidscreen. I didn't have to force the look much.

I welcomed my quest. It was more of an excuse than anything else, really. Work was so tedious, so repetitious, a numbing mindless mechanical routine. Ants conveying information instead of eggs from this place to that place. I might as well be a robot. Or a zombie. Rescue me again, Gabrielle, with your white flesh and your smell of candles, your eccentricities and your wild temper, your nonchalance about work and your love of the irrelevant! Work all seemed so meaningless, indeed ant-like, in the cosmic scope of things—so why not openly embrace the meaningless, the anarchy, as Gaby did?

I took a tube from my neighborhood directly to the B level of Morpha Street, without having to experience the carnival-like throngs and the colorful dangers of the upper Morpha Street. The subterranean version was actually more sedate. Relatively speaking. I pressed my forehead to look out as we pulled into our station. I hadn't been to this area in ten years . . . hadn't even been in any of the underground districts in a year or more, apart from tube stations and their adjacent gift shop/snack bar/waiting areas.

The ceiling was high above us, like a solid sky—with conduits and cables, pipelines and plumbing, hulking complex machinery in place of clouds. Lamps projected diffused light in place of Oasis' sun. An old shunt line whisked along a cable supported from the ceiling. The small train's passing sent a luminous rain of sparks drifting down, though most of it faded before it touched street level, or pattered harmlessly off the flat roof-tops of the smallish tenement buildings that were snugged shoulder-to-shoulder along either side of the street. Girders criss-crossed the ceiling, and skeletal metal columns like fossilized trees supported it at intervals. The overhead lights dimmed at night, but blazed half-convincingly now. At least it wasn't raining down here, except for the leaks that dripped here and there.

I disembarked, and wandered out from under the platform's little roof beneath the roof, refamiliarizing myself with the lay of things. Punktown was an ever changing, ever growing thing, but at last I recognized a vid store I used to go to back when I went through my Japanese movies phase before their misogyny finally outweighed the erotic charge for me (anime, and live movies with plenty of rape and horrifically real violent effects, with translated titles like *White-Stocking Girl 2: Die, Pink Flower Panties, Die!*).

14-B . . . I wanted 14-B . . .

I found it after only wandering for several minutes, and without even having to cross the street. It was housed in a building of pale violet bricks, the top of which uncharacteristically tapered jaggedly to a point just short of impaling the concrete sky. I couldn't go in, at first, because I'd purchased a bad coffee from a vendor robot who could probably do my job better than I did (selling coffee down here might be a welcome change for me). I had this thing about throwing away coffee, though, however poor in quality, so I paced the sidewalk and finished it off before I slipped between the young Choom prostitutes who lingered outside the purple structure's front step. I tried not to look at them, especially the one who was entirely naked except for some black barbed-wire tattoos that wound like diseased ivy or diseased veins around her flesh as white as a cave lizard's. Chooms, of course, are one of the most human-like of all humanoid races—the native people of Oasis—and these prosties would have been indistinguishable from Earth colonists if not for the wide mouths that split their heads from ear-to-ear, their jaws full of rows of heavy molars evolved for the chewing of the tough native roots they still favored. Their considerable mouths were painted bright red upper lip and bright blue lower lip (indicating, I guess, what pimp they belonged to).

"Hey, handsome, where you going?" one diminutive girl asked me, not the nude one, touching my elbow. "You think old books are more interesting than me?"

That was a good question. And I was flattered by the "handsome" line, even coming from a prosty, but I felt my face flush and I only smiled back at her before ducking into the shop which a sign identified as DOVE BOOKS.

Inside it was quiet, and gloomy like when the ceiling lights were dimmed for night, and the air had that pleasant musty/mildewed smell of old books.

And there directly facing the door, behind a counter, was Mr. Dove in the gray translucent flesh. He lowered a book with a tattered cover he'd been reading, and I caught the title: *The Thackery T. Lambshead Pocket Guide to Eccentric and Discredited Diseases*. Maybe he was trying to diagnose himself.

"Hello!" he said. "Can I help you with something special today, sir?"

"Ah, well . . . " I didn't like to be helped or even talked to by store people; I liked to browse on my own. But in this case I gave in and asked, "Do you have a book called the *Necronomicon*?"

"My goodness," said Mr. Dove, and he came out from behind the counter. "Wherever did you hear of *Al-Azif*?"

"*Al-Azif*?"

"It's another name for the book you mention. It has various translations."

"Oh. I read about it a little on the net . . . "

"I see. The net. Well, that book is exceedingly rare, and sorry to say I don't have a volume of it to sell. I myself have only seen portions of it."

"All right . . . well . . . do you have anything similar to that?" I felt like I was reliving our previous "conversation", and hoped he'd be more helpful this time. So far, not so good.

"Are you a collector, Mr. . . . "

"Ruby. No, but I'm interested."

"Well, I have a special collection of extremely rare volumes you might care to look at. I'm afraid they're behind a protective screen—this is a bit of a rough neighborhood, you understand—and can not be casually handled, but if you think you might still be interested after you've assessed my offering I can show you individual books while in my presence."

I shrugged. "I'd like to see what you've got."

"Very well, Mr. Ruby . . . this way . . . "

The beautifully tailored alien or mutant led me behind his counter, where there was a small back room with one circular table in its center. He drew back a curtain embroidered with intricate Tikkihotto designs of humanoid ancient warriors with eyes like the tendrils of sea anemones, doing battle with devils that looked like big white crabs with sea anemones instead of heads. Behind this tapestry was a series of shutters, and without Dove pushing any buttons that I could see one of these shutters slid aside to reveal a row of obviously very old books, most with crumbling leather spines. They were shielded behind a clear protective screen, as he had said.

"I'll leave you to your examination, Mr. Ruby. I'll be right up front should you require my assistance."

Good. I could browse. "Thanks," I dismissed him.

Many of the volumes didn't have printing on their spines, but the titles were projected onto the spines in blue glowing letters by tiny lenses along the shelf that housed them. I still had to angle my neck sharply to read them. My first thought was that a non-scholar like me—without any foreign languages residing in a memory chip implant—would not only need to put these books under a translator scan to read them on my computer, but I would need a translator just to decipher their titles (which weighed as much as the books no doubt did). Why couldn't the little shelf lenses translate them for me right now?

There were *Liber AL vel Legis* by Crowley, *De Furtivis Literarum Notis* by Giambattista Porta, *Daemonolateria* by Remigius, *Kryptographik* by Thicknesses.

But there were titles in English as well, thank the Daemonolateria. But the titles seemed just as impenetrable: *The Keys of Solomon* by S. C. Sargent, *The Magus* by Barrett, *The Metal Book* (with hinged metal covers) author unknown, *The Book of Awe* by Louis Marotta (which appeared to be triangular in shape), *The Secret Lore of Magic* by Shah, *Books of Power* by Abdul-Kadir, *Visions of Khroyd'hon* by William Davis Manly, *The Book of the Dominion of Mysteries*, *The Book of Night*, *The Zhou Texts* . . .

I had to straighten my already cramped neck. Where to begin in such a tangle of syllables and obscurity? Trying to get a grip on some of the titles reminded me of the garbled spells Gaby had read that night from her palmcomp.

Then Dove was at my elbow, leaning toward me stiffly but gracefully like a butler. He smelled like aftershave, though he had no hair to shave. Maybe cologne to mask a fishy smell. He purred, "So . . . do you need some guidance, Mr. Ruby?"

"I'm not sure. Which of these might be the most like the

Necronomicon?"

"Ohh . . . well . . . that depends on your precise area of interest. I have several other books as well, that I feel are of particular interest because they take some of the ideas of *Al-Azif* further. They concentrate on the geometry, the mathematics, of certain types of formulae found in *Al-Azif*, and . . . "

"I was never good at math. But what are they?"

"There is a book by a Choom alchemist, Wadoor, translated as *The Atlas of Chaos*. And a manuscript by the Tikkihotto author Skretuu, which translates as *The Veins of the Old Ones*."

"Varicose veins, then?'

Dove gave a little chuckle to indulge me. "Both books are similar in that they acknowledge the meticulous pattern that exists even in chaos."

"But are they spell books?"

"Yes. Wadoor's *Atlas of Chaos* concentrates primarily upon a god known as the Crawling Chaos, also as the Messenger. You will forgive me if in our conversation I do not name any of these gods directly. Even their names can be invocations . . . "

So, I thought, he not only sells this dung but he buys it, too.

He continued: "This god is a forerunner of the other gods. They . . . "

"Is this a bunch of gods, then, like Greek gods?"

"Well . . . in a way. It's a polytheistic system. They're called the Old Ones . . . or the Outsiders, Mr. Ruby, because the Elder Gods locked them out of our dimension in a battle for power which took place long before the birth of any living sentient race."

"So these Elder Ones that defeated the Old Gods—are they supposed to still be around?"

"Old *Ones*. Elder *Gods*," he politely corrected me. "No . . . they departed, to wherever gods go."

"Is there any historical proof that they existed? Could real alien races have been these so-called gods, and they were simply deified by primitive people?"

"I imagine they could be interpreted that way. As aliens. As beings.

But to us—in comparison—they are gods that dwarf the concept of any imaginary deities like the Greek gods you mention."

"Aren't all gods invented?"

"Such an atheist, Mr. Ruby!" Dove chided teasingly. "Ancient people worshiped the sun. They might have misinterpreted it, but they didn't invent it."

"So . . . *The Veins of the Old Gods* . . . I mean *Old Ones* . . . "

"Skretuu took Wadoor's theories even further. Wadoor used geometric formulae to open windows into other realms. The angles and curves of certain patterns can bend space and time, distort their flow, be manipulated so as to pry open rents in the cosmic fabric." He added after a pause: "So Wadoor tells us. In any case, Skretuu built upon Wadoor's idea of mapping these patterns, which exist invisible all around us, waiting to be traced. Waiting to be reconfigured to our desires. His attempt to chart these invisible patterns is the subject matter of *Veins of the Old Ones*. He was likening his research to the dissection of anatomists."

"Hm," I said, nodding like a thoughtful professor in discussion with a colleague. "Um, so these two books are fairly new, not as rare . . . since they furthered the studies of the *Necronomicon*, the books are obviously post-colonization . . . "

"Ah, not so. Both were written before Earth colonized Oasis. The Tikkihotto had come to Oasis already, and that was how Skretuu encountered Wadoor's book, written a hundred years earlier, but . . . "

"But you said they read the *Necronomicon* . . . "

"No," he corrected. "I said they took some of its concepts further. Both came upon some of the same concepts of *Al-Azif*, but independently of it. Some concepts, Mr. Ruby, are universal amongst sentient beings."

"Well, yeah. Like you said about the sun. Primitive people try to get a hold of their terror of the unknown by explaining it away with superstitions . . . "

"Mr. Ruby . . . that is not always so. Some of these books you were perusing contain sheer science of the highest order! May I ask you

. . . you're so skeptical . . . what made you come to my shop?"

"My girlfriend is into the occult." I thought of lying, for some reason. Thought of telling him I was shopping for a present for her. Instead I told him: "I just want to get an idea of what it is that she's so caught up in."

"She won't show you, herself?"

"No."

"And what materials does she already possess?"

"She has the *Necronomicon*. On a disk, at least. She . . . "

"Your girlfriend has a copy of *Al-Azif*? Complete?"

"Well, I don't know complete . . . "

"And where did she get this?"

"From a friend of hers. Maria something. She was murdered, apparently a drug related thing, and my girlfriend took some disks out of her apartment. The *Necronomicon* was on one of them."

"And where did this Maria get it, in the first place?" Dove sounded less dry, less like a butler, suddenly. There was a hint of the collector's hunger in his tone.

"No idea."

"How was she killed? Did they catch the culprit?"

"Apparently not. She was decapitated. I guess they never found her head."

Dove snorted. It sounded like a cynical laugh. "Interesting."

"What?"

"It's just that it sounds like a trademark killing by a Hound."

"What's that?"

"An alleged extradimensional entity. One that can be summoned by tracing various patterns into the corner of a room."

"It's a demon? Because my girlfriend said Maria claimed to have successfully called up a demon with that dung . . . I mean that stuff that my girlfriend attempted."

"Demon is an interpretation. As is Hound. Some literalists try to visualize these beings as dog-like, when the moniker is actually more symbolic." Dove straightened up taller, stiffer, suddenly. "Did you just say that your girlfriend has attempted to summon these beings, also?"

"Yes. Sort of as a joke more than anything else. She messed up her own attempt, so then she played a recording of Maria saying it. But she didn't draw any patterns on the wall . . . just said some invocations. Oh, and she burned eight candles in my bedroom. It has eight corners."

Dove nodded very, very slowly. "Not a Hound summoning, then. But a chant of Opening. Of Reconfiguration."

"Whatever."

"I imagine that since she won't let you see the recording of the *Necronomicon*, she wouldn't consider selling it to me. But do you think she would let me copy it, at least? If she doesn't trust me to handle the disk, she could even copy it herself. I would be willing to pay her handsomely for this, Mr. Ruby. I would even pay you a nice little sum, if you would pursue this acquisition for me."

"Well . . . hey, that's nice, but I don't know how much luck I'd have. Frankly, we're not too close all of a sudden . . . "

"Would you mind giving me her number, then? Perhaps she'll be more receptive to the idea if I approach her personally. If you can do that much for me, Mr. Ruby, I will still pay you that fee I mentioned. Say one thousand munits?"

One thousand munits! Just for giving a book dealer Gaby's number, even when she might tell him to go open a door to hell and walk through it? "Sure," I said. "Do you have a pen?"

I scribbled on a piece of paper he handed me. He folded it up and slipped it into a jacket pocket after giving it a quick, satisfied glance.

"So . . . how much are these books here, anyway? The prices aren't listed."

"Several aren't for sale, Mr. Ruby, though I do allow the occasional scholar to peruse or even scan them. But those that are for sale vary in range from twenty thousand munits to four million munits, in the case of *The Metal Book*, for instance."

"Four million munits? Jesus Weeping Christ!"

Dove held up a gray hand, as if to ward me off. "Please, Mr. Ruby

. . . no names of deities and their ilk. Invocations, remember?"

"Oh yeah . . . sorry. Well. Wow. Guess I won't be buying any rare books today."

"You could still find a smattering of related topics in our general section. But might I ask you, Mr. Ruby, what brought you to my shop in the first place? Did someone tell you I had a collection of such books?"

"No, actually, I ran a netlink search. Not a very detailed one—I just found out that you sold occult books. Your place was the first one I looked at."

I think Dove's black lips attempted a human smile. "Ahh . . . you see, Mr. Ruby? Some call it fate, or destiny. Synchronicity. But I think of such things as the patterns within chaos."

"Yeah, well, good luck with Gaby. Her name is Gabrielle, by the way. Put in a good word for me, will ya?"

"Here, let's go up front now so I might transfer that thousand munits from my card to yours, Mr. Ruby."

"Sure," I said, following him. Behind me I heard the protective shutter slide back into place over the museum-like display of rare—shockingly rare—tomes. Well, I sort of gave up on my original half-hearted quest, and didn't even bother to check out his general selections, but I had made a thousand munits for my trouble. And I imagined Gaby would make more, perhaps even a lot more, than that. No four million, because hers was only a copy on a cheap red disk, but it might be enough to put me back in her favor. And back in her bed.

* * *

I spent a quarter of my thousand munits right away.

The Choom prosty's flat was upstairs in the same building that housed Dove Books. She was short, slim as a boy and nearly as breastless. Her long straight hair was dyed dark purple and as shiny as the dark purple satin sheets on her bed; the whites of her eyes were dyed a lighter purple, as if she were color coordinated with the brick building. Her eyes were slanted with the Oriental fold, but this was just cosmetic, a recent fad; it was more common for Chooms to have their mouths made smaller, so as to fit in better with the people who had pretty much claimed their world as their own. This was the one who'd called me "handsome".

I was in her within the first few minutes. I was relieved that I was up to the task; I hadn't had a prosty in ten years, not since that Japanese girl I rented back in my Japanese phase, and so I was nervous and shy.

"Take me in the ass," she cried, slipping slickly out from under me, rolling fast onto hands and knees and looking over her shoulder. "You wanna take me in the ass?"

"Uh, no thanks, not this time," I said a little shakily, but I snugged up behind her and guided myself into her more conventional receptacle, then held tight to her slim waist as I ground myself luxuriously against her hard little bottom, so unlike Gaby's more cushiony but no less appealing model. I stirred her guts, so it seemed. She moaned. It was convincing enough to suit my needs. I liked the way her silky purple hair spread across her albino-white back. Gaby would fit in well down here, amongst the troglodytes. Couldn't stop thinking about Gaby. That made me guilty. I tried not to think of Gaby.

Sweating profusely from the strain of my churnings, the sweat of my mental churnings, slick with the girl's sweat too, and straining all the harder because I was finding it hard to come, finally I came, scrunching my face as if in pain, shuddering in hard jolts against her, my heart ready to tear itself free from its moorings. I slipped out and collapsed on my belly on the sheets. She stretched out beside me and started rubbing my back until I guess she felt the sheen of sweat and didn't like it, withdrew her hand.

"I have a disk of me and my roommate doing it. She's a girl. You want to buy something like that? I have a B and D disk of me you might like. For a souvenir."

"Maybe next time," I panted. I traced a finger between her slight breasts, made even slighter by her lying on her back with arms flung above her head as if to cool her underarms. "What's this mean?" I asked, circling a black tattoo there. It was a kind of crude star design with an eye in its center, and the eye's pupil looked like it might be a flame.

"A friend gave it to me. She said it would protect me. It does, too. I used to have these horrible dreams . . . horrible, horrible nightmares . . . they were driving me crazy . . . ever since I moved into this building. I complained to Ric—Ric is my pimp—but he didn't do anything, but my friend Rosa is like a witch or something . . . she's a prosty, too . . . and she put this tattoo on me."

"Like a good luck charm, huh?"

"Yeah. This building is haunted, you know that? At night I hear something in my wall. Like clawing behind the wall. Ric said it was just rats or bugs or drugs or something, but Rosa . . . she lives in the building, too . . . she says it's a spirit. Maybe even a demon. Rosa says that book store downstairs is the problem . . . Rosa says it's evil. She has this same tattoo as me." She touched it, as if kissing a crucifix.

I nodded my head on her pillow, staring at her, but my thoughts hovering outside me.

* * *

I tried calling Gabrielle over the next three days. She never replied to my messages.

Finally, I called Dove Books on Morpha Street. B.

"Ah, yes, Mr. Ruby!" exclaimed Mr. Dove, looking exactly as he had in his net page recording. For a second I wondered if he truly were live now. "Thank you so much for putting me in touch with Gabrielle . . . "

"So . . . so did she sell you her disk of . . . "

He held up a finger. "Ah—no names, please, while we're being transmitted. Yes, no, well, she made me a copy of it, in fact, which is wonderful. I'm very grateful to the both of you."

"I was just curious. How it went, you know . . . if she talked to you . . . "

"Yes, of course."

"Sooo. All right, then. I was just . . . curious, I guess."

"Certainly."

"Well . . . so . . . do you think I could get a copy of the disk from you?"

Dove squirmed uncomfortably in his seat. "I'm terribly sorry, Mr. Ruby, but that's just not possible . . . "

"Not possible? You've got to be joking!"

"I'm so grateful to you, as I say, but I'm afraid that's one of the stipulations Gabrielle made before she gave me a copy. That I mustn't sell a copy to you."

"Oh, great," I hissed. "Damn her. Who does she think I am?"

"I take it she doesn't feel . . . if I might venture to say this . . . that you are receptive to her beliefs, Mr. Ruby."

"Well she's right there, Mr. Dove, she's right there." I huffed again, and then said, "Hey . . . you said she 'gave' you a copy. You don't mean that she gave it to you for free, do you? You paid her, right?"

Was there just a half beat of hesitation, or was it my imagination? "Yes . . . of course, Mr. Ruby . . . I paid her quite nicely for the copy. But again, I'm afraid that matter is confidential."

"Thanks a lot, Mr. Dove—helpful as always." I reached out to banish his image from my screen. It was my work computer, anyway, and I was anxious not to let my boss catch me—she was less than thrilled with me, lately.

"I hope one day you can be more open-minded about these subjects, sir," Dove went on. The glow of his vidscreen was reflected in his metallic silver eyes without lids. "You could see things more clearly. See things you can't possibly see now. Or even conceive of . . . "

"You ought to date Gabrielle, Mr. Dove—you were made for each other." And now I did cut off our connection. My screen returned to my desk page image, which was a photo of Gabrielle with long black hair. The lighting was low and ambery colored, intimate and warm. It was a close up, so you couldn't tell that all she had been wearing when I took the picture was the black plastic masquerade mask she wore over her eyes, those eyes staring mysteriously out of the holes.

I went to her apartment that night. Banged on the door. Rang the buzzer. An elderly Choom woman crept around the corner of the hall on all fours, startling me when I looked down at her and saw her advancing on me.

"Looking for my beads," she croaked. "My necklace broke."

I sighed, and immediately squatted down to run my hands over the carpeting, which I regretted profoundly when I felt its greasy texture, like the hide of some animal. Rotting animal.

"You looking for the girl in that apartment?" the old woman asked.

"Yes. Gabrielle."

"She moved out, dear."

I sat up on my knees. "Moved out? Jesu–when did she move out?"

"A few days ago. Sorry I can't say where. I never spoke to her. But I saw her carrying out some boxes."

So. So, that was it then, wasn't it? And she hadn't even told me. Perhaps, she had even done it to get away from me. If she had stayed in town I might still never find her; Punktown is a big place. She had disappeared, perhaps like her mother.

Something small rolled under my palm, which I had forgotten was still sweeping. A tiny crystal bead, which I blankly handed over to the old woman. "That's all I could find," I droned, and I rose and then took her arm to help her to her feet as well.

"What a dear boy," she told me. She was as small and thin as the prosty I'd rented several days ago. Someday that young girl would look like this. Transfigured.

I sighed, glanced down the hall, and saw a door hanging open. It was the door that the immense, blue-faced man or woman had lingered in that time, peeking out at me.

Why was the door open that way? I expected to see the huge, balloon-like face float into the opening at any minute.

Instead, I saw the elderly Choom woman shuffle toward the doorway, and begin to pass through it.

I darted down the hall to catch up with her. As I whispered intensely to her, I flicked my eyes repeatedly into the apartment behind her.

"Hey . . . I'm sorry, but does another person live with you? Very . . . um, large. No hair? Blue skin . . . maybe?"

"Blue skin? No, dear, no one like that lives with me. In fact, no one lives with me at all."

I straightened up slowly. Had I been mistaken, then, about which door this was? I could have sworn that it was the same . . .

Reluctantly I backed away from it, muttering thanks. She thanked me again, and closed the door between us.

* * *

Gabrielle called me in the small hours of the morning. I had to get up for work in just three hours more, but I scurried bleary-brained to my computer when I heard her voice.

She was on the screen, but the light was dim on her end. Just the glow of her own vidscreen on her face. She looked terrible. Her eyes were not only narrow, as usual, but squinted. Her face was bloated and doughy. And now she had shaved off her eyebrows as well. It was not an appealing development.

"Thank you for putting Mr. Dove in touch with me, Christopher," she whispered, as if afraid someone else would hear her . . . someone there with her, "but never, never ever again tell anyone about me. About what I do. About that book I have. You know the one I mean."

"I'm sorry . . . it's just that he said he'd give you a lot of money for it."

"I didn't charge him for it. He's like me. He's a priest. I'm a priestess . . . "

"He didn't pay you? What the hell—Gabe, he told me he paid you! Do you know what he sells the originals of these things for? He could have at least paid you ten thousand munits . . . a couple thousand . . . Christ, I'll give you the rest of what he gave me. He gave me a thousand munits!"

"I don't want your money. I didn't want his money . . . "

"Where are you, Gaby? Why did you move, huh? Why didn't you tell me?"

"Don't tell anyone about me, Christopher. I'm warning you."

"Listen . . . Gaby . . . I love you. All right? You hear me?"

"Remember Maria. Remember what happened to her. Maria was stupid. Maria talked about these things. Showed them to people. It isn't smart, Christopher, to talk about these things to just anyone . . . "

"Gabrielle!"

"I can't talk to you any more, Christopher . . . "

"Gabrielle!" I shouted, as if she were falling away from me down a deep, deep well. I wanted to reach into the screen.

The screen went dead.

"Fuck!" I hissed, whirling away from the desk, pacing about the room. My huge VT was dead, too, except for a banner ribbon that never went away, scrolling across the bottom. Right now it asked me to try *Phixitol*, to combat depression, to alleviate anxiety, to bring calm and balance and make me able to face the day with a smile . . .

* * *

"Mr. Dove, do you happen to know where Gabrielle is living now?"

"No, Mr. Ruby, I'm sorry . . . I don't."

"Are you ever in touch with each other?"

"No, Mr. Ruby, we are not."

"She says she gave you the disk. For free. That you didn't pay her for it."

"I'm sorry, Mr. Ruby, I have a customer . . . "

"You lied to me, Mr. Dove."

"I have to go, sir . . . "

"You're making her delusions worse!"

"That's quite enough, Mr. Ruby."

"Should I call you Father Dove? She called you a priest. She says she's a priestess. Do you ever do your cute little rites together? Huh?"

"She told you that? That I'm a priest?"

"Yes, she did . . . "

"You both talk too much, Mr. Ruby, if I might venture to say so."

Then my screen went blank. Again.

* * *

It was my work computer. My boss walked past my cubicle and glanced in. I considered smiling over at her, decided to ignore her instead and look busy. I quickly opened a call from the customer service queue. "Hi, this is Chris," I said, "how may I help you today?" I distractedly took in a face on my vidplate; a blocky male face, little features clustered toward its center, a crew cut dyed metallic silver. Some sports star was wearing his hair like that, prompting such imitation, but I took no interest in sports. I took no interest in this man; instead, I found my eyes drifting out my window.

I was quivering very subtly but very consistently, as if an electric current flowed through me. Mr. Dove had been rude to me. In fact, if I wasn't being too paranoid, I thought maybe his tone, at the end, had been somewhat menacing. It wasn't like him. Or was it?

Down in the street, I watched a robot hovercleaner move along the gutter. Programmed to follow its maps of the city, never ceasing in its labors as it zapped the litter and garbage it consumed, never stopping to rest. As it turned from Grid Street onto Avenue K, I saw that two little black boys rode on its back bumper.

"Hello?" said the silver-haired young man. "Hey?"

I looked directly at him. "Yes—how can I help you?"

"I have a net page with your service . . . a game page, where I put a bunch of games I got off the net. And I used the game tools you offer to make a couple of my own games . . . "

"Yes, that's fun, isn't it? Do you need some game-making tips? We have a special crew for that kind of . . . "

"No . . . well . . . I don't know. My game is acting funny. The one I call *Sweet Revenge*. It's a first-person hunt-and-kill, and I track down these girls through Punktown . . . "

Sounded all too typical to me. I glanced out the window again, without even meaning to. I rubbed at my chin absent-mindedly, and felt rough stubble there. I had slapped on hair gel hurriedly that morning, running late for work; it had smeared and dried on my upper forehead, which now felt varnished and constricted. I craved another coffee. I vibrated.

"I used my past four girlfriends in the game . . . I scanned in some photos and vids of them, and made them into the four girls I'm tracking down to kill . . . "

"Hence *Sweet Revenge*," I said, nodding, not looking at him. "And?"

I narrowed my eyes. Every day this same view was presented outside my window, churning with life but unmoving, differing for the most part only in its lighting, in its weather. Because it was so unchanging, I barely dwelt on it consciously, only dreamily. I could really say the same about the city even when I walked its streets, interacted with it. Of course, part of me was always alert and on guard for danger; you had to be. But I didn't take in the details directly. It was like I saw and experienced most of the city peripherally, subliminally. My focus was narrow. Ant's eye view, low to the ground. Not even a bird could fly high enough to take in the whole of Punktown.

Maybe that was why I had never noticed the purple building I saw outside my office window now. At least, I had never consciously noticed it. For a moment or two I wondered if it were new, but it didn't look new, and I couldn't recall whether I had seen any skeletal framework of a building under construction in the past year or two.

" . . . I tracked down two of the girls into an alley near Oval Square," the young man was continuing. "I'd already killed Aymee and Breeze . . . those were my first two girlfriends in college . . . "

The purple building was actually more of a pale violet. It was quite tall—though there were certainly far taller buildings in view—and tapered jaggedly toward the top like an old step pyramid. A silvery spire topped it, gleaming in the sun like a thin blade. I thought maybe it was one of those buildings that are grown around a metal framework rather than assembled, because it had a sort of organic look, at least from my position. The purple bricks or tiles that either composed it or at least formed its outer skin looked large and irregular in shape, and I was reminded either of the cracked mud of a desert or the scaly hide of a crocodile.

"Well, I saw Jen and Breeeanna at the end of this alley, and they were sort of hiding around the corner of a big old trash zapper. I started sneaking up on them, but I took my time, because I wanted to scare them. To savor it, you know? Because this would be the end of the game. But I heard them whispering. And they were even giggling . . . "

"It's nice, the AI characters you can make for these games," I muttered.

"Yeah, well, I didn't like it. They weren't scared. I thought, do they have guns? Why aren't they afraid? What are they whispering about?"

"Did your program allow for them to protect themselves, fight back?"

"Sure . . . I wanted it to be a challenge. Breeze had clawed my face pretty good before I nailed her. But anyway, I moved in carefully with my shotgun ready . . . "

"Shotgun's always my favorite gun in a game," I murmured. I watched a helicar float past the windows of the purple building, reflecting the sun like rows and rows of mirrors.

"Yeah, so I could see them now around the end of that trash zapper . . . only it wasn't just Jen and Breeeanna. I saw a third girl with them."

"Yes? You had programmed the game to have incidental characters, right? Background filler?"

"Yeah, and there were interactive characters too, but this was different, man. I don't know. This other character was acting like my main characters. She was just more . . . alive than the background characters. And she was whispering with them. And giggling with them. I knew they were talking about me. And this new girl was *scary*, man . . . "

"How's that?" I asked. I saw clouds reflected in the windows on another face of the purple building. Clouds slowing moving. It made it seem as if you were looking at fog or steam rolling around inside a vast container.

"She was bald, and she . . . "

I looked into the vidscreen. "Bald?"

"Yeah, and she was fat. Fatter than dung. And her skin was like . . . "

Blue, I thought. Or did I say it out loud?

" . . . like a corpse, man. I brought up the shotgun and fired, I was so mad. I hit Jen in the shoulder and she went down, but Breeeanna and the fat girl ducked behind the zapper. I moved in and finished Jen off before she could get up. But she wasn't screaming, man—she was still laughing at me. Looking up and laughing at me like crazy. I blew her face off, that bitch. She used to laugh at me when I dated her, too . . . "

"The other two," I prompted him.

"They were gone. Turns out there was another alley that branched off to the right . . . I couldn't see it before because the zapper blocked it. I guess. I could swear there wasn't another alley there before. Anyway, they got away."

"Had there been any other unusual or uncharacteristic occurrences in this or any other game?"

"Well . . . sometimes in *Sweet Revenge* I hear weird music. Not like a soundtrack, but coming out of windows. Maybe it's just background detail. Mostly the whole background I got straight off of other game templates. It's just kind of . . . weird. I didn't used to hear it. Oh, and sometimes I get lost in places I know very well . . . and then when I get back to those places later, they're normal again. It's like the game moves the buildings around on me sometimes, or confuses the layout."

I nodded. I vibrated.

"Um . . . what did you say your name was?"

"Marrk."

"Marrk, would you mind giving me your pass code, so I can get into your game-building page and your finished games myself? I'd like to look into this for you."

"All right. Sure. My password is *killallbitches*."

I wondered why my new friend had such poor luck with the ladies. "Thanks, Marrk . . . I'll call you back with my findings as soon as I can.

You can continue to access your site, but please don't add to it or alter it in any way until I've concluded my diagnosis—all right?"

"Sure, thanks, man."

A shadow fell over my face and a large dark form lowered into view outside my window. Peripherally I saw an insect-like arm reach toward the pane. I flinched hard and swivelled in my chair to see a hovering robot running a soapy squeegee down the outside of my window. I nodded at its single staring lens, gave it a tattered flicker of a smile. I vibrated.

* * *

While a quick dinner heated up, I punched in the information to access the netlink page for Marrk Argent. I ate the dinner from a tray in my lap as I began his game, *Sweet Revenge*. It began in his apartment, which was too sumptuous to be based on his actual apartment, and I certainly hoped he didn't really own that arsenal of guns. I ignored the slithering advances of his two gorgeous room mates (based on popular VT actresses Jessika Heart Thatcher and Angelah Lee Henderson), which I'm sure would link into a sex game (perhaps a VR), and picked out a nice pump-action shotgun and a handgun from his vast collection to bring with me. Then I hit the streets. It was raining and night time. Irritated at the poor visibility, I had to go back to START and figure out how to make it sunny and day. Then I hit the streets.

To check out Argent's comments on how familiar surroundings had seemed to become confused, I headed for the nearest location that I myself would be familiar with—my workplace. I rode a tube and got there within several minutes (the game was totally real time). I found the outside of my workplace without any confusion, but the game wouldn't allow me to enter the building itself. I cranked back my virtual neck so as to stare up, up at my high window, as if I thought I might see my own face looking out of it, looking down at myself.

As I started away to take a tube to my apartment, the next location I intended to experiment with, a thought leaped to the front of my skull and I whipped around to examine the skyline as seen between the towers looming before me.

Yes—there it was, seen in the distance between my office building and its neighbor. The pale purple building with its gleaming spire and its pebbly scaly skin. Somehow, seeing it in this game seemed to reassure me of its existence more than gazing at it out of my office window had, earlier that day.

I rode the tube home like I would after any working day, except for the shotgun I carried (not that I hadn't felt like bringing a shotgun to work a few times). A Tikkihotto woman on the tube stood beside me holding the overhead bar, so that I caught myself peeking at her bared underarm. As if I needed to steal peeks at a computer construct. She was short and cute with her pale skin and plump curvy shape and little black dress, and I liked the flourescent lime green dye to her bobbed hair, but I could never get past those swimming clear tendrils they have instead of eyes. They wavered at me like plants underwater.

"What's that for?" she asked me, staring at my shotgun.

"Do you want to fuck?" I spoke out loud to the screen.

"No thank you," she said.

"Can I shoot you?"

"Please don't. You would get in trouble," she said calmly.

"What's your name?" I asked her.

"What's that for?" she asked, writhing sea anemone eyes directed toward my shotgun.

I disembarked at my regular stop, and again found my way across familiar sidewalks, up to my apartment building, without anything out of the ordinary. Maybe there was less graffiti on the Art Deco-like angels that flanked the front steps, abstracted and skinny and tall, holding swords in front of their nude androgynous bodies. There'd been more graffiti added since this scene had been recorded for use in such games. I wondered just how much of Punktown was available for exploration in this game. Well, it wouldn't let me inside my apartment building, so I couldn't find out if I were home.

So . . . what next? Should I start using his portable tracker to begin hunting down—what was the surviving girlfriend's name? —Breeeanna? Breeeanna and the fat bald woman who looked like a "corpse"?

I had a whim. I was still unsettled by my exchange that morning with Mr. Dove. I decided to check out one other fairly familiar location. I decided to go to Morpha Street. Subterranean level. Level B. 14-B, I wanted . . .

The tube let me off at the same platform as in my actual quest. Just as then, the high roof was like a fossilized sky. A shunt rattled by on an overhead vine of cable and a phosphorescent snow of sparks drifted down. I headed along the sidewalk. I remembered what 14-B would look like: a building with walls of pale violet brick, with a jagged crown that nearly stabbed the ceiling . . .

I stopped in my tracks. Pale violet bricks. Jagged, tapered summit. The building that housed Dove Books was like a miniature version of that building I had only just noticed outside my office window. That distant, larger edifice had seemed to me to have more irregularly shaped bricks or tiles for its hide, but the similarity was still there in shape and color. Synchronicity, I thought. Coincidence, was more like it. It was no doubt nothing more than 14-B having stuck in my mind, making me notice the larger building where I had never had reason to focus on it before.

Resuming my walk, I craned my neck to see if I could spot my destination. It must be right up ahead now, but I hadn't caught sight of it yet . . .

I had passed the Japanese vid store (with its various categorized sections such as *Yakuza*, *Anime*, *Rape*) and a robot vendor that I almost wanted to buy a coffee from, until I remembered I wasn't really on Morpha Street B. I walked on. And, finally, I came to a street corner.

I turned, looked back the way I had come. I had gone too far.

There was no 14-B.

The building hadn't struck me as a new one. Could it have been built, however, after this area had been recorded as a game template?

To be sure I hadn't passed it (maybe it had been painted another color?), I retraced my steps. But finally I stopped at the mouth of an alley where I realized the building should have been. Like a hole it had been extracted from. I saw a big old trash zapper back in there with filth-streaked sides, a few miniature shelters fashioned from shipping pallets. Spray-paint graffiti glowed in neon colors, so that the alley was bathed in blue, pink, green and yellow pastel light as if the sun beamed through stained glass windows. Several young prosties lingered in the throat of the alley, and one of them noticed me staring . . . moved toward me in an unsteady manner as if she might be drunk.

"Hey, handsome," she purred. There was a phlegmy rattle in her voice. She was small, thin, scantily dressed, and as she came out of the soft-colored gloom I saw that her long straight hair was dyed dark purple. The whites of her eyes were dyed soft violet. She was a Choom, but she had had her eyes made slanted like a human Asian. And I knew her.

"Take me in the ass," she gurgled in what was meant as a coo. She turned her back to me, spread her cheeks with her hands, smiled her huge Choom smile at me over her shoulder.

But when I had met her . . . when I had taken her to bed . . . the young prosty had not had four bony extrusions branching out of her skull like malformed miniature antlers. Raw pink skin peeled from them to show bone white beneath. Another of these forked growths sprouted from a shoulder blade, and another from one elbow. Yet another was beginning to sprout inside her mouth, pushing out her wide lower lip.

"Take me in the ass, handsome," she gargled.

I backed away from her. But I spoke to her. "Do you remember me?"

"Don't be shy . . . "

"What happened to you?"

"My dreams change me . . . "

"What happened to the place that was here?"

"It will be back . . . "

When she faced front again, I saw that she didn't have the tattoo on her chest that was meant to protect her. The star with the flaming eye her friend had put there. I backed away to the edge of the curb. She took one lurching step toward me, her arms moving weirdly in order to balance her.

"Tell me what's happening!" I demanded.

"There's someone at the door," she said. I heard my door buzzer sound. I flinched. As if amused, the prosty smiled so broadly that the new stump of an antler popped out from behind her lip and glistened with saliva.

I paused the game (afraid of what the mutant prosty might do to my character in my absence), got up from my desk and crossed to my door. There was a small security monitor beside it but it hadn't worked since I moved into my flat. Close to the panel, I called out shakily, "Who is it?"

"Gabrielle," a muffled voice said.

But for several moments, I didn't believe it. The voice had seemed to be that of a man. Deep, chesty. Then again, it was distorted through the door. Maybe I simply couldn't believe that Gaby would want to seek me out again.

I reached out and unlocked the door.

A sliver of a second after the lock came off, a mass of flesh exploded through the doorway, squeezing rapidly through as if it had no bones inside to impede it. It was a man or a woman, grotesquely obese, but moving with shocking speed, and it closed its hands around my throat and drove me back with its great bulk. It nudged the door closed with a thrust of its backside. It was a mountain of blue-tinged flesh in a smock like a black parachute. It was totally bald and without eyebrows. It was the creature I had seen standing on the tube platform. It was the creature that had been peeking at me in the hallway outside Gaby's abandoned apartment.

It was Gabrielle.

Her hands were powerful. I couldn't get a breath past them. She had me pinned against a wall now, and slid me up, up, until my feet kicked at the air, kicked at her immense breasts inside her smock. My feet danced like those of a hanging man; my heels caught in the front of her smock and tore it.

I saw the window that looked into her chest. It was nearly healed up, just a small puckered opening like an infected anus. But the pane itself was gone; the hole opened directly into her. It was black in there, and empty.

She snarled in my face, showing yellow, yellow teeth, and in a deep voice I didn't recognize rumbled, "You're too curious, Christopher. It wouldn't be a problem if you were curious like I am. But you aren't. You have a big mouth. You got Mr. Dove angry. Now he blames me. Now he might hurt me."

I clawed at her wrists. I clawed at her face. She squinted her eyes to protect them. She was enormous. There was no way for her to have gained such a vast amount of weight since I'd last seen her. But comically—or pathetically—she still carried her same old pocketbook . . . only her fatty arm was much too gigantic to get the strap around. The strap of the handbag was instead knotted around the sash of her black smock, so that she wore it like a pouch at her waist.

I was sure my face was black. The air prickled and fizzed as if it were full of fiery-colored swarming microorganisms. I couldn't even say her name to beg for mercy. I dug and pushed at her with my heels. I raked her face with my nails. I tried to pry my fingers under her lids to gouge at her eyes but she rumbled and pulled me away from the wall so she could slam me back into it. My left leg shot out straight in more of a spasm than an attack and struck her pocketbook. It came undone from the mile-long sash around her waist and dropped to the floor. It sounded heavy.

"Idiot!" she roared, and flung me down in contempt. I thudded more heavily than the pocketbook. Like a man resurfacing after nearly drowning, I sucked at the air in a pitiful whine. Tears filled my eyes and my fingers now clawed the floor. I felt myself teetering on a rail between consciousness and oblivion.

Gaby stooped to retrieve her fallen pocketbook. Through my tears I watched her; it was too horrifying to be humorous that she could not kneel down on the floor, but had to lean down past the obstacle of herself instead. The thick stubs of her fingers caught the strap, but as she drew the handbag toward her I saw her palmcomp drop out.

Her palmcomp. Was the red chip, Maria's chip, with the *Necronomicon* still inside it? No wonder Gaby was so frantic to protect the thing . . .

I got my knees under me. I reached to a chair to hoist myself up . . . held it to keep from falling back down. Those microorganisms still seethed, each one aflame. It was as though these bright flecks made up the air, made up everything, but only now could I see them.

The palmcomp had been rescued. Straightening up, leaving the handbag where it lay for the present, Gaby glared over at me again, clutching the palmcomp close to her chest. No . . . not just that. She was inserting it into herself. Into that orifice where once her tattooed heart could be seen through a clear window. She tucked her precious device with its priceless contents into her very body for safe keeping.

"You're blind," she snorted. "You might as well be dead, too."

"Gaby," I choked. I was able to stagger out of her lumbering path, now. But she was taking her time. I had seen how fast she could move.

"You're lucky, Christopher. You'll die now. You won't be here when all the doors open. It would make you insane. It would make a blind man like you tear his own eyes from their sockets . . . "

She extended those huge meaty hands in front of her. It felt like they had never left my throat. As she came, I smelled the stink of her insides from the gaping hole between the swaying planets of her breasts.

Circling away from her, I sobbed, "Gaby, please don't!"

"Death . . . "

"Gaby . . . "

"Death, sweet death for little Christopher," she whispered as if to soothe me.

I circled until I stood over her handbag, and then I dropped to my haunches to plunge my hand into it.

"Die!" Gabrielle bellowed, and it sounded like a dozen men had shouted the sound out of her one throat. An avalanche of corpse-blue meat in a blur of black. I tore from her handbag the small illegal handgun Gaby had taken to carrying after having been raped several times before I knew her.

The avalanche was nearly upon me. I thrust the gun up at her. I fell onto my back. I hesitated for several seconds. The hands followed me down. Her eyes looked so small, so lost in her face now. Her face hung over me for all time. Time had stood still. Time. Somehow, it was Gaby herself who had peeked at me in that hallway outside her apartment. On the tube platform. The future Gaby, having stepped just far enough through the veil between now and then.

It's all about time. Time and space.

The pistol was a gay yellow ceramic. It looked like a toy. It made a snapping sound when I pulled the trigger. I thought it was misfiring or clicking on dead cartridges, so I kept pulling the trigger again and again and again. I didn't realize I'd been hitting Gaby—I saw no blood against her black smock—until I saw the neat black hole that popped open on her forehead. Another one opened right beside it. They were like new eyes.

She lurched backwards like a dinosaur rearing up. She made a horrible liquid sound in her lungs, in her throat, a gurgle that seemed to go all through her, into her bloated limbs. She flopped back, one great arm smashing across my computer. It fell from the desk. She fell atop it. She did not rock comically. Instead, she seemed to spread amorphously across the floor, a gelatinous puddle.

"Gaby!" I cried out. But I kept the gun pointed at her. As agonized as I was, I would shoot her again—again and again—if she so much as raised her hand.

She didn't.

"Gaby," I sobbed. And then, without warning, I vomited. It sprayed my chest and her bare feet. I dropped to my knees and vomited again. But I didn't let go of that happy yellow gun.

At last, dry heaves like forcing broken slate through my throat. A pool between my hands. After my throttling, and the vomiting, I had nearly blacked out again, but another ghastly burbling made me look back to Gabrielle. Made me rocket to my feet and point the handgun again.

Just fluids moving from here to there. No real movement. No breathing. She was dead. I had killed her.

Did I really have to do it? Couldn't I have run away? Had I really been in mortal danger, or had I only been afraid of her? Repulsed by her?

"Gaby," I whispered, and crept nearer lightly as if afraid I might wake her from a nap. Gaby was a grouchy riser.

Her eyes were closed, thank God. A little blood had seeped at last from the holes in her head, but it was more like a thick gray sludge; brain matter, then? I saw another hole in one of her bare arms. More of that gray porridge. Not brain matter, then. I spotted a fourth hole in one of her half-bared breasts.

A new alarm filled me. Her palmcomp, inside her. What if a projectile had struck it? Ruined it? With the *Necronomicon* inside it?

Part of me asked, What does that matter, any more?

And another part of me knew I had to reach my hand into that puckered wound in her chest and pull the palmcomp out of her.

I knelt down beside her, again smelling her internal stink through that opening, so much uglier than the little holes I had made. I continued gripping my pistol in one hand, while I positioned the other over her. My stomach roiled as I bunched my fingers together, then guided them into her, trying my best not to touch the sides. But I had to, of course. As she had squeezed her impossible bulk through my threshold, so did I squeeze my hand through that fleshy ring. Her skin was cold against mine. When my hand was through, the lips of the wound closed again around my wrist, and I had an irrational fear that it would close and close until it had bitten my hand off.

It was even colder inside. Damp, slick. But I didn't have to probe deeply before I encountered the palmcomp. Anxiously I closed my hand around it. The lips of the wound had to stretch even further to permit my rude extraction, but I tore the device free without fear of hurting her.

On my feet again, I backed across the room. At last I lay the pistol down, so I could operate the small device in my hands.

It came on. I called up the contents of the disk currently inside it.

The opening screen came on. A few recipes Maria had stored on the disk, either before or after. And—the *Necronomicon.*

Another glance at her body. My computer pinned under her, my game interrupted. I would have to return to it again later on. If I dared to. I could use the palmcomp for that. But right now I had to get out of here. The neighbors might be calling the forcers even now. I was a murderer, you see. I had murdered my own lover.

I changed my clothes hastily, panting in between sobbing. I washed my hands vigorously, especially the one that had been inside her blackness. I tucked the sunshiny gun into my waistband, then slipped into a jacket. The palmcomp went into my jacket pocket. Without packing a suitcase, except to almost blindly fill a plastic shopping bag, without having any idea of where I was fleeing to, I left my apartment. Locked it behind me. Locked Gabrielle still inside.

PART TWO: SALEET

Pimp Mama T was sitting naked astride Slut Master E, when Bitchoney J burst into the room and stopped dead in the threshold, letting out his classic, much-imitated line, "God slap me dead!" The live audience roared. Slut Master E and Bitchoney J were played by two tremendously heavy black actors, OmarBlast M and MikeyMikey K, respectively. Slut Master E was Pimp Mama T's cousin, and Bitchoney J was her son. But in tonight's episode, Pimp Mama T was played by the diminutive white actress Jessika Heart Thatcher, who was probably younger than both male actors. In every episode of the sitcom *Pimp Mama T*, the title character was portrayed by a different actress (or actor, sometimes). Many famous movie actresses enjoyed guest-starring in the role, trying to outdo each other in their interpretations of the zany madam of a cheap Forma Street brothel. Her kooky family and friends were always played by the same cast, however..

While Pimp Mama T scrambled and stammered and tried to explain to her staring, gaping son what she and her cousin had been doing, clumsily putting his gigantic clothes on instead of her own, I slouched watching the wall-length VT with a warm Zub in my hand and an ache packed solid behind one eye and the bridge of my nose, brought on by too much Zub and not enough food.

It was a two room apartment. One largish room served as

livingroom/kitchenette, with a kitchen counter functioning as a partial partition between the two sections. The sofa folded out into a bed. The other room was a closet of a bathroom. The bathroom walls, floor and ceiling were scaled with aqua tiles, the grout between them a grimy black. The walls, floor and the ceiling of the livingroom/kitchenette were tiled a pale banana yellow. When I had woken that morning—my first morning in my new flat—I thought I was staring down at the floor instead of up at the ceiling, and I gripped my ratty blanket in my fists as vertigo yawned through me.

There was a small kitchen table beside my armchair. That was the extent of the furnishings, besides the aforementioned sleeper-sofa. The glossy top of the table was sunflower yellow. So were the refrigerator, sink and cooking/cleaning units in the kitchenette. Happy, sunshiny yellow. Like Gaby's gun.

On the table at my elbow rested three empty bottles of Zub and the messy paper that had wrapped a gyro eaten hours before. An open can of mixed nuts was the rest of my groceries; the fridge held more Zub and creamer for coffee. Oh yeah, I had a can of coffee, too.

Also on the table beside me was my palmcomp. Gaby's palmcomp, that is.

I hadn't wanted to bother with closing my account, so I had withdrawn all my money from the bank except for the bare minimum required, and had then printed it out on paper bills. I had bought a cheap printer and hooked it up to the palmcomp on the table.

I had called the candle shop at the Canberra Mall, and talked to one of Gabrielle's coworker/friends, Ebonee. First, though, I angled the palmcomp so she wouldn't see my apartment windows behind me. I didn't want her or anyone to know I was calling from a new flat. If she saw the windows, she might see just enough through the yellow translucent curtains to know that my apartment was in the subterranean section of Punktown. B Level. One street over from Morpha Street B.

"Hi, Ebonee," I said, smiling into my vidscreen at the lovely young black woman. She had short straight hair dyed metallic red. "Is Gaby there? I haven't seen her in days. I think she's avoiding me . . . "

"Aw, honey, didn't you know? Aw, Topher . . . Gabe quit her job. She said she was moving out of her flat, too. Maybe even out of Punktown altogether. You mean she didn't even tell you none of this?"

"No," I said, trying to look hurt. I *was* hurt; I imagined I looked quite tragic. "My God . . . no, she didn't say anything! *Why*? Did she tell you?"

"No, Topher. But she's been acting real strange. Shaved off her hair. Missed a lot of work. Gaining a lot of weight . . . I hate to say it . . . "

"She's been avoiding me totally."

"I think she's taking too many drugs, Topher. I'm real sorry to tell you this."

"Wow. Yeah . . . well, thanks. I'm glad somebody told me. If you do hear from her, or if the other girls do, will you call me?"

"Sure. And you do the same, all right?"

"I will. Thanks again, Ebonee."

I felt repulsed with myself when I switched the vidphone feature off. But I had to make it look like I hadn't seen Gaby. That she couldn't be found at my apartment. That I hadn't murdered her.

I put it off for as long as I could, stalled, paced, at last called my boss.

"Where have you been, Christopher?" she huffed. "Half the day is over and you're just calling in now?"

"I have a personal emergency, Julie . . . I'm very sorry . . . "

"Well, are you coming in?"

"I can't, I'm afraid. I don't know . . . I don't know when I can. I was hoping I could take a leave of absence, or something . . . "

"What? What kind of emergency is this?"

"A family thing."

"Look," she sighed, "you'll have to call Diane and explain this to her, if you want a leave of absence. But she isn't going to be happy, unless you can explain your situation a little better than that."

Diane was her boss, the office manager.

"Yeah, all right . . . I'll do that. But I am sorry, Julie, really . . . "

"All right," she sighed again irritably, and cut off the connection.

I stalled, paced. I never called Diane the office manager. I went out and bought Zub and my gyro and nuts (and coffee) instead. And now, as evening fell, and the lights beneath Punktown dimmed appropriately, I sat and watched mindless comedy on VT to deaden myself. Distract myself from the liquid vortex that had once been my brain.

During my shopping trip (when I'd also picked up the printer), I had bought a hair styling kit and a tube of hair accelerator. After I ate and before *Pimp Mama T*, I buzzed all my hair down to just a dark stubble. Then, I carefully painted the hair accelerator cream on my chin, over my upper lip, with the little brush in the cap. Rubbing my chin now, already I could feel the whiskers broken through the skin. By morning I'd have a full mustache and goatee. I had made sure to make my vidcalls *before* I changed my appearance.

Tomorrow, a few more errands. I couldn't envision a long-term plan. One errand at a time. I had to get rid of the yellow gun. I found I had emptied it into Gaby, anyway. Then, I wanted to buy a new gun. I'd discreetly ask around on the street. It would still get me in trouble if caught, but at least it wouldn't be the gun that killed Gabrielle. Then I thought maybe I'd get some tattoos, to make my appearance all the more different. I could always have them removed in the future. If I had a future.

I didn't know much about guns. I had fired a friend's pellet gun in an alley with him, but never a real gun. Real guns had always frightened me. Now, other things frightened me more. I'd do some research on the net. Read up. First thing in the morning, before I went shopping for one. I might want several, now that I thought of it.

I glanced at the palmcomp now. I was tempted to check that game again. I was afraid to check that game again. Had I only imagined that last bit? The Choom prosty? Misinterpreted her, misheard her words?

Had the man who'd called me for help done so just to set me up? Had he tricked me into playing the game, knowing that it contained a personal connection to me? No . . . that was ludicrous. Paranoia was fine, as long as it was realistic paranoia. But what had happened, then? Had I only been conversing with a computer construct, or had some other person or being been speaking through her, acting through the game?

How would anybody but me know that I had ever met with that girl?

Her apartment was in the same building above Dove Books. Had Mr. Dove seen me talk to the girl, go upstairs with her?

Mr. Dove had not been happy with Gaby or me. We both talked too loudly.

Mr. Dove. Mr. Dove. Mr. Dove.

* * *

Morning came, the constellations of artificial suns gradually dawned in the concrete sky, and I lay on the sagging but hard mattress of the sleeper-sofa staring up at the pastel yellow ceiling tiles. Idly, I started trying to count them, by counting the tiles along one edge of the ceiling, then by counting those along another edge, and I would multiply the two numbers, but the tiles were too small and some were fallen away here and there and I gave up on the exercise. Also, the walls were not square, which complicated things. On either side of the large single room there were two alcove areas, facing each other, and each had one window in it.

Sitting up sharply in bed, I went from counting the tiles in the ceiling to counting the corners of the room.

Because of the two alcoves, the livingroom/kitchen had eight corners. Eight corners like the bedroom of my old flat. Eight corners for eight of Gaby's perfumed candles.

Synchronicity, I thought. Or maybe it wasn't some mysterious cosmic design; I imagined a lot of rooms had eight corners if you bothered to notice. I just never noticed these things, as I never noticed the city around me much beyond what was in front of my nose.

I inspected my new goatee and mustache, actually had to trim them a bit with scissors from the styling kit. Then I showered (hating for my bare feet to touch the stained, aqua bathtub) and dressed in my most casual clothing (I hadn't even bothered to take with me any of the suits I wore to the office). Gray t-shirt, black jeans. Onto my newly shaven head I pulled a gray visored cap. I would wear dark glasses. I tucked the small yellow pistol into the back of my waistband and let my untucked baggy t-shirt hang over its protruding grip.

Errands to give me some sense of purpose. Errands to take my mind off the fact that I had murdered my insane, perhaps mutated former girlfriend, and sent my entire life whooshing into oblivion. First errand: coffee. I'd buy a better one somewhere than I could make here.

I found a fairly good large hazelnut with cream and sugar at a little stand that also sold doughnuts and hotdogs and native deep-fried dilkies, but I had no stomach for food. I had less luck buying a gun that day. The first man I asked recoiled a bit from me and said, "What do you take me for, Mr. Enforcer?"

"I'm not a forcer," I assured him, but he snorted and walked away.

I wandered more or less aimlessly, sipping my coffee, hoping to find a tattoo parlor. At the tube platform I sat for a few minutes and watched people funnel into or out of the sleek bullet-faced machines as they glided in for a stop. I felt like I was ridiculously disguised, as if I wore a Halloween costume, but had to remind myself that I actually looked quite natural. Other people wore shades underground, as well. A man in a dark business suit passed close by my elbow and I flinched. For a moment, I thought it might be Mr. Dove, whose shop was just down the street, but when I looked up at the man as he waited to pile into the tube he had a human head. He looked as numbly discontented as I must have looked to others when boarding the tube for work.

I had forgotten my other errands. Tried to pick them like pebbles out of the bottom of a muddy pool. Yes . . . the gun causing my lower back discomfort. I had to dispose of it. I found a men's room adjacent to the tube platform, and went into it. I ignored the two men in one of the stalls and what one was doing to the other (they ignored me, as well). I urinated, waiting for a third man to leave, then moved to the sinks. Looking in the mirror, and making certain the two in the stall couldn't see me at this angle, I quickly slipped out the gun, wrapped it in some paper towels, and dropped it into the trash. There wasn't much I could do or at least bothered to do about fingerprints or skin cells left on the grip. I was mostly just going through the motions of self preservation. For the most part, I assumed my recent actions would destroy me, that it was only a matter of how long it would take before I was caught.

Back on the street, the high ceiling reflecting the roar of traffic confined in these vaults. Traffic from above moving below, traffic from below moving above. Great ramps communicated between the two worlds, though there were none within immediate view of Morpha Street.

A billboard screen on the flank of one building showed a gigantic Jessika Heart Thatcher being interviewed, asked how she had enjoyed guest-starring on *Pimp Mama T*. She giggled that she'd been shy about doing her nude sex scenes with OmarBlast M, but he was quite the gentleman about it. But OmarBlast leaned into view and said it was necessary for Jessika to be on top so he wouldn't crush her. They both laughed. The interviewer asked if they had really had sex, as it had appeared, or if they had faked it (as some guest stars did). Jessika said she didn't believe in lying to the audience and OmarBlast chuckled deeply and patted her knee, saying, "Me either, Jess."

I wandered on. I drifted past a robot vendor selling coffee and decided maybe I'd get a fresh one on the way back. I wandered past the Japanese video store. Outside it, on the sidewalk, a holographic samurai with an insect-like robotic head—an advertisement for a new release—spun his sword around him in vicious arcs, as if to slash at the passing pedestrians, most of whom ignored him and walked right through his ghostly blade. A little Choom boy pretended to duel with him. I smiled at the child and walked on, and then realized where I was unconsciously wandering to.

There it was, the purple brick building. Not missing, as on the vidgame. On the ground floor: Dove Books.

Several young girls loitered outside the front steps, either nude or mostly so. One girl had tattoos that glowed like neon twined around her bare limbs, and her breasts were outlined with luminous red hearts. I didn't see my little friend . . . but I recognized one of the girls from my previous visit to that building, and I approached her. As I did so, I stole peeks at the lower windows of the building through my tinted lenses, half expecting to see a fishy gray face peering out at me, but the windows had all been adjusted to a full tint of opaque blackness.

"Hey, hey, lovey," this girl said as I approached her, stepping forward to meet me half-way.

"Hi," I said. "Hey, I'm looking for your friend . . . this girl with dark purple hair? Long hair? Choom girl? She had an Asian thing done to her eyes? A star tattoo on her chest?"

"I have a star tattoo on my chest," one of the other girls announced proudly, opening her shirt to show me. It was indeed the same design my girl had worn for protection, applied by one of the other girls. Rosa, my girl had said the tattoo artist's name was. Sort of a witch, but a prosty, too.

"You're looking for Jelena," replied my girl's friend. "She's gone—sorry."

"Gone? Was she . . . sick?" I thought she meant she had died. I remembered how she had looked in the game.

"He's afraid he caught something from her!" the other prosty with the star snickered.

"No, she just quit," laughed Jelena's friend. "She just couldn't take the life anymore, y'know?"

"Yeah . . . it's tough," said the star girl. "This ain't no *Pimp Mama T*."

Her comment made me embarrassed for having rented Jelena's services the last time. I stuttered, "Well, okay . . . I'm glad she got out of the life, then . . . "

"She was having weird dreams," said the star girl. "So do I. I think it's this life. It gets to you."

I nodded sympathetically, then I noticed something about this prosty. A bump on her head, protruding through her sleek black hair.

"What . . . what's that?" I asked, pointing.

Self consciously she clapped her hand over it. But before she did so, I noticed that the lump was pointed and distinct. It looked raw and pink, and as if it had begun to peel.

"It's nothing!" she snapped defensively. "Don't worry about it. I'm clean. Ric makes us all get check-ups, once a month. We're all clean."

"I'm sorry," I muttered, backing away.

"Where you going?" cooed Jelena's friend. "Jelena's not the only fish in the sea, honey."

I glanced at the black-tinted windows of Dove's Books. I wasn't ready to go in there today . . . but I knew that I must, as if it were my destiny, preordained, part of some invisible scheme of things. Another errand . . . but not for today.

"I'm sorry," I repeated to the prosties, and turned and headed back the way I had come.

* * *

I spent the rest of the afternoon reading about guns on the palmcomp, only leaving my flat again to buy another sandwich and a few snacks to keep in the apartment. Based on what I read, and what guns I had used in vidgames, I thought I had an idea of what I might seek out on the street, depending of course on what was available.

Vidgames. Dare I try that game again? It was beginning to grow dimmer outside with the approach of artificial night. It might be noon upground for all I could tell, though I knew it wasn't. For some reason, I wanted to look at that game now, quickly, before it got dark out, if I was going to look at it at all.

It started out in the apartment again. I remembered the man's name was Marrk Argent. Greeting me in his flat was Jessika Heart Thatcher and Angelah Lee Henderson, playing his room mates. I was tempted to check out Argent's sex program as it linked from *Sweet Revenge* (though I didn't have a VR set for the full effect)—I much preferred the cute Jessika to the plastic blond Angelah—but I was too unsettled to pursue it. Again I selected my weapons (a few more this time around), again I took to the streets. I almost trotted to the tube station.

Belowground, I passed the building that contained my new flat, and paused to gaze up at its windows, as if I were inside that building even now staring at the game on my stolen palmcomp. The two mes contemplating each other in an infinite Escher loop . . . Moebius strip.

Down the street, around the corner: Morpha Street B. I wanted 14-B . . .

Would the building be there this time?

It wasn't. That alley, instead. I gripped the double handles of a fully auto assault rifle loaded with flesh-dissolving plasma rounds in a fifty shot banana clip. If that purple-haired prosty, with her antler-like growths, stepped out of the alley I thought I was more likely to shoot her on sight than question her again. I tried to control my fear. I must question her. Her name was Jelena . . .

There were indeed several girls in the alley, though they didn't seem to correspond with the pimp Ric's girls I had seen in my actual visits. They didn't have the red and blue painted lips that seemed to be Ric's brand. When I tried to converse with them, they spoke in the sleep-walker's voice of computer constructs, not programmed for much interaction. When they began to repeat themselves I gave up on them.

So—had I hallucinated Jelena into the game, after all?

I was about to leave the program—with a good deal of relief, despite my failure—when I noticed a design spray-painted on the tiled alley wall I hadn't noticed before. It was quite large, done in a softly luminous purple paint, and it was almost a cross between a spider web, a mathematical equation, and a map or blueprint. Very intricate. Others had since spray-painted over parts of it.

"What's this mean?" I asked a Tikkihotto prosty, gesturing at the design with my gun barrel.

"Want some sugar, baby boy?" the prosty droned.

I exited the program.

* * *

The gun dealer's name was Rabal, and he was a Kalian. I had been sent to him by a gang of twelve-year olds I questioned in the street about where to buy guns (I figured they might know, since a couple of them openly wore pistols in holsters).

The boys directed me to the Subtown Library a few blocks from Morpha Street B, on Obsidian Street B. If Rabal wasn't in his van, in a vacant lot behind the library, he might be inside as he frequently was, in the Kalian Reading Room. I was instructed to look for a gold hovervan or a "fat Kalian in red pajamas". I gave the boys a ten munit note to split. "Zat all?" one boy barked in what I hoped was mock indignity, slapping his hand to his holstered handgun.

I joked to change the subject. "You buy that from Rabal? Is his stuff good quality?"

"It'll kill," he said with a shrug.

I walked the several blocks to the subterranean version of Obsidian Street. The Subtown Library was a smallish building of only three stories, its hide fashioned from blocks of pale greenish marble with glittery veins of gold. It rested in a largely Kalian neighborhood; I could tell not only by the numbers of Kalians who bustled around me, but the smells of their food (I loved Kalian food) and the sounds of their music coming from open windows and passing cars (I liked that, too). No wonder the library had allocated some space for a Kalian Reading Room. It was very hot, muggy in this section of subtown, and I didn't know whether that indicated faulty climate control or if the climate had been adjusted here more to the taste of the Kalian majority.

Nearly all of the Kalians I saw—male and female—wore turbans, which might be silken or rough, wrapped close to the head or piled high into cones or thickly coiled into bulging globes. These were always blue. Anything from powder blue to deep indigo, but blue. Their clothing varied from business suits to loose pajama-like affairs to robes (always long-sleeved robes on the women I saw), and metallic gold appeared to be the preferred color; even suits of red or green silk tended to be heavily embroidered with gold thread. Between their dress and their physical appearance, they were a strikingly handsome race. Their skin was a glossy gray (ranging from light to charcoal), their lips tending to be very full, their eyes slanted in an oriental fold. The eyes themselves had no whites, were entirely black like volcanic glass.

I skirted around the library to the fenced-off vacant lot in the back; stalks of a brittle, albino weed grew from cracks in the surface. There were a few vehicles parked here and there, though half of these were stripped skeletons. I thought I heard a baby crying from one of these shells; I half-started toward it, thinking an infant had been abandoned, but I heard a shushing woman's voice, so instead I walked toward a gold-colored hovervan.

After rapping on its sliding door and waiting a minute or two, I decided to check inside the library instead.

It was no cooler inside the library. As with all the buildings belowground, I felt I was entering a building inside the belly of a much vaster building. I supposed that sensation would go away as I became more acclimated. I removed my dark glasses.

The Kalian Reading Room wasn't very large; four longish tables in the center, and a small desk at the end of each aisle of books. The shadowy-musty smell of old books in here reminded me of Mr. Dove's place, a smell I had once loved but which now had an unpleasant connotation. There were computers at each of the tables and desks. I felt better that there were two other nonKalians in here as well, though these two looked like college students and I looked like a guy who wanted to buy guns.

Picking out a book at random (it was a child's picture book of the home world, I found), I stood at the mouth of an aisle, cracked the volume and over the top of it scanned the Kalians around me. One man read a Kalian newspaper. Two others played a kind of game like dominoes, but using thin yellow sticks. With grim calculation they were forming some sort of weird geometric pattern between them, as if they were mapping out the destiny of the universe rather than playing a game.

But the Kalian who quickly attracted my gaze was a woman seated alone at the end of one of the central tables. What seized me was the fact that she wore no turban.

Kalian hair is black as their eyes. Hers was long, falling below her shoulder blades, very thick and wavy, parted in the center. It was like a dark hood and cape in itself. It framed a high, smooth forehead. Her gray skin was as pale and colorless as ash.

Traditionally, I knew, Kalian women were not permitted to bare their hair in public. I thought I remembered hearing that women had been stoned to death for this, had even had acid thrown in their faces. A woman's hair was for the eyes of her husband only, because it was the alluring, tempting weave of lust and evil personified.

So, we had a modern girl amongst us. I wondered if the men at the other tables peeked at her with murderous scorn, or secret hunger. Both, I was sure.

She was very, very pretty. She had a layer of youthful baby fat I found appealing; I guessed her to be in her late teens to early twenties. Her lips were compressed into a subtle unconscious smile as she perused a massive book open before her. The lips were very full, the bow-shaped upper lip perhaps slightly fuller than the lower, and these were a darker gray than the flesh of her soft face. Those almond-shaped, glistening black eyes. Though her black eyebrows were not excessively heavy, they met into one unbroken line over the bridge of her nose, putting me in mind for a moment of the ancient Earth artist Frida Kahlo. Traditionally, Kalian men and women shaved their brows at this mid point to separate them. So, we had another perhaps defiant gesture.

But there was one very obvious brand of conformity upon her. She had the ritual scarring that every Kalian woman simply must have, and she had received hers upon the day she began her first period, as they all did. These scars varied, I believed, very little, at least to my untrained eye. They were on the face only. Three lines began just above the central point of her eyebrow and fanned out across her forehead into a three-pronged fork. They almost looked like an exaggeration of wrinkles of intensity or concentration.

In addition, she had a scar on either cheek. These were V's resting on their sides, a > and a <, pointing inward toward the nostrils, so that the top branch of each design curved along the cheek bone, the bottom branch running down to the edge of the jaw.

These scars were squiggly, and raised like keloids. They were as dark as her lips but had a kind of silvery sheen to them, too. I understood that when a Kalian girl first menstruated, her soiled clothing was burnt, and then the ashes were rubbed into the wounds that were carved into her face, so as to form the particular look of the healed scars.

The lovely young woman's markings were both horribly disfiguring, a kind of stamp of contempt upon her, but at the same time added oddly to her beauty.

She wore a black t-shirt. Her arms were bare, unthinkably: pale gray and soft-looking. The tight shirt made evident the heavy thrust of her breasts. I saw a tease of midriff, then her lower body was wrapped in a long, metallic gold skirt. Her feet were bare.

When I looked up from her toes to her eyes, I saw they were upon me. There were no whites, irises or pupils for me to know for sure that they pointed my way, but I could *feel* them on me. Maybe she had felt mine on her.

Awkwardly, I smiled at her.

I thought I saw her lips, already subtly smiling, stretch a bit more at the corners.

Before I understood what I was doing, I started toward her. Then I realized that I meant to ask her where I might find a man named Rabal. She might know of his reputation, and be aghast at the mention of his name, but it was the only excuse I could think of in an instant.

Before I reached her table, a hand lightly caught me by the elbow. I turned to see that a shortish, plump Kalian male in red satin pajamas had taken my arm. He grinned at me, his teeth bright in his slate-colored face, and whispered, "Hi, friend . . . hey, you mustn't talk to any girls around here, buddy. Not allowed. I mean to say, *they* are not allowed. I don't mean to tell you what *you* should do, my chum . . . I only don't want you to anger some jealous husband."

I recalled, then, that Kalian women were not permitted to speak outside the home. Even, sometimes, within it. The female voice was "lewd".

"Anyway," the man went on, "she's trouble, that one. Look at her; a disgrace. It's being on another world; in her homeland, it would never be tolerated. No offense to your people, sir." Grin.

"You're Rabal."

"Yes."

"Did someone say I was coming?"

"Someone told me you were knocking on my van. Should we go there, now? I'm done here for today. I'm reading the great Kalian novel, *Qubutstu*. It's in fifty-two volumes. I'm up to book thirty-seven now!"

"How is it so far?"

"A little slow. But the love interest was just introduced. Shall we go, friend?"

I glanced at the girl, hoping she'd still be watching me. She wasn't. She pored over her book again.

"All right," I muttered, and though I had come to find this man, I was disappointed at following him from the library.

* * *

When I stepped up into Rabal's van and he slid its door back into place, I saw a Kalian woman seated at a small table reading prayers from a computer monitor with a split screen. The other half of the screen showed her a loop of various security camera angles of the parking lot in which the van rested. She must have called Rabal in the library to let him know I'd been to the van earlier. She looked up at me, gave me a shy smile, and returned to her prayer reading. If she were ever to speak one word of those prayers aloud in her lewd voice her husband was allowed to execute her on the spot. She wore her hair cocooned inside a blue turban.

There was a kitchenette smaller even than mine, and a bed in the far back, I assumed, hidden by a curtain richly embroidered with metallic thread. Its design showed a kind of weirdly-spired palace. A row of people walked into its front door, hunched and using canes. Out the palace's back door filed a procession of small children. Rabal saw me admiring it.

"That is the demon-god, Ugghiutu," he explained proudly. "Ugghiutu takes many forms, pal, and often appears as a house or even masquerades as a temple to himself, to lure inside unwary souls so as to test them. Sacrifices to him were sent into such structures."

"But what's happening here?"

"This is the endless cycle of life, death, and renewal, my good friend. Ugghiutu feeds on life to create new life."

"God slap me dead," I said to myself.

"Hm?"

"Nothing." I turned to him. "Can I see what you have?" I was willing to bet I'd passed through a scan on the way in, so he knew I wasn't carrying a weapon—as a forcer or a robber—already.

Rabal stooped to slide aside a panel in the floor, then rose puffing from the mild effort. At my feet were row on row of guns large and small, dark and bright and colored. Before I could settle my eyes on any one of them, he slid aside another panel in the wall opposite the door, revealing another impressive, museum-like display. A library of weapons.

There were replica old Earth guns; everything from flintlocks to Thompsons, but which very well might fire ray bolts instead of musket balls and bullets. There were Kalian and Tikkihotto weapons.

Assault rifles . . . I enjoyed using them in games, but knew they were too big to be practical for my needs. Shotguns, also a satisfying weapon in virtual battle, posed the same problem—but ah! I pointed to a sawed-off version. "Can I handle that?"

Rabal passed me the gun. It was heavier than I would have expected, metal rather than plastic or ceramic like the pistol I'd disposed of. A pump-action, with a pistol grip in place of a full stock and a strap at the end of the grip. Out of politeness, I made sure not to point its barrel toward Mr. or Mrs. Rabal.

"For this baby, amigo, I can give you lead shot or crystal shot." He tapped the shotgun's truncated barrel with a finger.

"What does crystal shot do?"

"A lead ball makes a big hole, but a hole can be sealed. Crystal shot makes a hole but then shatters against bone; it turns to shrapnel, and sends sharp dust all through the tissues, into the blood, where it will be carried to the heart." He spread his hands demonstratively, grinning all the while.

I shrugged. "I'll take a box of both."

"You want a smaller piece, too, sir? A nice handy handgun?"

"You must have read my mind, mon ami," I replied dryly.

"Ray blaster or projectile shooter?"

"Um, projectile, I guess."

He waved an arm at the floor display. I pointed at a smallish automatic with mean lines and a nonreflective matte black finish. He retrieved it and handed it to me.

"A Thor .86 . . . it's a small version of the Thor .93. A beautiful baby, huh? Thirty bullets in a staggered clip, or sixty plasma capsules."

I hefted it. Ceramic, like Gaby's gun, but still it was heavier. The black color alone made it seem heavier. I liked it well enough, I supposed. It looked efficient, all business. "Can I have a box of bullets, and a box of plasma?"

"What kind of plasma?" He pulled open a drawer from the wall, touched cartons with a finger. "Usually plasma is color coded. Red eats a fairly small, limited hole before it stops dissolving. Blue is stronger but only eats organic surfaces, like flesh, though the projectile will penetrate cloth to get to the flesh. Green will eat anything . . . green can eat through a wall, or a car, before it burns out. With a couple of green caps, maybe even one good hit on a small body, it will eat the whole corpse. No body left. Very handy, good buddy."

"Very expensive, too, huh? What if I miss and hit a bystander? A bullet and they might have a chance. Green plasma and they're eaten alive."

Rabal shrugged. "Hey, you hit a bystander either way, it's bad news. Don't shoot near bystanders, if you're worried, my friend."

I straightened. "I'll take a box of the green plasma."

* * *

Rabal gave me a big plastic shopping bag which advertized a woman's clothing store, in which to carry the shotgun and ammo home. I doubted he let his silent wife shop there. The handgun went into my waistband, unloaded. (I had asked him to show me how to load it, and he had explained it, but apologized that he couldn't allow me to actually load any weapons inside his miniature gun store). I was terrified of being detained by a forcer on the walk home, but despite my fears, I stopped again inside the Subtown Library. The Kalian Reading Room.

As I had fatalistically expected, the exotic gray-skinned girl was gone. Idly I wondered what she'd been reading.

Before I left, I saw that those two men still played their game with yellow sticks. The web-like pattern between them had now covered almost three quarters of the long table. I wondered how far it would spread before they were finished.

* * *

The weather channel said it was raining, upground. It seemed like another lifetime since I'd been upground.

I stayed in all day, as if it were raining down here, too. I snacked on junk food. I watched VT. I paced. I made coffee. I played with my new guns. The green plasma scared me even to look at the gel capsules ranked inside their box, so I loaded the handgun with solid bullets.

I sat and read from the *Necronomicon*.

Could I really believe that Gaby had opened some inter-dimensional portal, just by lighting some candles and playing a recorded chant? The Coleopteroids, that unpleasant beetle-like race, had to ride in great black train-like machines around and around upon train-like tracks laid out in odd geometric patterns in order for them to travel to our dimension from theirs. I couldn't think of an extra-dimensional race that could enter into ours without use of some sort of technology. But did that mean it was impossible?

After she had performed the ritual, Gaby had realized that the "ascending mode" had been said twice—once by her, and once by the recording of Maria—but the "descending mode" had only been said once. When I'd suggested she play the descending mode again, she'd said it was, "Too late." Assuming some door truly could be opened in this way, as she—and Mr. Dove—believed, would it hurt for me to play the recording of Maria reciting the descending mode for a second time, anyway? Or, instead of closing the portal, might that just make matters worse? Ultimately, I didn't dare play any more of Maria's recordings until I knew more.

Aside from the spells themselves, some of which required the prerequisite bizarre ingredients and occasional sacrifice, and which generally consisted of a lot of unpronounceable gibberish, the book read like a mythology written under the influence of hallucinogens. Cosmic battles between monster-gods. And the defeated race of monsters scratching in their sleep at the barrier that separated them from us. Influencing our dreams with their dreams.

As skeptical as I was, I dared not say the names of the beings out loud; I tried not even to say them in my head. I made my eye skim over them. I thought of them simply as the Others. Even their names, Dove had said, were incantations.

Yes. I admitted to myself once and for all that I did believe. Even if one opposes a faith, sometimes, one must first have faith in it. A Satanist is a Christian inverted. I had been converted. A fresh acolyte. How else could I explain Gaby's tricks with time and space, the horrible change in her?

Gaby. Did she still lie, even now, on the floor of my upground apartment?

If this book really could open doorways to other worlds, to let in the Others or at least to let in a greater degree of their influence, then no wonder the book was so difficult to obtain. I imagined that it had been repressed, sought out and destroyed, for generations. It should be. And so should those other books at Mr. Dove's shop . . .

What did he, a "priest" as Gaby had called him, intend to do with the *Necronomicon* himself?

Someone should suppress him. Get a hold of the copy Gaby had made for him and destroy it.

I remembered the two books he had mentioned to me which took some of the more mathematical ideas of the *Necronomicon* further, focused and improved upon those approaches. One by a Choom author, one by a Tikkihotto. Those sounded like especially dangerous books that should be sought out and destroyed, as well.

Gaby still lay on the floor of my apartment. A victim of my past life. I couldn't exorcize the image from my mind.

I switched off the *Necromomicon*, and used my computer to call the candle store at the Canberra Mall. I spoke to Ebonee. Any word yet on Gaby?

I expected, by now, that I'd been found out. I had murdered Gaby. Ebonee would be horrified. She'd curse me, try to have my call traced (though I used a blocking feature).

She only smiled sympathetically. No . . . no . . . still no word from Gabrielle, she apologized. But what had I done to my hair? She almost hadn't recognized me.

Oops.

To hell with my new look. I called my boss, Julie.

"Christopher," she fumed, "you said you were going to call Diane! You never did! She won't give you a leave of absence now, you know . . . whatever your personal emergency was, you should have talked to her before it was too late!"

"I know," I stammered. "Um . . . I realize I'm terminated. But I just wanted to call to apologize to you. To say I'm sorry about all this. You can just, uh, transfer my last check to my bank account . . . "

Julie did not say, "My God, Christopher, why are you calling me? You're a murderer! They're looking for you!"

No one was looking for me. No one was looking for Gabrielle, I realized. Poor, forgotten Gabrielle. Missed and mourned only by her murderer.

Dare I return to my old apartment, then? My old life? Put all this furtive, fugitive dung behind me?

I couldn't. Like Gaby, I had been changed somehow. Not just in appearance. It was both terrifying, and oddly exhilarating. I hated to admit it to myself, but there was a kind of freedom in walking away from my ant-like past self . . . a kind of liberation in self-destruction.

But more than that, I felt I should try to do something to avenge Gabrielle. To protect other foolish people like her and Maria. To protect everybody. It would be easy enough, wouldn't it? No great heroic sacrifice. I wouldn't have to battle cosmic monster-gods. Just burn a couple of books. Maybe, at most, one book store.

No, I wouldn't return to my old life. Not just yet. But if Gaby's death hadn't been discovered yet, perhaps it never would be. If I handled it correctly. As much as I dreaded it, I had to return to my old apartment and take care of this before my next rent came due, and the landlord let himself inside.

So I turned off the palmcomp right then and there, extracted the clip of ammo from my gun, removed a few solid bullets from that, and inserted three green plasma capsules instead.

* * *

It was evening by the time I arrived upground; the rain continued to smash to the streets. In the tube station where I disembarked there was a row of shops not yet closed, and in one of them I purchased a poncho-style purple rain slicker with a hood, which would protect me from the elements and help obscure my face. Purple was the big fad color lately, I noticed, so I was nondescript.

Entering my apartment building, I felt as jumpy as if I were on a mission to assassinate a new victim. Don't they say that murderers are compelled to revisit the scenes of their crimes?

This was the exhilarating freedom I mentioned before? To be going to view the corpse of my former lover, whom I had killed?

I thought of the gun seller Rabal's tapestry, showing people consumed by the chameleon-like yin/yang devil/god, master of life/death Ugghiutu . . . his worshipers killed and ground up and digested and then shat back into a new existence. Yeah, that was me. From one hell reborn into another.

I feared confronting a neighbor who might know me, or even the landlord. Forcers, detectives, outside my apartment door in the middle of their investigation. But I met no one in my hallway. My hand trembled as I tapped out my password on the keypad. Like an impostor of my former self, I got the password wrong, had to try it again. The door opened inward. It opened half-way, at least, then was blocked.

A locomotive of stench struck me dead on, nearly flattening me.

It was dark in the apartment, but I plunged into it and shut the door hurriedly before more of the stench escaped. Before someone happened along. But a panic washed over me, worse than the reek, to be closed in the darkness with Gabrielle, and I clawed at a wall switch to turn on the overhead lights.

Oh, if only I hadn't.

Bodies can bloat with decomposition, fill balloon-like with the gases of corruption. But could such a phenomenon account for *this*?

The door had been blocked by Gabrielle's body. But Gabrielle had fallen more toward the center of the livingroom. In death, she had spread out from that center. She had reached all the walls, and her belly was pressed flat against the ceiling, and I wondered if she had even bulged through the bedroom doorway.

The ceiling lights shone through the purple-black translucent flesh of her abdomen, making her seem to glow from the inside. And the light passed directly through the crater of a hole where her chest window had once been.

Through silhouetted nests of veins I could see organs inside her, seeming to float in an aquarium of cloudy liquid. I couldn't distinguish her swollen limbs from her torso, except I thought I recognized an immense, distorted foot squashed up against one of the walls.

That smell . . .

I clamped a hand over my nose and mouth, fought back a rattling gag. With my free hand I fumbled the Thor out of my waistband. I had to burn this blasphemy, burn the witch, burn it from my sight before I lost my nerve and my mind . . .

There was a muffled sloshing sound. A kind of gurgle like a stopped drain might make. And then I saw one of the murky organs move inside Gabrielle. At first I thought it was merely drifting, but I realized it had paddled itself along, trailing jellyfish-like arms of various lengths and thicknesses.

It wasn't an organ.

I lifted and pointed and fired the Thor at Gabrielle's belly. At the thing swimming inside her.

Just a sound like a door slamming, from the gun. The pellet pierced her. The entrance hole was so small that only a trickle of clear fluid ran out, down the glossy stretched skin. But the smell that was released was like a waterfall crashing over me, and I dropped to my knees and vomited.

Above me, I vaguely saw the light inside Gabrielle turn greenish, and fluttery.

A sizzling sound. A bubbling. Now I looked up and saw the green inferno boiling inside the blackish balloon. I scrambled to my feet and pressed myself back against the wall as the fire spread to the skin of the balloon and holes began to widen and a flood gushed free. It lapped around my feet, my ankles. I quickly slid along the wall and sprang up onto a small chest of drawers, kicking aside the table lamp there. I didn't want the fluid—or the fire that suffused it—to touch me.

The great bulk began to recede from me, to hollow itself out. I aimed a bit further back and fired a second plasma round. More green fire spread. A sort of cave was being tunneled back through the corpse. It was not a cave I wanted to explore. I saw organs drop to the floor in the rush of fluid, melting into red-black puddles. I saw no trace of the swimming thing I had glimpsed vaguely through her skin.

I fired a third shot. My last gel cap in the gun.

The flood on the floor began to recede, as well, replaced by a curling, churning fog . . . perhaps of evaporation. The ebbing tide left the carpet eaten and sodden. That would come out of my security deposit, I thought madly. I started to laugh, vomited again instead, falling from the chest. My hands pressed flat to the floor and I expected plasma traces to corrode their palms but the fire was short-lived and already spent here, the last traces of it chasing the hulk as it attempted to flee to the bedroom.

Lifting my one-ton head, I saw the last of Gabrielle. Her own head, larger than my body, compressed into an hour-glass shape, half of it in the livingroom and half in the bedroom. Thank God there was enough life left in the last gel cap to consume it. Thank Ugghiutu for his greedy consumption . . .

She was gone.

I retrieved my dropped gun and regained my footing, though I staggered forward several steps. The vapor around my feet was dispersing, fading away like a ghost. The green fire had even eaten the stench. Most of that was gone, as well.

Gun held before me, I explored my apartment, as if I feared that the swimming thing had somehow escaped her, taken refuge in the bathtub, or under my bed. I didn't find it. It was a relief.

I thought of the ritual we had playfully performed; to conjure a demon to do our bidding. Had she succeeded, after all? But done *its* bidding, instead? I despaired to think of Gabrielle as completely controlled, possessed, by that thing. Perversely, I preferred to think that she had mostly chosen to give herself over to this path. As shameful as the feeling was, I preferred to believe I had killed a person who had become evil, than a primarily innocent victim trapped within herself. That, then, would be like shooting through a baby in order to kill its kidnapper.

I blotted out that possibility as if slamming and bolting an iron door. Gaby had invited their influence, I told myself, melded with it willingly. The doorway she had opened was within herself. Perhaps literally. And their power had suffused and seduced her. These forces, these entities, had cultivated her own potential for evil. But listen to me. Evil. Demons. They were not Judeo-Christian demons. And evil is subjective. No more terrible demon ever existed than a man looming over a pig in a slaughterhouse.

I returned from my inspection of the rest of my flat. Except for stains on the floor and to a lesser extent the walls and ceiling, the apartment was restored. A tomb containing my former life.

Since I was here, I decided to take some more things back to my new apartment, and filled a large plastic trash bag. My computer was beyond salvage—it lay in the center of the floor where Gabrielle had fallen upon it, crushed and partially melted. I stuffed its pieces into the trash zapper and vaporized them entirely.

I had an inspiration. I would write a suicide note, then leave my gun on the floor. When the landlord summoned the police, they would think it was I who had melted here, marring the floor. My freedom would be complete. Christopher Ruby would be officially obliterated.

But what if it were possible to return to this life, should I want to one day? What if I needed those abstract numbers of identification that proved I was a legitimate physical entity? My money wouldn't last forever. Much as I rejected so ridiculously prosaic a concept as a job, I would need to work again one day. No, I didn't dare murder Christopher Ruby.

Would the landlord call the forcers anyway, to complain about the stains? If they came, would they bother to examine them closely? I couldn't be sure, but at least it was better than them finding Gabrielle's body.

Gabrielle's body, which I had once kissed, caressed, entered. I had expected to feel more remorse, pity, but I mostly felt revulsion just then. She had been so transformed. The Gabrielle I mourned was another body than the thing I had disposed of here; a body made from memory. It's all about time and space.

I fled my apartment, fled to the underworld, for a second time.

* * *

They kept the heat high in the Kalian Reading Room. The humidity was tropical; I thought I might faint in one of the suffocating coffins of an aisle, and had to go quickly sit down at one of the central tables with a few books I'd pulled from a shelf at random. It was like sitting near to an oven at the height of summer. But I knew there was a fever inside me as well.

There was a deep stink of sweat plastered thinly with a too-bright layer of cologne, like makeup on a decaying corpse. Had it been this hot in here yesterday? Yesterday I had wandered here as if sleep- walking, had seemed to wake up in this room. I didn't stay, yesterday—I simply browsed for a few minutes, scanned for a familiar face. But it had not appeared.

Today I had sleep-walked here again. This time I'd decided to stay. Where else did I have to go?

With a start I realized a figure stood over me; glimmer of gold fabric out of the tail of my eye. I twisted and looked up anxiously to see a gray face with a subtle compressed smile. The characteristic brand-like scars. But this woman was older, thinner than the young woman I'd admired previously, and she wore a blue velvet turban. She proffered a tray covered in miniature tea cups like a doll might drink from. In her other hand she carried a steaming spouted kettle.

"No thanks," I said, smiling.

I saw men look up sharply from their books and newspapers and their games with the yellow sticks, at the other tables around me. Did the woman's carefully sculpted smile flick at the corners? Had I erred by talking to her, or declining the offering? Embarrassed, flushed even hotter, I nodded and selected a dainty cup. The Kalian woman filled it with a clear tea, then floated away. Eyes were still on me. I sipped the tea tentatively, as if I expected to be poisoned or at least scalded. It had a subtle hint of an anise-like flavor. Good. I sipped it again. The looks subsided.

The books I'd chosen were in Kalian. No wonder no one had seemed to object to my taking them. Not even pictures in them. I closed them and pushed them aside.

The wood of the table was a whitish-yellow, bone-like color, and varnished to a high gloss but with the grain of the wood still clearly visible through the sheen. A Kalian species, perhaps. I rubbed my hands across it but they were sweating and squeaked, resisted, smeared moisture stains. I removed my hands and watched the moisture stains grow smaller, smaller, fade. Fade away like Gabrielle. Like me.

She had not only died, a tragedy enough, but it was as though she had never existed, which seemed to me even worse. Father dead—a suicide. Mother lost somewhere in the city, presumably dead as well. Her friends would forget her after a time.

Could I be the murderer of a person who had not existed? By not being recognized for my crime, it was as though I myself did not exist. No forcers seeking me out. My loss at work an irritant but not crippling; I would be replaced and forgotten.

My parents were divorced. Mother, a veterinarian, lived with a man in Miniosis, close by and even greater in size than Punktown but not nearly as—colorful. My father, an art history professor at Paxton University (good old PU), lived with a woman in an apartment off Oval Square. Mother administered to her pampered small animals. Father administered to his wealthy, large children. I hadn't seen either of them since Christmas. I had an older brother. He'd moved to Earth.

I wanted to call them up. "I'm a murderer," I'd tell them, like another son might announce his engagement or job promotion. I wanted to run through the streets, shouting it. But people wouldn't pay any more attention to me than they did the old Choom I'd passed on my way here, shambling along the sidewalk in filthy pajamas, bellowing something about winged whales that were coming, like someone who'd been awakened by a traumatic dream and had never recovered from it.

There was a knothole in the wood near my right hand, a large darkish whorl, like a whirlpool or vortex that had solidified, frozen in time. It had the shape of a miniature, fossilized galaxy. I was put in mind of that old chestnut about a whole universe existing inside a dust speck. I wondered if the cells had grown out uniformly from the center of that knothole, or if they had slowly, so slowly grown around and around in a spiraling shape. Nature loved a spiral. Like a sea shell. The maze-like whorl of my thumb print. It connected me with this dead thing. I looked down the length of the table. A single piece of wood. How many minute units, once alive, composed this slab? And it was just a small part of a larger whole, cut down and sliced up to make that other table there, those shelves, someone's house. How long had it taken for this bone-like dismembered slab to grow to this length, microscopic cell upon cell like brick upon brick? An intricate structure . . . a mind-boggling composition. And me hovering too high above it to grasp its inner patterns, dead but still intact like microorganisms fossilized in rock. Me like some mindless god unable to comprehend the world he had fashioned . . . unable to lower himself close enough to see the particles of life within the grain . . . to see that the lines in the grain spelled out mysteries that might be translated if one knew the key to break their code . . .

"Hi," said someone at my elbow. I saw peripheral gold. More tea being offered, perhaps, and I looked up to see a subtly smiling gray face. But this woman wore no turban; her thick black hair fell behind her shoulders. It was the face I hadn't found yesterday.

Again, around me, the heads coming up. The hot glares. I tried to ignore them.

The young woman wore a gold sarong-like skirt wrapped around her ample hips, and a tight indigo blue top with long sleeves. This time, when she smiled, I saw a hint of bright teeth against her charcoal gray lips. Unthinkable. Blasphemy.

"Interested in our culture?" she asked in a near-whisper, nodding at my unread books and my tea.

"Um, yeah," I said. And I was. In a specific aspect of her culture. *Her.*

"Is there—something I can help you with?"

"Well, uh . . . sure . . . I . . . "

"You began to approach me the other day, when you were here."

"Yeah, right . . . I did . . . I was looking for someone . . . I was going to ask for help . . . "

"Did you find them?" Her voice was not "lewd". It was indigo blue, and gold.

"Yes. All set, thanks."

"That's good."

I nodded. "So . . . ah, would you care to sit down? I'd like to ask you a few questions, if you don't mind. About your people. Your customs . . . "

She lowered herself into the chair to my left. The chair was also of bone-like wood. Her skirt seemed to bind her legs, mermaid-like. "Are you a student?" she asked me.

"No. I'm, um, unemployed right now. I'm just interested in your people. You have a very intriguing culture . . . "

"Perhaps you're as drawn to the similarities between us as to the differences. You've heard of the story of Ugghiutu, and how he seeded the universe with our peoples?"

"A little. Maybe not that part."

"My name's Saleet Yekemma-Ur."

I shook her hand. More glares, some stealthy and some open, burned me hotter than the air. I expected someone to leap up from one of the tables and swing his chair over his head at any moment. But Saleet seemed much less concerned than I.

"Friends call me Sal, or Sally," she went on. "Or Emma."

I preferred Saleet. Much more exotic. "I'm Christopher Ruby," I told her. "People call me Chris." I didn't mention how Gabrielle had called me Topher. Later on I'd realize that I could have made up a new name for myself, seeing as how I was a nonentity, a feeling that was both vertiginous and weirdly liberating. Since I had self-obliterated, I could self-invent. Well, I'd design a brand new Christopher Ruby. I just wished he was less shy.

"Well, Chris, on Kali it's believed that the devil-god Ugghiutu created all the universe. There are various groups who believe different things, as in any religion, but most of them agree Ugghiutu at least created the Kalians and those who are like them. Some say he didn't form the universe itself. Others say the universe is a living being even greater than Ugghiutu, in which we all dwell. Some say Ugghiutu was merely one of a group of gods who came into this universe from another one. Those believers are called the Cult of the Outer Gods."

"Which schism do you subscribe to?"

She smiled. "I'm an agnostic."

"I'm an atheist."

"Well, you shouldn't entirely close your eyes to the mysteries of the universe. An Earth man named John Muir, in 1869 AD, said, 'When we try to pick out anything by itself, we find it hitched to everything else in the universe.'"

"Very nice. You have a good memory."

"I have a good memory implant—a Mnemosyne-998."

"Ah. That must come in handy in school? Work?"

"Work. I graduated from PU. I'm twenty-two." She smiled knowingly. Knowing that I wanted to know. I felt more bashful still.

"So—you were saying that Ugghiutu seeded human-like races throughout the galaxies . . . "

"Yes. That's why Earth humans, Chooms, Tikkihottos, a few other races so closely resemble the Kalians. How else could we all be so humanoid? What are the odds? Each seeded race adapted to our various environments, but . . . "

"What about evolution?"

"It was guided by Ugghiutu. Directed by him. When I say he seeded the planets, I don't mean to say he set down a Kalian Adam and Eve here, a Choom Adam and Eve there, fully developed . . . "

"Ahh . . . "

"I'm just relating the myths. It doesn't mean I subscribe to them."

I nodded, and got past the woman's amazing looks to digest some of what she'd told me. One piece hadn't dissolved, stuck in my brain like a splinter of bone. "This Cult of the Other Gods . . . "

"Outer Gods."

"Do they believe . . . do they believe there was a war between two races of gods? A race maybe called the Outsiders, or the Old Ones . . . and another race, who defeated them, called the Elder Gods, or the Elder Ones?"

"Yes, yeah, something like that. The Outer Gods did battle with a race of deities called the Nameless Ones, or the Shadow Gods, because there's no image or idol or name for any given one of them. After they put Ugghiutu and his brothers down, buried them and put them into comas, apparently, the Nameless Ones left our universe without a trace."

I nodded again.

"So, you've heard that story before?"

"I read something like it, in another book. Not a Kalian version, but very similar. Too similar . . . "

"A lot of religious themes are very recurrent. They often involve celestial power struggles. Battles between gods. Gods mastering the destiny of their subjects." She shrugged.

I grunted in agreement, but I was less inclined to dismiss the similarities between this version of the Ugghiutu myth and what I had gleamed from the *Necronomicon*. Was it coincidence that had drawn me to Rabal, the Kalian Reading Room, Saleet, and now this information? Or was it destiny? I remembered the quote from John Muir that Saleet had just recited. Everything connected . . . some sort of pattern . . .

"One of my favorite stories from childhood was 'Zul and the Black Temple'. It's an example of the belief that Ugghiutu is still with us, even though he's sleeping under the spell of the Shadow Gods. He can influence our lives, through his dreams . . . "

"What do those people believe who don't subscribe to the war with the Shadow Gods bit?"

"That he's awake and undefeated . . . but distant, behind the curtains, like your Christian god."

"So how does this 'Zul' story go?"

Again, the flash of white teeth between dusky lips.

* * *

ZUL AND THE BLACK TEMPLE

Zul Tubal-Zu was a girl with a beauty greater than the two moons combined, but her tongue was as black as her hair. When Zul was ten, her hair was bound in her first *tevik*, but her tongue should have been bound or hidden away as well. For when her hair, which hung to her seat, was cut so as to better fit within the shimmering *tevik*, her mother by accident tugged on that ebony curtain, and Zul let out a curse. Her mother fainted dead away, but the servants seized upon the fiery-tongued child and dragged her to her room in the house of the farm where her father raised a fine herd of glebbi.

Three years passed, and Zul obeyed the law of silence that she had donned with her *tevik*, speaking only within her father's house, never before company, and always in tones of respect, as befitted a child on the doorstep of adulthood. But when the time of staining came, and Zul woke one day to discover herself a woman, it was soon found that her black tongue had merely hibernated like a durbik these past years, waiting to again spew its venom.

For when Zul was given the Veins of Ugghiutu . . .

("The what?" I asked.

"Our scars. They're called the Veins of Ugghiutu. To indicate that his presence flows through us, and that we bear his mark. That he owns us."

"Doesn't he own the men, too?"

"Of course. But I guess . . . I guess they don't like having their faces sliced up.")

. . . when Zul was given the Veins of Ugghiutu, at the touch of the blade she let out a curse that might have made the strongest herdsman on her father's farm faint dead away. But the priests held her steady, and despite her wails and sobbing they completed their task, ashamed that they should sully their blades with the blood of such a creature. One priest even offered to unburden Zul's father of so horrid a child, by using his blade in another manner, but Zul's father apologized and told them that he hoped Zul was not yet hopeless.

Still, now that she was of age to marry, Zul's father grew greatly anxious, hoping that Zul would not disgrace a future husband's family, and thus bring dishonor upon his own.

Zul returned to her silence as her scars healed, and attended her labors about the farm. One morning she rode on the back of one of the glebbi, guiding a group of twenty to the farthest reaches of her father's land in search of fresh grazing. She had been forbidden to do this, for their farm was on the edge of the Outer Land, and only the most seasoned herdsmen were to venture to these fields. But it had not rained in many days, and the greens that the glebbi favored were dwindling, so Zul thought she was doing her father a favor by disobeying his commands. Still, she knew full well that there was never a good reason for disobeying the orders of one's father.

The mountains of the Outer Land loomed dark purple against a pale gray sky, and silhouetted thus, put Zul in mind of some fantastic city of castles. She was sorely tempted to leave the herd to graze here, and ride her glebbi to the foot of those mountains where they thrust abruptly up from the soft earth. But she was able, at least, to resist that impulse. For she knew that in the Outer Lands, Ugghiutu's dreams wound through the crags, and slithered along cliff faces, and wailed and howled, all in the guise of black winds.

Still, she pushed the herd nearly to the foot of the mountains of the Outer Lands. And in the deep, cold shadow of those soaring purple peaks, she found a building that she had never seen before, or heard her father speak of. It was too large to be one of his sheds or barns, and it did not look like a dwelling. As she drew nearer, Zul saw that the building, being black and eight-spired, was a temple to the demon/god Ugghiutu.

Zul marveled at its solemn beauty. She had seen temples in the village and in the city when accompanying her family to market, but being a female, she had never seen the interior of one of these glossy black houses of worship.

Zul dismounted, and left her glebbi to feed amongst the others. She cast her gaze around her, but saw that she had not been followed. Who, she thought, would know if she peeked inside the black temple? If she saw a priest inside, she would duck back. If he pursued her, she would claim to be lost, and weep for assistance. Her father would defend her. His love had proven that foolish and overly forgiving in the past.

And so, Zul crept up to the front portal of that edifice, which loomed taller and more majestic as she approached. The eight spires were slim and polished, jutting their spear-like points at the sky. There were few windows. The walls of the temple were not formed of block upon block, but were smooth, so that Zul imagined the entire temple had been carved out of a single great mound of volcanic glass.

There was no door at the front portal, just an oval opening through which Zul peered, craning her neck. She discerned little in that murky interior, though a faint light filtered through a few small windows. But she strained her ears, and heard no chants, no music. She smelled no incense. Was this temple now disused, long abandoned?

The girl stepped across the threshold.

The interior of the temple was as cold as one of her father's barns in the winter. Zul hugged her arms tight to her young body. She shuffled timidly across a floor apparently formed from one unbroken sheet of obsidian blackness that looked like a pool of tar, looked like it might swallow her and drown her at any moment.

Off this main entrance hall with its high ceiling and odd supporting arches there branched several other hallways, round in shape and narrow. Zul gazed into each of them. Like the entrance hall, they bore no decorations. She chose the corridor in the center. At the end of this tunnel there was an ebony curtain hanging over the opening. She reached to it, and found it was leathery and heavy. She pushed it aside just enough to spy into a new chamber, but seeing no priests there, she entered it. There was a ramp here, winding in a spiral around and around to a high upper level. Several round windows let in misty rays of gray light.

Zul ascended the spiral ramp. At the top of this small tower there was a larger window, and from this she looked out upon the pasture where her glebbi had been left to graze.

Where the plump, dull glebbi had been passively munching their greens, there were now scattered withered carcasses like animals dead of starvation or thirst. At first, Zul believed she was seeing the remains of a herd that had become lost out here and died perhaps months earlier. But as she stared, she saw that one live glebbi remained. And she saw a great black form lower from the sky toward it. A great black boneless limb with a point at its end, which speared the plump glebbi, and lifted it into the sky. Its fat legs paddled the air and it let out a small, forlorn moan. Though the animal was raised high out of her sight, Zul knew that it was being drained like a fruit squeezed of its juices. And she knew that the vast limb she had seen, glossy and black, was one of the eight spires of the temple.

Madly, Zul raced down the spiraling ramp, tears flowing over her scars. She tripped and fell, and in so doing her *tevik* became partly unraveled. She tore it from her head and her long hair fell free. She raised herself to run again. She burst through the slick, leathery curtain. She hurried through the narrow tunnel. She ran into the entrance hall.

The front portal was gone. But she saw, when she drew closer, that it had not vanished but instead closed to a tight pucker.

Crazed, she darted toward a small window at ground level. Yet even as she neared it, she could see it, too, beginning to grow smaller, to pucker closed.

Just before reaching it, through this window she saw one of the outermost of the eight spires. And it was writhing, fluid and alive, as she knew all eight spires must be doing. Ugghiutu was rejoicing in the sacrifice which Zul had unknowingly brought him.

The orifice sealed up, and shut out the last rays of light. Zul was plunged into a darkness as black as her hair.

And when Zul's father set out with his men in search of her the next morning, he found a herd of twenty glebbi mummies, rotting at the foot of the forbidden purple mountains.

But there was no trace of Zul. Nor even of a temple there.

* * *

"Very good," I told Saleet, grinning.

She tapped her temple. "Mnemosyne-998."

"That was the most blatant morality tale I've ever heard."

"Fairy tales often are meant to intimidate children."

"It's so anti-woman, why did you ever get so attached to it?"

"Because I related to Zul! I thought she was great. Rebellious. Brave. Curious."

"Look where it got her."

Saleet shrugged.

"Someone told me before that Ugghiutu can masquerade as a temple to lure people inside."

"It's one of his favorite forms, for some reason."

"What's his actual form?"

"Formlessness. Chaos. Chaos needs a form. So—although he initially made us—now he imitates the forms we make."

"Do you want to go get something to eat?" I whispered without segue. My style with women was chaos.

Saleet glanced around her. "Yeah. Let's get out of here."

"You're a bit rebellious yourself. Untraditional, shall we say. So why do you come here?"

"Chris, just because I reject aspects of my culture doesn't mean I reject my entire heritage. I wouldn't want to color my skin like yours, or get rid of my scars. I don't want to disown being Kalian. I just want to redefine being a Kalian."

"Sounds good to me, Zul."

Saleet stuck her tongue out at me. It was pink, not black.

* * *

I had never been to the *Café Quay*—it was a small Morpha Street restaurant with a menu that aspired to represent a dish from every race that had settled in Punktown. The walls and ceiling were covered in brown wallpaper with a velvet feel, and unfocused black and white photographs of rusting machines and broken dolls hung in overwhelmingly ornate copper-colored frames. But the artsiness and over-lush opulence seemed more satirical than pretentious. The menu was shown in luminous white letters which scrolled, at my touch, across the black table surface. I could also, at a touch, find out what artist had recorded the jazz track currently playing over the sound system (Lech Jankowski). I played with the table and nursed a beer until Saleet joined me. Irrationally, I had feared she might not show up—that her sending me ahead of her might be a ruse to get rid of me.

Back at the Subtown Library, she'd told me, "We'd better leave separately . . . you go ahead. Do you know the *Café Quay*?"

"Been past it, never inside. What's wrong?"

She had leaned forward, lowered her voice further. "My people will tolerate a degree of nonconformity . . . here on Oasis, at least—they'd have put me in line a long time ago, on Kali . . . but if we leave together it would be too scandalous. Complaints could be lodged with the Kalian Embassy. I knew a boy in college who was deported back to Kali—I hate to think what happened to him."

"What's the matter . . . he didn't wear a *tevik*, either?" I joked bitterly.

"He was a homosexual."

"Ugghiutu forbid."

I savored watching her approach my table. She was barefoot again today. Her steps were short and rapid, bound as she was in that awkward gold skirt. Her entirely black eyes looked eerily like empty sockets, from across the room, but when she sat opposite me the lighting was such that they were filled with broken flecks of light like stars in space.

"Don't be alarmed," she told me, "the food in here isn't as expensive as you might think. Just that the owners have artistic tastes. I went to school with them."

"You ever have lunch with an Earth man before?" I asked nonchalantly, perusing the menu.

"Yeah." Then she added, "Never on a date. Just friends from school, friends from work."

"You only date Kalians?" I pretended to be reading the appetizers.

"So far."

"It didn't work out?"

"They didn't approve of me, it would turn out, much as they thought they were untraditional Kalian men. What initially attracted them to me ended up repelling them. They didn't like it when I argued with them."

I looked up. "How does one break off with a Kalian man? Sounds like it could be messy."

"One boyfriend cried and pleaded with me, actually. The other one grabbed me by my hair and dragged me out of his apartment and threw me down in the hallway. So I got up, went to his door, knocked on it, and when he opened the door I chopped him across the throat like this." She made a knifing move with her right hand, and I flinched even though it stopped an inch from my Adam's apple. "That took the wind out of him, so I could get him on his face and pin him. I had handcuffs in my purse."

"Handcuffs?" She was more liberated than I'd dreamed.

The biggest grin I'd seen from her yet. "I arrested him for assault.

I'm a police officer, Chris."

"You're a *forcer*?"

"Yeah. I graduated from the Law Enforcement program at PU at twenty-one, so I only had to take one year at the Academy. I got my badge this year. See?" She rummaged through her purse, and when I leaned toward her I saw a gun inside, in its own leather pocket. Matte black, like mine.

But it was a billfold that she withdrew, flipping it open so I could see her metallic blue shield, and her photo ID. In it, she wore her hair clenched back in a tight bun.

"Wow," I stammered. "Officer Saleet Yekemma-Ur."

"I'm not a patrol forcer, if that's what you're thinking . . . "

What I was thinking was that the other day, I had nearly asked her if she knew a man named Rabal. A seller of illegal firearms.

What I was thinking was that I was carrying my illegal Thor .86 in my waistband right now.

What I was thinking was that I'd shot my girlfriend dead. And dissolved her body.

Saleet was still talking: "My boyfriend was my first and only arrest to date!" She chuckled and leaned back as a waitress put a glass of wine in front of her. "I'm in the Sex Crimes unit in Precinct 9-B." She grew more serious. "We investigate rapes, sexual child abuse, even work with Vice on prostitution, when a prosty seems to be in it against her will, or has been abused by a client . . . "

"So you're a detective?"

"I'm an 'investigator' . . . I can't be a 'detective' until I put some more time behind me, move up in rank. Politics, you know. I have to work with a senior partner for several years before you can call me Detective Yekemma-Ur."

"Wow . . . wow . . . jeesh, I'm really . . . impressed . . . wow."

"I know two Kalian men who are forcers. They're good men, liberal-minded. One wears a *tevik*, the other doesn't. I had a crush on one of them until he got married." Grin. "But I'm the only female Kalian police officer in Paxton, I'm told. There are a few in Miniosis, but they're lab techs . . . don't do field work . . . "

"Are you on duty now?"

"No. You think I could chase a rapist in this?" She swept a hand over her gold-sheathed legs. "My day off."

"Have you chased any rapists yet?"

"In a vehicle. Not on foot. But my partner made the arrest. I haven't had to draw my gun yet."

I wagged my head. "No wonder your two boyfriends couldn't handle you."

Saleet's expression turned more serious. A bit disappointed, maybe even on the verge of anger. "Does it intimidate you that I'm a forcer, Chris?"

"No . . . no . . . I mean, them. Them, being Kalians. No, I think it's great. It's just a surprise because you're young. And, of course, because you're a Kalian woman."

She seemed to grow less defensive. "I think it was Zul that did this to me. Nosy, curious Zul, so eager to investigate that Black Temple."

"She should have got a search warrant first," I joked.

We both laughed. And I was proud of Saleet. And I liked her all the more . . .

. . . and I wondered if it would be safe to ever see her again.

* * *

At home, I sat reading from the *Necronomicon* while slathering hair accelerator lotion across my prickly head. Shortly before we'd parted, over coffee, Saleet had told me, "You know, you'd be even cuter if you had some hair."

I figured I'd keep the mustache and goatee, at least. A happy medium between the old and the new Christopher Ruby.

But I didn't know if I would call Saleet, though she had given me her number, and I had traded her mine. I didn't know if I'd take her up on her suggestion that we see a movie sometime.

So why was I growing my hair back?

I'd told her where I had worked, as though confessing to her in an interrogation room. But I had lied and said I was laid off. I had lied and said my girlfriend had dumped me. Well, not a lie. But leaving out the real conclusion of our relationship was a lie.

I didn't have time for an infatuation with a new woman. I had to avenge the corruption and destruction of my ex-girlfriend. I had to find out about the mysteries that might corrupt and destroy many, many other people.

But Saleet knew about some of these mysteries, superficially at least, didn't she? It couldn't be a coincidence, about the Kalian god of creation and destruction. Who was both god and temple to that god . . .

My hair grew back overnight, and in the morning I shaped it with obsessive precision, until it was short and neat. I trimmed my goatee. I looked less feral than I had, of late. I was glad I hadn't gotten tattoos, after all. Didn't want to look like a thug to my new forcer friend. But I still looked haggard. My cheeks were sunken and my eyes dark and puffy. I'd been having bad dreams; I knew this though I could almost never remember them in the morning.

But last night, it had been something about a pod of whales, swimming closer, closer from the horizon. Only they weren't swimming on massive fins, but flying with slow-flapping immense bat-like wings. And as they began to drift nearer, leaving shadows like clouds across the city they dwarfed, I saw that they were much, much larger than whales. And though they were shaped rather like sperm whales, I saw as they approached across a purple sky that they had no jaws, and no eyes, and their great faceless heads terrified me, because it made them seem all the more implacable, and immune to my sobbing prayers and chants for mercy.

* * *

I had settled on the belief that I must murder Mr. Dove.

I had gone upground for the day, hoping the sun and the change of scene would bring clarity. I needed a firm destination. A decisive course of action. Disembarking from my tube, however, I found myself too close to Paxton University, where my father taught art history, and so I wandered from the campus toward the oldest part of Paxton, which was actually what remained of the Choom city that had occupied this spot before it had been buried under millions of tons of colonist city. I had to pass by Oval Square, and this was where my father had an apartment with a girlfriend, so I walked briskly and kept my head down and I wore dark glasses. After I had left cobble-stoned Oval Square behind I felt more comfortable, and I allowed myself to enjoy the cool of the autumn air, the bright blue of the sky as filtered through my lenses. The buildings were shorter here, opened up to more of that sky; the sunlight could actually fall all the way to the streets.

The streets were narrow, in this area, many of them still cobblestoned. The crowded rows of smallish buildings were largely faced in brick and stone. Expensive gift and antique shops, quiet little book stores and coffee shops occupied the ground levels. There were even small trees growing at intervals along some of the sidewalks. Coffee in hand, I stared through a window into a tiny art gallery. I wandered on. There was one central lane, Salem Street as it was now called, again cobblestoned, where vehicles were not permitted to pass even though it was fairly wide and long. It was almost an open mall, lined with the greatest concentration of shops in the area, and bustling with people on their lunch break. Somewhere ahead a small group performed live music. Water splashed in a fountain, and children went barefoot in its pool. There was a good museum on this street; I'd been in it before. I saw no derelict passed out across the sidewalk. No skeletal teen slunk up to beg me for a munit. There were still some unsavory people I passed, but this was as nice a spot as you would find in Punktown. There were, of course, isolated Choom structures still scattered here and there throughout the city, but this was the largest single concentration of such buildings. It felt like the calm eye of a hurricane. A pearl lodged in the bile-filled stomach of the whale that had swallowed it.

Clarity. I could think. I thought about burning Mr. Dove's store . . . all those potentially dangerous volumes on scientific magic and magical science. But I couldn't endanger the prosties who also lived in that building, or anyone in neighboring buildings. I envisioned myself, instead, going into the bookstore and firing hungry plasma capsules at the shelves . . . watching the glowing corrosion quickly spread.

But first, I'd shoot a plasma capsule into Mr. Dove. I couldn't entirely blame him for Gabrielle—she had innocently, half-playfully embarked on her own destruction before meeting up with him. But they had interacted somehow, and he had furthered her poisoning. And he was a priest. He was a threat to other innocent Gabrielles. And I wanted one single flesh and blood face I could confront. And shoot.

I was an underworld dweller, now. Morpha Street and its tributaries were my neighborhood. I was nervous about killing a person so near to where I lived. Afraid to burn his books despite my fantasies, that shop being so close to my apartment. And now there was Saleet living and working down there, close by as well. Saleet the enforcer . . .

If I could arrange to meet Dove elsewhere. Lure him away . . .

On what pretext?

Well, I wanted to see more of the books he offered, anyway. Specifically, the ones he had mentioned to me which furthered certain ideas found in the *Necronomicon*. One by a Choom author, the other by a Tikkihotto. I'd tell him I wanted to buy them, after all. Ask him to meet me for lunch somewhere. Somewhere non-threatening, where violence was less expected. Like this quaint little district I was in right now. What more innocuous a setting could one choose in Punktown? Here, one hated even to say Punktown. It became Paxton again . . . its real name. The Town of Peace.

I'm turning psychopathic, I thought, milling with others in front of a Choom trio who played that live folk music I'd been hearing. What will I gain from killing this man? I should forget him. Forget Gabrielle. Saleet liked me. Saleet was a door to another direction.

But I was already a murderer. Even if it had been in self defense. I had fled, disposed of the body. I had changed forever, regrown hair notwithstanding. Saleet was a door to law and order and sanity that would ultimately not open to my hand, I told myself. She was attracted to me, that was plain. But if she only knew the truth . . . would she go so far as to arrest me, or only be repulsed by me? Either was equally horrible to me. Better not to see her again at all. Better to let myself continue the descent I'd already begun . . .

Besides, those whales were coming on great, black wings. Maybe not looking like that. And coming from where I didn't know. But I felt the beat of their wings in my every cell. I heard their soundless sonar calls, a static in my veins. Gabrielle had opened a doorway, and given Dove the means to do the same by handing him the *Necronomicon*. He must not be allowed to open any more—any larger—doorways for these beings that some worshiped as gods.

I listened to the crisp tinkling of instruments, the soft peaceful voices of the singers, the laughter and shouts of the children like live cherubs in the fountain behind me. So brittle. Fragile. Why must I be the one to know how endangered they were? Why must I be the one to defend them? I couldn't even fare better in life than a customer service job. I couldn't even save my own girlfriend.

Look at me behind my dark glasses, like a celebrity, I silently invited the performers. I am the salvation and the way.

I must kill Mr. Dove.

I neared PU again on my way back to the tube station. The sun was lowering and slanted golden across the green park of the campus. I gazed off at the university's buildings rising above the park. Saleet had studied to be a police officer there. Law and order and sanity were preached in there. But they didn't have the *Necronomicon* on their shelves, did they? In their med classes, they didn't dissect immensely bloated mutant corpses to get at the floating jellyfish-like beings inside . . .

I felt utterly alone in my knowledge. It was for the best, in a way.

* * *

Today during my excursion I had worn a backpack slung over my shoulder. In it were my pistol and my palmcomp. Riding the tube back home, I opened the palmcomp on my lap and did another search on the *Necronomicon*.

I found stray references, scanty mentions, even a couple of the more well-known passages (much as anything from its pages could be considered well-known), but again, it was not available in its entirety on the net, nor did any listed book seller offer it for sale. But glancing at several articles, I saw how the few copies of the book that existed had been hunted down and destroyed over the years, usually by religious fanatics or at least disturbed individuals. One scholar who had been given permission to handle the tome in the rare books room of a college library had set himself on fire, and clutched the book to his chest while he sat on the floor and burned.

I also read a line or two in a couple of the articles about a group who called themselves Children of the Elders, who claimed to have destroyed three copies of the book themselves and had hacked into a net site that had presented the full text. They had obliterated the site, and even sought out the site's owner to steal an original volume from his house. The owner of the book and of the net site in question wasn't described or named, unfortunately.

I was under the impression that this organization was a contemporary one. What would they think of Mr. Dove, for owning that book? Or me, for that matter? Though I would hope that in me they would see an ally . . .

So I did a search on the Children of the Elders, but mostly it just pointed me back to the same articles I'd already seen. They seemed to be situated on Earth, only. Well . . . at least they had Earth covered. But I would have appreciated some assistance on my end of things.

One brief piece that did mention them noted that they hadn't been heard from in a while, and jokingly suggested that they had been hunted down themselves and spirited away by the demons from the very spellbook they sought to erase from existence.

I tried to find out more about those two books that Mr. Dove had mentioned, but couldn't locate anything without remembering their titles or authors. At last, as I neared my stop, I packed the palmcomp away, the red disk containing the elusive *Necronomicon* housed inside it.

When I stepped onto the tube platform, belowground once again, I saw that the streets were flooded with water six inches deep. Wheeled vehicles plowed through the dark liquid, hovercars skimming above the oily-looking rivers but disturbing the surface in their wake. Pedestrians ran along cursing, as if hurrying to their destinations would keep them drier. I asked a man waiting on the platform what had happened.

"A helicar hit an overhead water main," he sneered. "A big one. Stupid kid was speeding. They think he was drunk. Killed his passenger, but he's alive, of course—the idiot. I never feel sorry for losers who get killed drunk driving."

I often didn't either, though I supposed I'd feel different if it were my friend. In any case, I thought of hailing a cab, but it didn't look favorable, as a lot of other people already had that idea. I finally just stepped off the platform into the ankle deep water—cold!—and started slogging my way toward home.

I passed an old Earth man who stood in the middle of the sidewalk staring up at the ceiling and muttering to himself. He was entirely soaked, and I imagined he was a derelict who'd been sleeping on the street when the tide washed in.

There were sirens ahead, deafening for being contained down here, and I saw colored flashing lights from around the next corner. The roar of the escaping water could now be heard, like a waterfall crashing to the street below. I gazed up at the ceiling like the derelict. Crisscrossing pipelines, conduits, a seeming chaos of conveyance. But there had to be order in it, patterns in the web. This cable had a specific starting and ending point. That main took sewerage to a certain destination. Maybe it hadn't all been blue-printed from the start, every single pipeline charted in advance, but plans had been written upon plans, and webs woven through existing webs, and the anarchy was actually a system.

I was reminded of what a friend who studied at PU to become a doctor (he had succeeded, and I'd since lost touch with him) once told me, after he'd performed his first human dissections. Inside the body looked so—messy. The organs weren't color coded, neatly outlined and self-contained like in text book illustrations. It was all so soft, so gray, so formless looking. Like a congealed soup of protoplasm. Instructors spoke of the glorious human machine, but this didn't look mechanical. "It shouldn't work!" my friend had laughed in awe. It was just this . . . mess. Where he had always been a staunch atheist before, he told me this experience had actually started him wondering about God. Presumably, only a god could animate such clay.

I wondered if this religious awe had grown since we'd last talked, if he still marveled, or if he were now a jaded surgeon who could clearly discern the patterns, the structure, the machine in that gray chaos.

Patterns. Structure. Order and purpose. But it could be broken. It could bleed. I heard that water gushing.

And as I stood there listening, watching the colored lights of the emergency teams flash between the buildings across the street, I felt my backpack torn off my shoulder.

From behind, the fleeing thief looked like a skeleton in bulky, shabby black clothes. A hairless bony head, weirdly metallic in color. A robot, then? Tribes of runaway, rebellious robots lived in certain abandoned sections of the old subway system that had been partially buried and never repaired after the great earthquake of several decades past. But when I lunged forward in pursuit—kicking up water in great splashes—I saw the thief glance back at me, and he was of an alien species I wasn't familiar with. He had huge black eyes that seemed to be covered in a silvery protective film or membrane, and a long pointed beak like a bird's projected from the front of his head. His skin had a silvery sheen, but like his eyes seemed black below the surface, so that it had an odd look as though his body were an X-ray or a photographic negative.

"Hey!" I shouted after him. "Give me that back, fucker!"

A good thing he didn't know I had a gun in the backpack. He could simply stop running, pull out the pistol, and threaten me with it. Maybe even shoot me with it. But that wasn't the only dangerous item in the bag.

My palmcomp. With the *Necronomicon* still inside it . . .

The bird man darted into an alley. Huffing, slower, I pursued him. I splashed water on a woman as I passed her. "Die, you wanker!" she snarled at me.

I nearly lost my footing as I turned into the alley. The street level must have inclined lower here, or else the flood was getting higher (would it rise and rise until it reached the ceiling, drowning us all in a tragedy of Biblical proportions?) . . . the water was nearly to my knees. I waded heavily through it. A massive, graffiti-covered trash zapper blocked my view of the alley's far end. It was no longer functioning, so it overflowed with refuse, and the stench of rotting garbage was great. Looking down, I saw the alley's flotsam and jetsam. A dead cat without any skin brushed against my leg. It wasn't dead, after all; its hind legs paddled weakly and its mouth opened and closed without sound. It drifted past me, flayed white, like a fetus in amniotic fluid. I wish I had my gun so I could kill it.

Blobs of decaying food—perhaps it was food—slimed the surface of the water. Sheets of cardboard were borne along like little islands. I reached the trash zapper. Beyond it, I saw a man lying on his back entirely under the water, eyes closed as if he were seeing how long he could hold his breath. A derelict, drowned in his drunken dreams.

At its end, the alley branched into two sub-alleys, to the left and the right.

"Dung!" I hissed. Looking down both these narrower, darker corridors between buildings, I couldn't see the bird alien. One alley had a roof-like grille that ran overhead. I chose this one, plunged unarmed but furious into that dimly-lit tunnel. I was desperate. I possessed one of the few surviving copies of the *Necronomicon*, me the reluctant one man army, and I had let it be stolen by a purse-snatcher. In that book were spells that could close the doors, if only I found out how to wield them. Formulas that could reshape the patterns of the universe. Stolen . . . stolen by a street punk so he could buy himself some drugs.

"I have money!" I stupidly announced to the dark tunnel as I raced along it, splashing filthy water, the pallid light from above sending the grille's pattern across me in a flowing tight web of shadow. "I'll give you all my money if you give me the backpack!"

I arrived at the end of the alley. It was a T, branching to the left and the right.

Looking down either alley, I saw no bird man. These alleys were narrower still, barely enough to squeeze through. I heard steam hissing from a vent in one alley, and the steam filled the passage, obscuring my view. Had the alien plunged through it? Was he even now lurking back there waiting for me to follow him, my gun in hand? I chose this path.

When the steam clouds surrounded me, when I could no longer see my hand in front of my face, I felt along the slimy-slick walls of the facing buildings more for a sense of the tangible than to guide my way. At any moment, I expected a blow to swing at me out of the fog, to crush my skull . . .

. . . but I emerged from the humid, billowing vapors into a small courtyard. It was like looking up from the bottom of a gigantic chimney, a chimney lined in rows and rows of windows. Many were boarded up. Some had been obscured entirely with graffiti, at ground level.

It was a dead end.

I lowered my forehead into cupped hands. Please, let that thief—or whoever bought the palmcomp from him—erase that red disk. Copy some stupid games onto it instead.

When I looked up, I saw a face staring out at me from one of the ground floor windows. A curtain quickly dropped back into place, hiding it. Graffiti on the window had obscured the face, but it had seemed to be a gray-fleshed, fish-like being. I had caught a glimpse of a neat white shirt showing through a dark suit.

Had it been Mr. Dove, or another of his race? Who were his race, anyway? I was no more familiar with his species than I was the bird man.

Maybe all the fish-men dressed as neatly as Mr. Dove. But if it had been him . . . was this his apartment? I had assumed he lived in the same building that housed his shop.

If it was him, had he recognized me in my dark glasses, my new goatee? He'd only seen me for an instant, and a thin mist from the steam filled the tiny courtyard.

I wanted to steal up to the window, peek through it. But I feared getting caught. I feared that even now, that gray face might be peeking at me through a chink in the curtains.

Turning, I retraced my way through the alley network, no longer running. My shoes were filled with foul black water. It felt like the apocalypse had already descended, though I knew this chaos was nothing . . . just one drop that precedes a downpour.

* * *

The ruptured vein was repaired, the blood stopped gushing. It was drained away, leaving wet trash in clumped ridges pushed up against the gutters. I looked out my window, down at the still-slick street. Tomorrow I'd have to wear my ruined shoes one last time when I went to buy a new pair. This was the only pair I'd brought with me. My apartment stank from them.

No palmcomp. What if Saleet tried to call me? She couldn't. That was no doubt for the best . . .

But from a phone booth, with water up to mid-shin, I had called Mr. Dove on the way back to my apartment. I located the number of his book store from a listing.

Graffiti on the vidscreen. Graffiti like there had been on that window. I had removed my dark glasses. Now, the screen filled with his gray face, his silver eyes and pink, subtly pulsating gills.

"Hello, Mr. Ruby," he said, recognizing me. Polite despite the tension of our last phone conversation.

"Hi, Mr. Dove," I replied, just as civil. "Um . . . I've been thinking about those two books you recommended to me. The ones that you said took ideas from the *Necronomicon* further . . . mapping the patterns in the universe, looking at things from a kind of geometrical view . . . talking about how to reconfigure those patterns to bend time and space . . . "

"Yes. Wadoor's *Atlas of Chaos*, and *The Veins of the Old Ones*, by the Tikkihotto Skretuu. But I thought you were profoundly skeptical about these concepts, Mr. Ruby."

"Well, Gabrielle is opening my eyes a bit. I'm trying not to be so stubborn about things I don't understand."

"So, you located your missing friend . . . "

"Yes!" I said, even sounding cheerful. "We're back together. So I thought I'd like to purchase those books, if they were available. For Gaby and myself. A gift for Gaby, mostly. If it's a gift I can afford!" I chuckled.

"Well, fortunately, these particular volumes are not nearly as sought-after as a *Necronomicon*. They don't have the same level of renown. Would you be interested in actual volumes, for their collector's value, or are you only interested in the text? Because I could supply both books on disk. A single disk, if you like."

"How about prices, first?"

"Wadoor's is older, and rarer . . . a copy would be twenty thousand munits."

"Jesus Bleeding Christ," I murmured.

"Skretuu's book was reprinted by a publisher of occult books, but is dismissed by many as mere quack science, didn't catch on with a readership. So there is actually a twenty-five year old paperback version of it, which greatly lowers the value of both the text alone and the original printing. An original would be worth five thousand munits, but the paperback version is only worth about ten munits."

"Oh. Wow . . . what a difference."

"Its information is superb, often better than that in *Al-Azif*, but again, it doesn't have the reputation. People are blind, as both books are superior, in some ways, to *Al-Azif*."

"How much for both on a disk?"

"I would cut the value of Wadoor's book in half, and give you the other for free. Ten thousand munits, Mr. Ruby."

"An expensive gift," I muttered.

"Indeed. A lot to pay, for someone who is still not entirely convinced of the credibility of the material."

"Well . . . it is very important to me to make Gaby happy. To patch things up with her . . . "

"Perhaps a ring would be a better investment."

I took this as a joke rather than sarcasm, and smiled. "Yes. But . . . you know, I'd really like to get her . . . to get *us* . . . both of those books. I think I'm going to have to say to go ahead and make that disk."

"Really? And you can pay me the full ten thousand?"

"Yes. I have it. It will break me, but I have it."

The amphibian-like head nodded slowly, in consideration. "You do seem seriously interested in the subject. Well . . . since Gabrielle allowed me a copy of *Al-Azif*—the *Necronomicon*—I'll take pity on you, Mr. Ruby, and reduce the price to five thousand munits."

"You will? Really? Oh my God, that's so generous! I know Gaby was indiscreet about you being a follower of these beliefs, and I know I was rude to you when I couldn't find Gaby . . . I'm so sorry, Mr. Dove. I'm so grateful for your help."

"There are a lot of very important things to be learned from these books, Mr. Ruby. It's good that you are opening your eyes to the larger view of the universe. Listen to what Gabrielle has to teach you. Together, the enlightened form a pattern themselves. You and I . . . links in a chain, Mr. Ruby. We can make each other stronger . . . "

"Yes . . . yes . . . that's what Gaby says!" I enthused.

"I'll make that disk, then. When would you like it by?"

"Um . . . three days from now?" I picked a number out of the air. Not tomorrow. Too frighteningly soon. I needed time to think how I might actually go about this. "Say, noon?"

"I'll be expecting you then."

"Ah, well, could we arrange to meet somewhere other than your shop? I'll be visiting my father in Oval Square, upground, for the next few days. You know where that is . . . "

"Yes, near Paxton University."

"Yes; my father's an art professor there," I revealed, to give myself credibility by association. "In fact, he'll be lending me the money I'll be using. He's hinted to me he'd like to have a look at the books himself. He may or may not be accompanying me, if that's all right with you. Anyway, could you meet me at noon at the corner of, um, Fassl Street? It's near Salem Street, a few blocks from Oval Square." I'd been there today. Between two buildings on Fassl Street there was a small courtyard with a fountain in its center. A nice secluded spot for our expensive transaction. "It's easy to find; there's a candy store right there . . . "

"I'll find it."

"Maybe we could have lunch together, after we meet."

"I appreciate the offer, Mr. Ruby, but that won't be necessary. So . . . three days from now . . . noon . . . meet you at the corner of Fassl Street, outside a candy store."

"You've got it. I appreciate the trouble."

"And you *will* have the full five thousand munits at that time, Mr. Ruby?"

He was suspicious. The location, however innocent (a candy store, even!), was nevertheless distant from where both of us lived. It struck him as unusual. I hoped involving my father in the scenario helped to temper his mistrust . . .

"Yes, of course," I reassured him. "And again, I can't tell you how grateful I am about the lower price. Um . . . and you know . . . I had my palmcomp stolen by a mugger today, and my copy of the *Necronomicon* was in it. Would it be possible to put that on the disk, too?"

"I'm afraid I couldn't do that for free, Mr. Ruby. Despite my gratitude for your help in securing my own copy, *Al-Azif* is of too much value to simply give away. We would have to return to the ten thousand munits . . . the best I could offer you, as a friend. In any case . . . I would assume it was Gabrielle who made you your own copy of *Al-Azif*, as I can't imagine she'd lend you hers. Can't she make you a new copy herself?"

The greedy fucker! Gaby had given him a copy of that book for free, and he couldn't do the same? But how could I argue with his logic? The other two books would have to suffice.

"Of course," I managed amicably. "Didn't mean to be lazy about it. All right. See you then?"

"Yes, Mr. Ruby. And have a pleasant stay with your father."

I'd have to keep a low profile on the street until then. If he spotted me subtown, when I'd claimed to be elsewhere . . .

"Thanks," I told him. And signed off.

* * *

With my pistol stolen, I couldn't burn away Mr. Dove's body with plasma, as I had Gabrielle's. Should I seek out Rabal again? Get a new gun? I still had my plasma ammo, at least, in the apartment.

The shotgun was still in my possession. To hell with it. I'd use that.

For the next couple of days, I didn't leave my flat. I tinted my windows full black so no one could see me inside. I wondered if Saleet had tried to call me. I wanted to see her badly. I kept telling myself it was for the best that she couldn't.

Tomorrow morning I had an appointment upground, where I would commit premeditated murder several blocks from where my father gave lectures on pursuits more creative than destructive, where he taught symmetry instead of obliteration, the order of line and perspective instead of anarchy and chaos. See? Even without the magical powers of spells I was reconfiguring destiny. My own, and that of others.

But, in a silent mantra, I repeated to myself, "I am a good man." It was because I was a good man that I must kill tomorrow. Wouldn't I rather not? But I had a burden of responsibility, and I must do something because it addressed my innate goodness, a goodness deeper than I had known I possessed. I was willing to risk death and insanity for the good of others. Who would have thought? I had a sense of what men must feel when patriotism impels them to join an army, to fight in a war. Knowing they might not make it back home. Maybe it was just an animal instinct, natural programming, protect the herd even at risk to yourself. More chemical than heroic. Whatever the tune of the trumpet, I must follow it. And all that sort of dung.

Gaby would tease me about being a customer service rep, and it would anger me, because it would shame me. My parents had done so much better. Over the past few years, they had subtly let their disappointment be known. But I had no talents, no special aptitudes. My ego was too big for me to be satisfied with my situation, but my effort too lacking to change my prospects. I envied people who could make peace with their insignificance in the universe, stuff pimentos in olives as placid as oxen pulling plows. But maybe I was, ironically, just the right kind of person to come upon this knowledge and responsibility. Without being filled up with something else, I could be filled with this. Without being focused elsewhere, I could see things that others did not. I thought of it in terms of this city. Most people only saw the stores, the offices, the places they had to go, and if they looked closely enough they might just glimpse the cracks in the sidewalk . . . but they did not see the lines of stress that made those cracks in the sidewalk, or the immense pressure of a heavy building resting on the earth, they did not see the winds that were directed and sculpted by the spaces between the buildings . . . all these forces that, in a sense, shaped an invisible city that existed conterminously with the visible one.

The day before my date with Mr. Dove, I sat watching the wall-length vidtank. It didn't have a vidphone feature, but I could still access limited, nonsubscriber netlink bands. I was doing random searches on various topics. Presently, I was trying to find out how many species of nonhumans had settled in Paxton. A lot. An example was given of each one. The people of Kali were represented by a photo of a man. I hadn't exhausted the list yet, and I had seen photos of a few races I'd never run into before, but so far I hadn't seen anything like Mr. Dove. Or, for that matter, that silvery-sheened bird-man who had stolen my backpack.

There was a knock on my door.

I sat up from the sleeper-sofa, startled. The landlord? A glance at the kitchen table, where my sawed-off shotgun rested openly like a book or a coffee mug. I jumped up, picked up the heavy black weapon, slid it under the sleeper-sofa. I shot more looks around me. Anything else that shouldn't be seen? Was I missing something? The ammo boxes were out of sight. The door knocked again.

I went to it. I opened it. Framed by the threshold stood a police officer in a severe black uniform, with glossy black boots, glossy black gun holster. Pouches for cuffs, other equipment, weighing on the belt. But the forcer was a pretty woman with her thick hair pulled back in a bushy ponytail. Saleet smiled bashfully.

"Wow . . . look at you," I said.

"You haven't seen me like this yet."

"Very impressive."

"I'm sorry to barge in on you like this, but I've been calling. You didn't pick up. I thought maybe you were avoiding me." She pouted her dark gray lips, but I could tell it wasn't entirely a joke.

"I was afraid of that. The punk who stole my palmcomp doesn't want to answer your calls, that's what it is."

"It was stolen? Did you have a break-in?" A forcer's angry determination narrowed her obsidian eyes. Her single brow bowed in the center. It made her face fierce.

"No, I was mugged. Not hurt. I chased him but he got away."

"Did you file a report? No? Want me to take a recorded statement right here? I can do that. I'm on my way to work, but it's early . . . I have time . . . "

"What time do you work?"

"Rotating shifts. This week it's second shift. I have time. Can I come in?"

I had been blocking the doorway. "Oh, yeah, sure . . . it isn't much."

"It sure isn't," she said, looking around her as she stepped in. Standing behind her, I breathed deeply the scent of her hair, clustered in a black storm cloud at the back of her head. She turned to face me and I took a step back. "Hey, I see you grew some hair!" She reached out and ruffled it with her hand. "I like it . . . much nicer!"

"Thanks."

Maybe she saw my discomfort and misread it. "I'm sorry I came here unannounced, Chris."

"How did you find my address?"

"You gave me your phone number," she grinningly apologized. "I used our computer system at work to find an address to match it."

"That's all right," I reassured her.

"What are you watching, here?" Nod at the VT.

"I'm trying to find out what kind of alien mugged me. I've never seen his kind before. Her kind. Whatever it was." I then described the being to Saleet. Her brow dipped intensely again.

"Can't say that it sounds familiar to me. There are always new peoples coming to Punktown . . . "

"Want to sit down? Want a drink of something? Coffee?"

"Coffee is good."

I brought her one. When I returned from the little kitchenette section, she was sitting on the sleeper-sofa. My shotgun directly beneath her. It had a smell of oil I hoped she wouldn't pick up on. I handed her the coffee and sat beside her. She had been continuing my VT search for the bird alien. "No luck yet," she announced. From her belt she unclipped a recording device. "Let's take that statement."

I held up a hand. "No . . . no . . . don't bother. It was my ex-girlfriend's machine, anyway. I'll buy a new one. How would we ever find this punk, anyway?"

"Well, if he's of an uncommon race, it might be a lot easier."

"I'd rather not. I'm all right."

"Chris, I don't see the point in not . . . "

"Saleet, I'd just as soon forget it." But I was ready to give in, to avoid a full-out argument. One doesn't argue with a forcer.

She gave in first, however. "I'm sorry, Chris . . . first I barge in on you, then I try to bully you into giving a police report. I guess my uniform goes to my head. But please let me know if you change your mind."

"I will." I sipped my own coffee.

"I should have you move into my flat," she kidded, looking around her again. "This place is dinky . . . "

I smiled inside, fluttered inside, felt a bit delirious. She had tried to sound nonchalant, but I realized then just how much she was attracted to me. She was letting me know, her comment calculated. What was it about me? That I had taken an interest in her people where perhaps other Earth men hadn't? Was I as exotic to her as she was to me? She looked back to me. "Any luck in the job hunt?"

"No. Well, I haven't been trying too hard. Not that I'm lazy . . . just . . . I guess I'm battle fatigued, from my work experience. I'm catching my breath."

"I understand."

"Wow," I repeated, "I still can't get over the uniform. Slick . . . "

"I work plainclothes, sometimes. I'm allowed to wear street clothes if I'm just doing the desk bit. Or if we're trying to blend in, on the streets. But I like the uniform." She smiled. "Is it sexy?"

"Not really," I confessed.

She pouted again. "Oh well."

"But very impressive. You make me feel safe."

"Good. Feel safe. I'll protect you." She sniffed, glanced around her. "What's that smell?"

"My shoes. I need to go out and get a new pair. They got wrecked in that flood the other day, when a helicar smashed into a water main?"

"Oh yeah. That was a mess. Do you want me to take you out and get a pair now? I have time . . . "

"No thanks." I couldn't risk Mr. Dove seeing me in the neighborhood, much as I liked the notion of shopping alongside Saleet as if we were a familiar couple. "Actually, I'm feeling a little sick today. A stomach bug or something."

"Aww. Sorry to hear that. Maybe the smell of your shoes?" she joked. "Do you want me to go so you can rest?"

"Not just yet. Let's watch VT." I switched off the netlink. Put on a documentary about animals. "I like animals," I told her.

"I do, too," she said, inching a little closer to me. Our shoulders and legs almost touched. We settled back, our mugs cupped in our laps, and were peacefully silent for nearly a half hour as if we were indeed a familiar couple. It was a good feeling. It was just a bad time for it. I had spent several days acclimating to the idea that I was a killer. Programming myself to become the avenging angel. Now, seated beside me, was my nemesis. And I was falling in love with her.

I woke to find I'd dozed off. Saleet was gone. On the VT, a bright green snake with a leafy frill around its head poised motionless amongst vines and leaves, watching and waiting as a three-legged insect drew closer to it. At last, it struck with a blur of speed. Three kicking legs dangled out of its smiling jaws. Camouflage, masquerade. It made me think of the fairy tale Saleet had told me.

A clink from the kitchenette. I sat up straight and saw Saleet smile at me over the counter/partition between the two room sections. She was at the sink, had just rinsed out our coffee mugs. "So, you're awake. How rude of you."

"Sorry." Stretching, I rose.

She came to stand in front of me. Playfully, she pretended to grind her black heel on my bare foot. Then she looked up at me. She was short, but still imposing in her uniform.

"I better get going. I hope you really aren't mad that I came."

"No, I'm not. Really."

"Get yourself a new computer. And it wouldn't hurt to give me a call from a phone booth, until then. We could see a movie . . . "

"I'd like that."

I walked her to the door. At the door, she turned, put a hand on my shoulder, drew me down a little and kissed me on the mouth. She didn't open her lips, and didn't linger long. Short and sweet. Very sweet. Then she slid her hand off me. "Call me," she repeated.

"I will," I promised, not sure if I were lying.

She stepped over the threshold. I closed and locked the door between us.

PART THREE: JELENA

I am a good man, I am a good man, I am a good man, I repeat to myself as I pace my small apartment. Good thing it rained up there today, I think. Good thing, so I could wear my poncho to hide the shotgun under. How else might I have hidden it? I could have worn it anyway, though it might have seemed odd. I'm still sorry I lost my pistol . . .

It is all over. It is done.

Mr. Dove was standing there in front of the candy store, as agreed, and he had a black umbrella folded under his arm. I suggested he follow me down Fassl Street a little, to an alley, to a courtyard. Though it had stopped raining, he seemed perturbed to be continuing our business outside, but we walked side by side like old friends. He was so polite. Polite to a dangerous fault. "Don't want anyone to see us," I told him. "This is a lot of money. I have paper bills; is that all right?"

"Certainly," he said. Having a lot of paper bills on me instead of transferring the amount from a credit card helped to legitimize the need for privacy.

"Sure you aren't hungry?" I asked as we entered the courtyard. I had noticed the other day that it was octagonal in shape. No windows on any of its eight walls. I couldn't imagine why the fountain in the center had ever been put here, but then again there were a few stone benches, and some overgrown flower beds. I could envision more than one marriage proposal here, maybe between long-dead Chooms. Had this courtyard been located at another point in town, derelicts would be sleeping on the benches and the fountain would be lost under graffiti. Even in this nice part of town, there was still some graffiti on the walls, and trash bobbing in the broken fountain's slimy pool.

"I've eaten," Mr. Dove said. He sounded a bit impatient, testy. Did my arrangements make him nervous? Did he have a gun on him, too? My shotgun's pistol strap was slung over my shoulder, so that the gun hung down my side. All I had to do was slip a hand under the purple slicker, swing the gun up into both my hands, level it and . . . everything went by so fast after that.

I remember that gray serpentine limb that reached toward me from the fountain as I fled the courtyard. He *had* been suspicious, hadn't he? I didn't find a gun on the body, but he had brought a friend. How had it known to be in the courtyard? Had he willed it there as we entered it?

It's a good thing I killed him. Someone with powers like that. I'm a good man.

From my pants pocket I take the little poker chip that contains both *Atlas of Chaos* and *The Veins of the Old Ones*. I wish I had a computer to view them on. I'll have to spend more of my limited funds on that tomorrow, damn it. I don't want to venture out again today. I'm too—charged right now. I need to pace. Just pace.

The disk is purple, like the building with the book store. Purple seems to be the big fad color these days. What will become of Mr. Dove's expensive collection now? Next of kin? Will they be auctioned? Dispersed throughout other colonized worlds? Spreading the disease? Maybe I should have put more thought into burning them after all. But I can only do so much. In fact, am I finished? Aside from studying these two books, what more can I do? How could I ever track down any of the other priests that are out there?

Well, I still need to see if I can close whatever portal Gabrielle opened. Dove, too. Maybe the books will help me locate those portals. That would be the first step, I should think.

I end up going out, after all. Just to a corner market to buy some

Japanese beer. I drink one after another at home. I fall asleep watching a documentary about animals, wishing Saleet was beside me. Ants carrying eggs in their jaws through intricate underground labyrinths . . .

I dream of giant ants coming from a far distance, ants with immense wings that are like sails catching the light of stars to convert into energy. These gigantic ants carry horrible, squirming fetuses in their jaws, fetuses with great bulbous heads and bundles of external intestines or perhaps tentacles clustered over their distended bellies.

* * *

I buy a new, full-sized computer. I pay for a cab to bring me home with it lest I get robbed again. I set it up; a nice big screen, no more squinting into that tiny palmcomp vidplate. The first thing I want to do is call Saleet. The first thing I do is pop in that purple chip I didn't have to pay a single munit for.

The books are dry, impenetrable at first, do indeed seem like the work of crank science. Not much talk of all those interesting demons from the *Necronomicon* that I dare not name. (Even a name can be an evocation.) But interesting diagrams. It is suggested that some of these figures, particularly drawn in the corner of a room, can open doorways to various alternate planes of reality. It is even suggested that a structure, built in a certain way, with certain angles to its rooms, built atop certain intersecting lines of magnetic force in the earth (I'd read about similar "ley lines" and "dragon paths" in Earth occult books), could serve as a kind of subway station to numerous alternate dimensions.

A news story on the VT behind me draws my attention.

Mr. Dove's body has been discovered.

The courtyard is shown. His body has been removed, but there's a nice close shot of blackening blood on the old Choom cobblestones. (A link offers to take me to photos of the body itself; I decline.) Mr. Dove, it is reported, was a mutation . . .

(Ah! So he wasn't an alien after all!)

. . . and his real name was Ben Chapman. Mr. Chapman owned Dove Books, on Morpha Street B Level. This buyer and seller of rare books had a collection estimated in the millions of munits. It is not known if Mr. Chapman had family, but if he didn't, local schools and scholars are hoping to acquire some of these texts.

Ants are crawling through my veins, stealing corpuscles in their jaws.

The motive for the crime is not known, but robbery has been suggested. Mr. Dove (his face easy to remember) was seen talking with a man in a purple poncho-style rain slicker . . .

I've got to get rid of that right away! God—what if the police run scans of the witnesses' memories? They could get a clear image of my face, broadcast it. And if Saleet were to see it . . .

I have to shave off my goatee. God, I might have to shave my head again. But what would Saleet think of all this changing of my appearance, back and forth? Better stick to the goatee. Anyway, I remember, I had the hood up over my head. That was good . . . yeah . . .

The news story ends. Another killing comes on its tail: a murdered prosty with a broom handle jammed inside her. (She's shown on a metal table spread-eagled, the broom inside her up to the bristles; is that the end of the handle coming out of her bloody mouth? God, I hope she was already dead before that happened.) If viewers blinked they'd have missed the Mr. Dove story. I can only hope that it isn't much pursued . . .

I take my new, shiny black shoes into the bathroom to examine them closely, wipe at what might be blood spatters. Well, I should buy new shoes again; even a minute particle of blood will show up if someone gets hold of these.

I shave off my goatee and mustache after all. I hope Saleet likes this look—if I let myself see her again. Now I look like I did when I still had my job. Respectable, bland. Camouflage, masquerade, like the green vine-like snake, smiling at the insect. That's me.

* * *

Poncho gone. Shoes, too. Second pair of new shoes in a week.

Saleet calls me. "So, you have a new computer. And why didn't you call me?"

"Sorry—still haven't felt well."

"You don't really want to see me, do you?"

"Of course I do! Look . . . let's um, let's go to a movie tonight."

"Are you sure?"

"Yes! Really! Look, Saleet . . . I'm just shy. Y'know?"

"Yeah, I know." She smiles, reassured. "It's cute . . . "

We see a film by Jason Torrey, a director we both like. I pay for her tickets and popcorn; I have a bag of fried dilky roots, that great greasy Choom snack. Afterwards, we sit in a corner café, in the window like fish in a glowing aquarium; it reminds me of that Edward Hopper painting (my father brought me up on art). We discuss the movie, then talk turns to Saleet's day at work.

When she starts to describe a murdered prosty with a broom shoved inside her, I tell her I saw it on the news. She's on that case herself, with her partner.

"Who could be so sick?" she fumes.

"Some men really hate women. Because they lust for them, and that makes them feel like they aren't in control of themselves. Like they don't have the power. Have you considered a Kalian perpetrator?"

"Very funny. This isn't a joke . . . "

"I know that!"

"This is just an exaggerated penetration, like an exaggeration of the contempt that all men feel toward prostitutes when they use them . . . "

I feel pretty guilty right now that I've rented prosties myself, between girlfriends. But I didn't feel contempt toward them at the time. Just stupid animal desire. Still, I can appreciate that it degrades the women, perpetuates their own self-abasement, and I'm not proud of it. But I can't tell Saleet any of this. I want to change the subject, but she feels passionate about her work and I do find it interesting.

"I helped arrest an exhibitionist today. He drove up to some teen age girls and asked for directions. When they looked in his car he wasn't wearing pants, and he was playing with himself. He said abusive things to them. They got his license number, the idiot, so my partner and I cuffed him at home. He has a wife and a teen age daughter himself."

"Pathetic loser," I say.

"I feel like I'm doing some good in the world."

Yeah. Me too, I say to myself. But your arrested pervert will go free soon, maybe after he gets some pills to take. Maybe it would be better if someone put a load of shotgun pellets into his head, instead.

"People are so sick, so diseased," she goes on. "It's like a plague. Like being all cramped up together in a city drives them insane. You know, like too many rats in a cage. I know this is nothing new, but still, as a forcer it really comes home to you. Really makes you feel helpless. But you do what you can."

"That's all one person can do," I agree. "It's human—humanoid—nature, though. You can't blame the city itself for it. Not like the city is possessing them."

"I know. Human nature. I read in a Kalian newspaper recently that twenty-four people were killed in a feud over the disputed ownership of a glebbi."

"Like our friend Zul had? What is a glebbi, anyway?"

"Sort of a lizard that looks like a llama. Not worth twenty-four people dying over."

"That was back home, on Kali . . . not here . . . "

"Right."

"Have you ever been to Kali yourself?"

"I was born there, but my parents moved us here when I was four. It was a business consideration; my father is an executive with Alvine Products."

"What products are those?"

"They genetically design and produce comestible life-forms. They farm them right there in the same plant. It's a big complex."

"I think I've seen it; in Industrial Square, right?" And I know what she's referring to so politely. I've seen documentaries that show rows of these big fleshy blobs, without heads or limbs (well, some have these stout stumpy flipper-like legs so their bellies aren't dragging on the floor), hooked up to cables pumping them with nutrients, pumping out the waste. Most are designed from cattle, pigs, Earthly domesticated animals. Chickens (with or without bones; take your pick) with no heads to lop off . . . but they still have those tasty legs and wings (mm, mm!). Even without heads, these creatures make you sad to see them on VT, so in a way I don't know that it's much of an improvement. Makes these zombies even more pathetic than natural animals, in a sense. But I don't criticize the practice because I don't want to make Saleet defensive, and anyway, I'm eating breakfast for dinner even as we speak: sausage and bacon with my eggs and toast. Mm, mm. But she brings it up herself, anyway:

"I love animals, so I don't ask him about his job much. Luckily he's not a designer; he's administration, upper management. I had a tour of the plant once, and that was enough for me. Reminds me of that poem by Thomas Hardy—*Bags of Meat*."

"Ah, don't know it, but it sounds tasty." I chew exaggeratedly. "I saw something horrible the other day. When I was going after that mugger. In an alley, in the water from the flood, I saw a cat with its skin pulled off. Its hide, you know? It was still alive. I saw a show once where some fucking cold-blooded fucker tossed a cat alive into a boiling vat to cook it for food, then pulled it out and peeled its hide right off like husking an ear of corn, only a lot easier, and then they tossed it back in and it was still alive, still trying to swim as it cooked, and trying to scream. It was the most horrifying thing . . . so unnecessary. It was like taking the time to actually kill the cat first wasn't worth consideration. What does that say about a person? But anyway, this cat I saw was just like that. It was near a trash zapper that was all overloaded with garbage, so I guess I thought it was . . . I dunno . . . garbage too. But still alive." I shrug.

"Sure it was really flayed? Maybe it was just a mutant."

"Maybe."

"That's sad. It reminds me of the Utalla."

"Which is?"

"A kind of hobgoblin in Kalian folklore. They're these big wingless birds that live in the mountains, and they love to eat cats. They skin them alive to torment them before they eat them, and make their nests from their pelts. I guess the fun of the myth is that cats usually eat birds—get it?"

I get it. And I'm also thinking that when I spotted that dying cat, I was in the process of chasing an alien with a long beak like a stork's. I can see that Saleet, watching my face, is realizing it now, too.

"Hey—maybe our mystery alien is a Utalla."

"Do Utalla have bodies like men?"

"Nnno . . . but. It's funny, isn't it? They're described as having skin like metal . . . "

"My guy had shiny skin. Like it was translucent silvery on the surface, but black under that."

"Huh," Saleet says, gazing down into her salad, poking through it intensely as if looking for something. She murmurs, "That's funny, isn't it?"

"The devils are afoot," I say.

She looks up at me. She looks grim. But can she feel as grim as I do? I figured I was merely the victim of some addict in need of drug money. But now I'm wondering if this creature knew about my palmcomp in that bag, and the chip that lay inserted within it. Was sent to retrieve it from me. That would mean that even with Mr. Dove dead, I still have active enemies out there, who know who I am, what I have, that I'm a threat to them. If I'm right about this, I assume the thing was in league with Dove, or at least had communication with him, learned from him about me. But . . . when I told him on the phone that my disk was stolen, he convincingly acted like he didn't know about it. So this being acted independently of Dove. Still, how did it know about my disk? What else might these forces have gleaned about me? Did I really kill that jellyfish thing I saw inside Gabrielle's body, the only witness to my deeds? If that thing escaped somehow, into some other plane, it too may have carried word of my activities. And that tentacled thing in the fountain. All of them bringing their reports back to . . . who? Is my paranoia getting too far ahead of me?

I try to get off the subject, so Saleet won't wonder why I'm getting so serious about hobgoblins, and ask her, "So why are you investigating this woman with the broom thing, instead of homicide?"

"We work in conjunction with homicide on sexually oriented murders; homicide needs all the help it can get, in Punktown. This is my first murder investigation." She munches some leaves thoughtfully. "I wonder if they'll bring us in on that dismemberment case, where they found the woman's body parts all over the city."

"I think I heard a little bit about that. They found her head in a laundromat in the suburbs, right? Inside a washing machine? And her legs miles apart . . . "

"Yeah—she was scattered to all the furthest points of the city, except for her torso, which was in the middle of the city, on a park bench on Salem Street."

"Salem Street, huh? I didn't know that." All nonchalant. That nice old Choom sector is getting more violent these days. Thanks in part to yours truly. "So, do they think she was sexually attacked?"

"Well, she was a prostitute. A young Choom girl. Besides being dismembered, her heart was cut out."

My fork has lodged in the air, half-way to my mouth. Saleet and I have definitely converged in the web of fate . . . if what I suspect is true. My intuition, my churning guts, tell me it is. I lower my bite of scrambled eggs. Must be nonchalant. I want to ask her if there were any traces of a star tattoo on the girl's chest, or did the removal of her heart obliterate that? But I must be careful what I ask. I could say I heard such and such on VT, but the forcers might be holding back certain details from the media, details I must not bring up lest she think I murdered the prosty myself.

"So they think a client . . . "

"Again, man hating women. Pathetic," she sneers. She's beautiful even sneering angrily.

I want to ask if the girl had purple hair. Eyes artificially slanted.

Saleet goes on: "I don't know why the sorry little wanker went out of his way to disperse her across the city like that, but who knows what fantasies drive these freaks. Head, torso, arm, arm, leg, leg, heart, and one finger. Index finger of her right hand. Go figure."

"Eight," I whisper.

"Eight?" she says.

"Eight pieces."

"Yeah. Eight."

Eight. Eight is the number. It's all about numbers. Math. Those body parts were not placed randomly. I want to know what other spots they were found in, but I'm afraid to get so worked up over this that it disturbs Saleet. She's smart, she's got that enhanced memory; I don't want her to turn her sharp mind on me in that way. I don't want to spoil what we have, whatever that might be.

Saleet looks like she's lost her appetite, too; she sets down her own fork, takes a sip of tea, then looks up at me. "The Utalla," she says suddenly, throwing me off, "are aligned with Ugghiutu, in the folklore. They're one of the groups of his servitor demons. Supposedly they know where to find his sleeping or hidden body—depending on your schism—and they feed some of his orifices the way birds feed their chicks . . . "

"Regurgitated cat," I try to joke. Stomach churning so loud I'm afraid she'll hear it, churning like a washing machine with a decapitated head inside it.

"You didn't really know about the Utalla before tonight, did you, Chris? I know you're interested in Kalian culture . . . "

"What? Saleet, you don't think I made up that mugger story just to play with you?"

"I'm not saying that. Just . . . "

"He really looked like that, I swear. Maybe it's just an odd coincidence." Though I don't believe in coincidence any more.

"Well, I just . . . it's just funny how you didn't want to file a report on the incident, and . . . " She stops. I think she can see the anger in my face as I turn my head away and sip my orange juice while I watch the traffic through the window.

"It's getting late," I say.

"Chris. I'm sorry." She puts her hand on my arm. I like the contact, but I can't break out of my chill that quickly. She thinks I'm a liar. "Chris . . . what do you want to do now?"

"Do?"

"Do you want to come see my place? You haven't yet. Or we can go watch some VT at yours . . . "

I know where this is going. My heart flutters above my roiling stomach, and the combination is a bit too much for me. Lust and fear don't digest well together, especially with sausage and coffee thrown into the mix. I want this . . . oh, have I ever wanted anything more? . . . and I've been wondering when it would come up. But I have to hesitate. Again, I'm not sure I can keep seeing this woman if I'm to follow the path I'm taking. And with this new information, which connects to me directly, how can I not? Plus I'm hurt, a bit angry. And I'm distracted; I want to look further into the matter of Utallas and this murdered girl on my computer at home, right away. It isn't the optimum time for this delirious opportunity . . . if any such perfect time could ever come. But even through all this chaos of feeling, she's impressed and excited me. How many Kalian women would be this forward, this brave? Braver than me, that's for sure. In a way, I wish she was addressing these matters instead of me. How I'd like to tell her, so she could help me . . . take over the investigation. But I can't involve her, endanger her. And I can't admit to my crimes, lest I end up trying to investigate these matters from inside a prison cell. Frankly, finally, I want Saleet so badly that it makes me overwhelmed, frightens me. But I'll bet she wouldn't believe that to be true.

"Not tonight, Saleet," I tell her. "I'm tired. It's late. Next time."

She slides her hand off my arm. "Right," she mutters, picking up her tea cup again.

I look back at her. "No, really. Next time. Just not tonight."

"I really am sorry I said that, Christopher. I do believe you. All right?"

"All right." I smile to reassure her, but it must look forced. I'm not feeling too smiley. May never, ever again.

We part solemnly. I give her a kiss on the cheek. I'm afraid she'll get sick of this distance I wedge between us, will give up on me. It would kill me. But it would be for the best.

* * *

First, Utallas. I find a few references, and one folktale in its entirety which reads a lot like Saleet's Zul story but without the benefit of being recited in her charming, slightly accented voice. Nest of cat pelts, skin like metal, pretty much the same stuff she mentioned. The things come across half whimsical in the tale, mischievous, not too scary for demon servants of the Big U. On another net site, an illustrated bestiary of imaginary animals, I find an artistic representation. It doesn't look very much like my mugger. A long beak, but too curved. Great black eyes, but my creature's eyes were bigger and his didn't have whites. The illustration's skin is too literally metallic (reflecting the crags around it). But I note the thing has arms and hands instead of wings. It holds a spitting cat in one fist.

Opening my eyes, I realize I dozed off for a while in front of my monitor. My cheek is sweaty from resting in my supporting palm. Sitting back from my position hunched over the keyboard, I check the time and see I was only out for fifteen or twenty minutes, but it was long enough to dream. In my dream, I imagined that I had stumbled upon a net site devoted to the Choom alchemist Wadoor, author of *Atlas of Chaos*, who according to the late Mr. Dove used geometric formulae to open portals to other planes. Suddenly Wadoor himself was there on the screen, speaking to me in an urgent tone . . . but I couldn't understand his native Choom tongue. The memory of the dream, its strong illusion of reality, actually gives me a brief shudder.

I get up to stretch, pace myself further awake for a few minutes, open a bottle of Chinese beer (the best thing about Punktown's cultural diversity is the diversity of beer), then settle in front of my nice new computer again to see what I can find out about this murdered Choom prosty.

I go to the official site of the Paxton Police Force. On their menu, I find public access file categories for HOMICIDE, SEX CRIMES, CRIME LOG BY DATE, and such like. I decide to try HOMICIDES first. On that page, I type in a search with the words, "dismembered Choom prostitute". I get a longer list than I'd hoped. But I click on the link for the most recent case, and I have found the one I'm looking for.

There is a photo ID of the victim staring out of the screen at me. (A police mug shot, I discover; she was arrested once for hooking.) A young, pretty Choom with her hair dyed snow white. But her eyes cosmetically altered to emulate those of an Asian human. One lip painted blue, the other red. And lest I have any doubts because of the different hair color, the name spells it out. Her name was JELENA DARLOOM.

The little creature I took to bed. Who lived in Mr. Dove's building and had bad dreams and got a star tattoo with a fiery eye at the center, to protect her . . . but who ultimately abandoned her pimp to escape her life of prostitution, according to her friends. Could her pimp, Ric, have tracked her down, killed her as a message to the others in his stable? I don't believe it. He wouldn't go so far to make his point.

I'm afraid to look further into the file, but I must. I must look at the link to CRIME SCENE PHOTOS.

Oh . . . God . . .

Best to get this first page over with. It's of her head. There are several photos of it. One was shot through the front window of the washing machine. Another was shot through the open top hatch. The clearest shots were taken of the head on a tray in the coroner's lab. Her hair, in these pictures, is a dark purple color, long and matted like a tangle of seaweed. Her altered eyelids are weirdly frozen half shut and her huge, gaping mouth has had its red and blue lipstick smudged and smeared away. But even in the laundromat shots, there is no real blood to be seen. Was the blood actually drained, or was it just that so much of it was lost through the sheer act of dismemberment?

The next page shows her left arm. It lies on the open side hatch of the mail box in which a postman discovered it. The letters around it don't look stained by blood. The flesh is as white and unmarred as wax.

Next, the right arm; crime scene, and coroner's slab. This appendage was discovered resting in an old flower box outside a suburban bakery. The palm is turned upwards, the fingers half curled like the legs of a dead spider, only the first finger is missing. I zoom in on the stump. Clean, neat, no blood.

Left leg with its dainty bare foot propped carefully on the outside window sill of a bank. Right leg found lying against the wall, conscientiously out of the way so as not to be under foot, in the vestibule of a small tenement house. The toe nails, like her finger nails, painted fluorescent orange.

Index finger of her right hand, pointing its orange nail at the sky. It was found with its end stuck atop a spike in a metal fence surrounding a smallish cemetery. I'm not only feeling sick, at this point, but increasingly angry. That finger touched itself, however unlovingly, to my flesh. Once it was the tiny, dimpled finger of an infant, whose mother had pressed her lips to it. Now it was a prop for a monster's self-amusement, as if it were made of rubber.

Resting on the hood of a hovercar parked in a condo complex, a shock to whomever had found it whilst preparing to head off for another seemingly dull day at the office, a smallish dark blob that had once been a pumping heart at the center of a vital, living being. I remember what my friend the doctor said, about organs looking like they shouldn't be able to work. This near-shapeless mass does not look like it was ever an efficient, life-sustaining machine, even when connected up to its valves and tubes. It is a sad symbol, as if Jelena Darloom's entire life and entire body have been reduced to this anonymous, compacted handful of bruised tissue. Reverted to a pitiful, formless fetus that will never be reborn.

The last page shows Jelena's still shapely torso, its purple-dyed tuft of pubic hair grotesquely challenging the world to view it, of itself, as sensual. Or *not* to view it as such. No bruises, no stains, such lovely alabaster skin made even whiter through loss of blood. Even the absence of head and limbs doesn't seem to mar its terrible perfection, at least not the way that hole does between her tiny breasts. Its edges are clean, it's almost a perfect circle, and the star tattoo is utterly gone as if removed with a cookie cutter. I'm reminded of Gabrielle's chest window, showing her tattooed heart within her, into which later on she hid away her palmcomp.

The torso rests on its back on a park bench, blanketing newspapers folded back from it, like a derelict who has spent the night there. Very funny. Very clever.

Thank God that part is over with. Now I return to the beginning of the file; I can either read or listen to the coroner's or investigating officers' reports on the case. I decide to just skim through the transcripts, not comfortable with having these lawmen facing into my apartment, seeming to talk to me.

Circumstances of death: HOMICIDE. Cause of death: UNKNOWN.

I know they did not try to extract memories of her last moments from her brain, even if her head was still fresh when they found it. She was only a prosty. A runaway, I see from the report, previously arrested as I glimpsed before. Wait. Her head. Her head . . .

I go back to the photos of her head, much as I hoped never to view them again. No bone-like, antler-like protrusions, as in the vidgame. But I saw the beginnings of such a growth on her friend when I went in search of Jelena that time. The lines between reality and unreality are blurring for me. I can't take it in. The lines and curves of existence are being bent beyond all recognition . . .

I skim the reports some more. The pimp, Ric, has been questioned but he has witnesses that can place him in a dance club at the time when Jelena must have been killed. Not to say he couldn't have had an associate murder her, but I for one don't believe that to be a possibility.

Again, I'm intrigued—as the investigators are—about the wide dispersal of the eight body parts. On the file menu, an overview of the city is offered to pinpoint the spots where all the fragments of Jelena Darloom turned up. I click on this link.

I view a satellite photo of Punktown which indicates the points of discovery, and also a street map with the same eight red dots. Punktown is so vast that from space it seems to sprawl like a continent in itself. Because it is always growing larger, larger, like a living thing (some believe one day it will merge with Miniosis into one megacity), it has an organic shapelessness. It does not grow out evenly in all directions. Around Punktown, in sparse fringes, are all that are left of the great forests that once surrounded the smaller Choom city it swallowed up.

I'm not surprised to see that the points where the body parts were found form a neat if obscure pattern. At the very center of Paxton: the torso. At the extreme northern point of the city, the head. To east and west, the arms and legs (right arm west, left arm east, as if a giant lay on its back, crucified across the face of Punktown). I'm reminded of that sketch by Leonardo da Vinci, a diagram of a man standing inside a box inside a circle, seemingly with four legs and four arms, limbs spread wide like Jelena's. I choose to view the pattern as a clock, however. Jelena's right arm at ten o'clock. Left arm at two o'clock. The heart at four o'clock. The right index finger at eight o'clock. I can't grasp the significance, but I do know that each of the body parts is precisely the same distance from that central torso.

A sacrifice. A ritual. I don't doubt, a ritual of summoning.

Did they (*they?*) already put their mark on her before I met her? After all, she was already besieged by nightmares. Tried to ward them off with a tattoo of some occult symbol. Or, did I doom her through my contact with her? I can't bear that thought. I have enough guilt about Gaby as it is.

I use my tool bar to draw lines connecting each point to the center. I end up with a pizza with seven unequal slices (unequal because there's nothing at one, three, six, nine and eleven o'clock). I try tracing a pentagram but that doesn't quite work. As I look for some clear system, and try to remember if the figure matches anything I've seen in the books by Wadoor and Skretuu, I can't help but notice the patterns in the street map of Punktown itself.

The central, oldest section is more organic, a little less systematized, at least less obviously so. As the city spreads out from there, a bit more mechanically ordered. Grids that run north and south, east and west. But still, that system is broken up where the city has overlapped the older city, and overlapped itself time and again, so that grids superimpose grids, blueprint atop blueprint, as if generations of spiders have woven their webs directly upon those of the spiders that preceded them.

Idly, I trace patterns in red, connecting this street to that street. It's like finding figures in the constellations; you can pretty much build anything you want from the possibilities. I see suggestive patterns in both the old Choom streets and the newer, Earth colony avenues, but again, it's like seeing animals in clouds. Or Don Quixote seeing giants in windmills. (But Cervantes said, "Fear is sharp-sighted, and can see things underground, and much more in the skies.") What am I suggesting to myself, here—that there is some vast conspiracy in the lay-out of Punktown, starting with the Chooms (perhaps begun as a curse, a revenge, directed at the invading Earth settlers), then carried on by the colonists themselves? Carried out over generations by some secret cult of Freemasons, devoted to the Old Ones? Hardly possible.

Well, perhaps not a conscious conspiracy. But could a silent, invisible hand . . . a vast, eight-fingered hand . . . have had some influence over the web-weaving? Some consciousness reaching out, whispering into sleeping ears, bending the lines and curves to its own advantage? Building a geometric diagram of its own brain in the very streets of this city? In effect, haunting every building with its essence, making each inhabitant a single cell of its titanic mind?

I sit back in my chair, to either clear my head or take this concept in.

It's insane. But I think about Ugghiutu, shaping his amorphous body into a temple to himself, to lure inside the unwary, the Zuls. Masquerade, camouflage, like the snake pretending it was a vine.

Hungry. Patient.

Insanity, or intuition? Do my very cells recognize the truth in my suspicions? Does this invisible presence that I suspect even have a strand of its web connected to my own soul? Do my very atoms scream at me in an attempt to wake me up to this invasion as last? Maybe this is how the Old Ones, or their servitors, or whatever I'm fighting, have learned certain things about me . . . because I'm threaded into the weave.

It's like an epiphany.

Thus begins hours of obsessive research that strays hither and yon, adrenalin counteracting my former doziness and the effects of my beer. I do a search on ley lines, which I read about in an occult book years ago purely for entertainment. I read about a Sacred Triangle in Great Britain that connected the ancient sites of Avebury, Stonehenge and Glastonbury. These ley lines or "straight tracks" are supposedly a pattern of magnetic earth force, and everything from prehistoric megalithic sites to less ancient churches were built upon them, as if to tap into their currents. The Chinese had their concept of "dragon paths". I read about the phenomenon of crop circles. Huge mysterious symbols appearing in fields; most blatantly faked, apparently, but others supposedly genuine and allegedly formed along patterns of earth force. The immense Nazca Lines. The Phaistos Disk of Crete with its maze-like patterns and strange hieroglyphics. The principal of Feng Shui.

I get briefly sidetracked reading about an ancient book called *Hypnerotomachia Poliphili* by an Italian friar, Francesco Colonna. Sounds like something Dove Books would have carried. It's a weird, symbolic romance. The author was obsessed by architecture, and sex, and the subtitle is: The Strife of Love in a Dream. I like that; it makes me think of myself, and Saleet. There is a basic, a crucial two-number equation between man/woman as simple as yin/yang, but so many people defile it, not just the Kalians but my own people, and no wonder things are in constant chaos when people can't even get that arithmetic right.

As if this is a segue from one's external environment to the inner landscape, I move from the outside to the inside. I read about the seven chakras, or nodal points of energy, said to reside within the human body. I read that we each have seven bodies: the etheric, the astral, the mental, the spiritual, the cosmic, and the nirvanic. A diagram of a man seated in the lotus position shows the position of these nodal points, following a column up through his center. And, da Vinci-like, geometric patterns surround the figure, are defined by his very form. A triangle is formed from the top of the head connecting with the two knees. Another, inverted triangle connects the shoulders with the groin. The concept of chakras is compared to the Tikkihotto concept of the inner "wheels" of energy housed in the body. One in the forehead, one in the throat, in the chest, the stomach, and in the genitals. These wheels of force mesh like gears with the clockwork of the universe; when the physical body dies, the forces of the universe keep these wheels of force turning, so that the spirit persists (a ghost in the machine?). From the body, back to the outer world again. The Golden Mean. Da Vinci used this mathematical concept of proportion, as did the Egyptians and Greeks to design their structures. The crucial, "irrational" number of 1.618 is at the heart of the Golden Mean. I read about the Golden Mean being seen in the ratio of growth patterns in living things, such as the formation of a sea shell's spiral. It gets very dry from there, and starts to read like Wadoor and Skretuu's mind-boggling spell books. Aperiodic tiling. Five-fold symmetry. Overlapping decagons. I skim over Fibonacci's sequence. Pythagoras' constant. String theory and supersymmetry. My brain starts to feel like it's unraveling and reknitting itself. I finish the dregs of my warm beer, am too absorbed to walk to the grimy yellow fridge to get a replacement.

With my head thus full, I go back to looking at street maps and overviews of Punktown, both upper and lower levels. I find charts of its major sewer lines. At the site for the Paxton Transit Authority, I view the arteries and veins of the subway system. On one site, which focuses on the great earthquake of twenty some odd years ago, I view maps that illustrate the areas of damage, primarily to the subway and subterranean systems, but also to the upper levels.

I find that at the epicenter of the destruction, a Tikkihotto church literally dropped into the subways below when the ground gave out beneath it.

The temple, I read, was for a minor religious faction called the Church of the Burning Eye.

I want to read more about this compelling development (a church sinking into the earth? . . . sounds almost Biblical), but finally I get up to use the bathroom, stretch my legs, back and especially my neck, tight and aching after leaning forward so intently into the screen for hours. Pacing in the kitchenette, I get myself a cold beer at last.

Hey, I realize. The Tikkihotto don't *have* eyes, burning or otherwise. Ocular filaments like tendrils instead. I hurry back to my seat, run a fresh search.

The official page comes up for the Church of the Burning Eye. On their main page is their logo. It's a five-pointed star, with an abstract eye at its center. The pupil of that eye is a column of fire.

It's the tattoo Jelena was given to ward off evil.

I go into the page. Read a bit from the link called WHO WE ARE.

Sounds very quackish, very cultish, very smiley and blissful. But something really stands out for me.

They worship a pantheon of gods they call the Elders.

I remember what Mr. Dove said about the Elder Gods, who defeated the Old Ones and imprisoned them in comas, before disappearing from our plane. Saleet described something similar in the nameless Shadow Gods. Is this a kind of archetypal concept that is bound to repeat itself in diverse cultures, or is there an actual connection here?

Their church has since been rebuilt, but—oddly—in the city of Miniosis. They mention the earthquake but don't suggest that there was any evil agency behind it.

Still . . .

A kind of cosmic revenge? I wonder. Does the ancient battle still rage?

I remember that mysterious group I read about, the Children of the Elders, who hunted down and destroyed copies of the *Necronomicon*, but they were on Earth, were not (apparently) Tikkihottos. Coincidence? Believing that there is only coincidence at work in all of this is more of a stretch than accepting it all as truth. In my research, I read a quote from the philosopher Schopenhauer that said, "Everything is interrelated and mutually attuned."

Suddenly I want very badly to know if the ruins of the original Church of the Burning Eye remain underground, sealed up in one of the numerous tunnels that were abandoned after the terrible quake. Suddenly I want to go there and see for myself.

But for now, I drink my beer, and absorb, and digest, and I feel myself changing, ever changing. Maybe it's called enlightenment.

* * *

I spend this morning casting spells to protect me from evil.

They're actually referred to as "formulae", as the computer translates the language of the books *Atlas of Chaos* and *The Veins of the Old Ones*. One formula, from the first volume, is called "Doors upon doors". It will block, redirect or reroute "the pathways of dangerous energies which might gain access through the dwelling's primary entrance". I use a bar of soap to draw: it needn't be the blood of a sacrificed goat, infant or virgin. It doesn't even need to be visible, as I interpret it—the patterns can be traced simply with a finger. But I like the idea of leaving some trace or residue which makes the pattern tangible, and since I don't have an indelible marker, which would be the best thing to use on these glossy pale yellow tiles, I come up with the idea of leaving a thin, waxy scum of soap (after considering but dismissing toothpaste). I outline a large circle around my apartment's door, and referring to the design on my computer's screen, draw various intersecting lines across the closed door itself.

I draw patterns in the corners of the room, following a recipe from the latter book, which cautions that the angles of corners can be utilized to open portals from one plane into another. In certain light, I can see the shiny snail-trails the soap has left.

All the while, I reevaluate my epiphany of the night before. Yes, I might have let my imagination run too far with the ball, but I don't think so. It feels too right. It goes beyond intuition into a realization, a knowledge that lies in my very molecules.

And I keep thinking about the Church of the Burning Eye. I want to find out more about it. If there are allies out there so I'm not so alone, overwhelmed . . . so helpless despite my knowledge.

But, as frivolous as it seems in comparison, I keep thinking of Saleet as well. The tension that seems to be eclipsing our attraction. Cosmic matters vying for my attention with bodily matters of the most primitive sort. No, but it isn't just a sexual attraction. I am falling in love with her, no question; none of the ambiguity of emotion I felt with Gaby. I decide I must take some incentive here; I must make a move, before she decides I'm uninterested, not worth chasing any more. I can't find her number so I have to look at my message log on my computer and trace her last call to me. This done, I leave her a recording telling her I want to see her tonight, tomorrow, whenever she's free. She must check her messages during the day, because only two hours later I get a call from her. She's at work, in some noisy office; I hear vidphones ringing, voices, laughter, someone crying. She's in uniform, her thick hair sleeked back and clenched behind her head. She looks warily pleased.

I smile and make my suggestion. She says, "Why don't we wait until day after tomorrow; I have the day off. You want to see my apartment? You haven't yet."

"It better be nice, after you criticized mine."

"Well, it's humble. But I like it. I couldn't afford it without Zoksa." Zoksa is her Kalian room mate, who works as a hostess at a Kalian restaurant. "You can meet her. She and I can make dinner for you."

"Wow—wonderful."

So, it's planned. That went well; her wariness faded pretty quickly.

I'm glad I made the effort. I play back our exchange, and freeze a certain image of her that I like, making it into my computer's desktop. Big smile white against her dark gray lips, eyes narrowed warmly. To think I used to find the black eyes of her people frightening.

I see figures frozen in their bustle behind her. A Choom plainclothes officer with his white sleeves rolled up, walking across the office. A uniformed human officer sitting in another cubicle; photos and memos tacked up on its gray partitions that remind me of my own honeycomb cell of old. Wait. I touch keys, magnify the image, closing in on the photos tacked in that other cubicle. Yes, as I thought. Crime scene photos of Jelena Darloom . . . the same I saw on the net last night. An image of her decapitated head fills my computer screen, as if she is a jealous lover who wants to take Saleet's place.

Reopening Wadoor's *Atlas of Chaos* on the screen, I peruse more formulae. I plan to stand on my one chair so as to draw a large warding symbol across my ceiling. I need to bury this room in a thicket of formulae, so that nothing can penetrate it or even find it, so that it exists beyond or behind the city which leans heavily outside its every wall. But I end up skimming around, reading longer passages in the book, and in so doing, I find this:

"There was one night, when rain-filled winds slashed at my windows, and serpent tongues of light flickered beyond my drawn curtains, that I found myself seeing more deeply than ever before into the catacombs that are burrowed through the ether all around us, connecting this realm with those too numerous to fathom, this greater clarity seeming to coincide with the force of the storm, as if the lightning itself lit these tunnels. As I sat gazing into the complex formula chalked onto the slate propped before me, my consciousness flowed forward, down this corridor and that, narrow passages that seemed carved through walls of solid light, and rooms branched off from them. Some of these luminous white chambers were filled with thick swirling mists, and offered nothing to my mind's eye, but in one of these rooms I found a small window or opening in the far wall. This window, when I approached it, gave me a view into a more conventional room in which a man slept at his desk directly in front of me, his head lowered with chin in hand, but I could see him clearly enough to note the unusual smallness of his mouth. I knew, without knowing, that I must awaken this man who was not a Choom, to warn him of a vast dark force I strongly sensed converging around him, that I must share with him the protective formulae I have learned, but when the man raised his head to listen to my words, I could see that he was both frightened and uncomprehending. And then mists rose up between us, and the man and indeed the window itself were gone."

After I read this, I sit blankly at my computer a long time, all but numb. But I do shudder briefly.

* * *

Saleet's place is nice, and so is Zoksa. She is a Sarikian, a Kalian tribe that primarily lives on a large island called Sarik Duul and which is much more moderate in its views than are the people Saleet finds her origins in. Zoksa tells me a bit about them. They wear red turbans rather than blue, and now I recall that I have indeed seen Kalians with red turbans in the past. Zoksa reveals that Saleet used to say she'd marry a Sarikian one day, because he'd more readily accept her. "But now, all I hear her talk about is you." Zoksa smiles and Saleet gives her a warning look. I like Zoksa, and she's very pretty, but no one is more lovely than Saleet.

Their apartment is in a nicer part of subtown than mine—on the fringes of the Kalian neighborhood—but it isn't a whole lot bigger than my flat, except that it has two individual bedrooms and is much cleaner. The walls aren't tiled like mine, and are painted a nice terra cotta color, with metallic gold stenciling applied around the edge at ceiling level (Zoksa's proud handiwork). There are tapestries, paintings, figurines that reflect their Kalian culture, but there is a bizarre co-mingling of funky plastic toys, fashion magazines, framed movie posters. Fragrant incense unfurls into the air, I sip tea such as was offered to me in the Kalian Reading Room, and tantalizing aromas drift from the kitchen partitioned off from the livingroom.

When Zoksa goes into the kitchen to stir something or other, Saleet and I smile at each other. This afternoon she wears a too-small black t-shirt which bares much of her midriff, so smooth, subtly rounded; I'm not crazy about women with hard washboard stomachs—too masculine. The short sleeves bare her full, soft arms almost up to her shoulders. She wears a pair of black pants of a shiny silken material, low-slung on her hips, clinging tightly to her thighs. Her feet are bare, as she prefers (I think if she could wear bare feet in her forcer uniform she would).

I drink her in, sip her like a wine, savoring a beauty that almost makes me panic; how can I possess this, hold onto this? I mustn't let this go. Her hair, so black it's almost a midnight blue, falls thickly down her back, parted in the middle to bare her forehead with its raised scars. Her nose is somewhat broad, her cheekbones strong though her face has that appealing layer of baby fat. She smiles so mysteriously at me, her full lips compressed together, like the haughty half-sneering pout of some exotic princess. The dark unbroken line of her brow dips slightly between her almond eyes, which seem to smile at me slyly out of their corners though without whites I can't say for sure. Her breasts are heavy as they strain against her little girl's shirt, seeming to aim at me, engorged. I'm feeling engorged myself. Swollen with something even more delirious than lust.

I go across the colorfully carpeted floor to her. She's still smiling that closed little smile which couldn't be more subtle or more plain. I take her bare upper arms in my hands, kneading my thumbs across their pale gray flesh. She tilts her head back; I'm nearly a head taller than her. Her lips part just a fraction, with the tiniest of moist sounds. I bend my head down and our tongues trade places, slither across each other languorously, like mating things independent of us. Slowly my arms slide around her, encircle her, her breasts pressing up against my chest. I slide my right hand down to her lower back, where it's deliciously bare under my palm. I want her with such an urgency, such a greedy hunger that I wish I could merge the atoms of my hand into the atoms of her back. I want us to swallow each other at our joined mouths. For our pounding hearts to rise up through our constraining ribs and blend and blur into one doubly-pounding organ. But it's more than the animal call to mate, to propagate the species, more than the jungle drums of hormones. There is a weave through all things, I've learned, and we are woven together, I have no doubt of it. Our destinies are written in the ley lines, in the constellations, perhaps even as an afterthought in the dreaming brains of the Old Ones.

I think I hear Zoksa come back into the room and I glance up, but she must have ducked back when she saw us locked in the center of the room.

Gently Saleet disengages from me (maybe she heard her room mate, too). She whispers, her voice husky, "Zoksa is going to a movie with two friends after we eat. We can be alone then."

"Nothing against Zoksa," I whisper back, "but I'm glad to hear that."

The food is a sensual overload all by itself; everything from our meal to the effects of the wine that accompanies it to the incense—the Kalian music playing in the background and the exotic surroundings—conspires to lift me into another, heightened state of consciousness. Another universe at the center of which, like an all-consuming black star, is my Saleet, still giving me those mysterious smiles across the table even as she chews.

I love every dish except the glebbi, which tastes like a llama-sized lizard. Saleet informs me that this specimen was one of those grown, butchered and packaged at her father's company. I don't imagine it would be any better had it been born and raised in the natural way (with those little extras like a head). After dinner we have a sugary kind of soup for dessert, along with some nonKalian espresso. As I blow on a spoonful of my hot soup Zoksa turns to Saleet and says something softly in Kalian. Saleet says something back and they both laugh.

"Hey, now," I scold them, "none of that stuff." Looking at both of them at once, it finally hits me. Zoksa doesn't have the "veins of

Ugghiutu" on her face, the ritual scarring that Saleet has. "Zoksa," I ask her, "what do the Sarikians worship? Don't you believe in Ugghiutu?"

"Oh yeah," she says, "we believe in him, all right. But we don't worship him. He's isn't both our god and our devil, to us, but just our devil. Ages ago, my people went out to the unoccupied island of Sarik Duul on great ships, and settled there to escape from the influence of Ugghiutu on the mainland. Our priests surrounded the entire coast of Sarik Duul with protective symbols they drew in the sand, and which are redrawn in the sand once a year, even today. We worship the Shadow Gods, who did battle with Ugghiutu and his brothers, and put him to sleep in chains of magic."

"I told him a bit about that," Saleet says.

I ask, "Well what more do you know about these Shadow Gods that Saleet's people don't know?"

"No more. That's probably why more people don't follow our beliefs—there's just so little known about the Shadow Gods, even what they looked like, even their names, so there's not a lot to get a handle on. But they beat the devils, and that's good enough for me."

"Do you yourself actually follow this religion? Do you pray?"

"Yeah, I believe in it. But we don't pray to them . . . we don't ask them for help and guidance. They're gone, they have no more influence here like Ugghiutu has. We just give our thanks to their memory, more than anything else. If they hear us somehow, great. If Ugghiutu were ever to break free of his chains and awaken someday, we want them to come back. We want to stay on their good side."

I turn to Saleet. "I think you should convert to Zoksa's religion, Sally."

"I told you, Chris, I'm an agnostic."

The Shadow Gods are the Elder Gods of the *Necronomicon*, there is no doubt. And the Elders worshiped by that obscure Tikkihotto cult, the Church of the Burning Eye. But those deities are gone. Are they, Gods forbid, dead?

I continue to tease Saleet. "My girlfriend, the devil worshiper."

"*Girlfriend*, huh?" Zoksa says, wiggling her long single brow.

"Your girlfriend, the forcer, who's going to hit you with her nightstick," Saleet says.

"Will you handcuff me first?"

Zoksa promptly rises from her chair. "Oh-kay . . . I'd better clear the table and get going soon."

Saleet and I smile across at each other again. I flush a little bit, that bashful streak rising, and avert my eyes to sip my coffee.

We help Zoksa clear the rest of the table, then move ourselves to the sofa while we wait for her to be off with her friends. As is becoming a fond habit of ours, Saleet and I watch VT. Girlfriend, I think. I can't believe I came right out and referred to her as my girlfriend. She doesn't appear to mind; her hip and outer leg are pressed almost too hard against mine, she sits so close to me. I ache to put my hand on her thigh under its blue-black membrane of silk, taut across its firmness like the skin of a fruit. I can't bring myself to do that, but I do something more significant. I reach over and take her hand, weaving my fingers through hers. It's warm. She squeezes back and I see her look over at me but I swallow and keep my eyes on the VT. Yes, there's an unspoken agreement which, in my heightened sensitivity of late, I feel profoundly in my molecules and in my chakras and whatever else is crammed inside me. Tonight is our communing.

Dropping my eyes idly from the vidtank to the carpet which takes up nearly all of the livingroom's floor, I admire the intricate embroidery in colorful and metallic threads. The carpet is shaped like a large cross with four equal arms. Thus, I realize, eight corners. In the central area of the rug, beautifully rendered hunters armed with something like spear guns, some riding large glebbis, chase after fearsome animals that look like manta rays with four lithe legs under their broad mantles. One of these animals, rearing up, is tearing a hunter's arm off with the mouth on the underside of its flat body. Huddled protectively in one of the four arms of the cross shape is a cluster of finely-garbed women, wives or admirers of the heroic males, watching the action. Another arm of the cross contains a miniature rendering of some spired city. A third arm contains an image of one of the manta-panthers roasting on a spit. And in the fourth arm is a black structure with eight tapered minarets or towers. Men are carrying one of the manta-things, trussed up but apparently still alive, to its yawning front door . . . obviously as an offering. Sacrifice.

"Can we eat one of those the next time I visit?" I ask, pointing to the carpet.

"A goloth? They're extinct now. Too much hunting, maybe."

I look directly at Saleet. "When will I meet your family?"

Now it's Saleet who avoids my eyes, turning back to the VT. "I don't know . . . "

"They won't ever accept me, will they?"

"They've been very tolerant of me. They're more modern than . . . "

"I don't expect you to have to make a choice between us."

"Shh, Christopher. Not now. We'll take it as it comes."

Zoksa returns brightly to say her goodbyes; I release Saleet's hand to rise and thank her. She unabashedly gives me a hug. I don't want Saleet to be anyone other than Saleet, but it would be so much easier if she were one of these Sarkinians. I suspect her family would accept me more readily. Especially since I'm sympathetic to their religious beliefs.

Now we're alone. We sit back on the sofa. I hope I haven't ruined the tone of the evening with my difficult question. I try to get us off into another direction. "How's your case with that . . . broom . . . thing?"

"Going nowhere yet. But my partner and I have been asked to lend some help on the case we talked about, with the prostitute . . . "

"Jelena Darloom?" I practically blurt. I think I even sat up straighter on the couch, just now.

She raises her brow at me. "You're really following this, aren't you?"

"Well . . . it's an unusual case. I read about it a little bit on the net . . . "

"Well, unfortunately, murdered and mutilated prostitutes isn't an unusual occurrence."

"So they must feel it was a sex crime, to bring you into it . . . "

"They found semen inside the body, as it turns out."

"Human? Choom?"

A hesitation. Then, "Kalian." Another beat. "That's another reason they want me on this."

"Semen from one person, or were there more?"

"Chris, I really can't talk . . . "

"Well, what about the parts being spread across town? Any ideas on that? What's with her finger, stuck on that spike on that cemetery fence?"

"Only the delusional fuck who did that to her could explain it, Chris."

Mm . . . this isn't a good line of conversation. I don't like to hear Saleet swear, and she's getting too intense, somewhat hostile. I've stained the mood a bit, maybe. I hope to learn more about the Jelena Darloom case from her, but I can't push it further right now.

"I'm proud of you," I tell her. "What you do. You're so strong. I worry about you, though."

"I'm pretty tough."

"And you're pretty, too." I take her hand again, bend toward her for a kiss. For a beat or two her lips feel hard, a bit resistant, but they soften pliantly under mine. She leans into me. Her body is very warm, seems warmer to the touch than an Earth person's; an inner steam rises through the tightly-knitted material of her skin and of her clothing.

I move my lips to her throat, just under her jaw, and she tips her head back to arch her neck invitingly. I move along its length, to where it sweeps into her shoulder. The scent of her hair is heavy in my nose, fills my head like a dark cloud. Her hand rests with feminine lightness on the back of my own neck. I take it, turn its palm up, and press my lips into its damp hot center where the lines cross and intersect in mysterious patterns some feel they can decipher. Rising, still holding her hand, I draw her to her feet. We drift lightly toward her bedroom together.

The door shuts with a secretive but decisive click.

Saleet turns to me, and we're embracing again, kissing deeply. I'm kissing her throat again. Whether it is her natural scent, or an oil rubbed into her skin, she has an earth-toned spicy smell that reminds me of sandalwood or patchouli. There's a faint, not unpleasant musk of perspiration. I'm rubbing her lower back, gliding my hands up under the abbreviated hem of her shirt. Then sliding them down to cup her full bottom. She copies me, squeezing mine in turn.

I disengage from her enough to take the edge of her shirt and begin to pull it up away from the flesh beneath, as if peeling a ripe fruit. She assists me, and skins the black membrane over her head. Glimpses of the intimate shaved bareness of her underarms. Her bra is dark purple. I cup her breasts and lift each of them slightly to plant a gentle kiss on the nipples that press at the restraining fabric.

Reaching around behind her, I unclasp the bra, and free her breasts. They are soft but hold much of their bound shape, in that gravity-defying trick of the young. Their aureoles and nipples are the same dark gray of her lips. Again I cradle them, again distribute slow, gentle kisses upon them, deeply inhaling their flesh. I take a nipple between my lips, and no suckling child was ever more contented than me. I could lay my head on her chest like this for eternity.

But following our telepathic program, we step away from each other so we can finish undressing. I remove my shirt, watching as she unfastens and works down her satiny black pants. Her briefs are of dark purple cotton. We embrace to kiss again and I feel and squeeze her full shapely cheeks through her soft panties . . . but I can only take so much of that before my hands are sliding beneath their elastic. I work her panties off her hips, down her legs, and she steps out of them.

Now reclining on her bed, her arms flung back behind her head, she watches as I finish my own undressing. Then I position myself over her lower body, begin exploring her almost daunting number of wondrous curves and planes. I stroke and massage her feet, the soles of which are tough and even calloused. She murmurs something self-consciously about not rubbing lotion into them often enough, but I kiss them to reassure her and work my way up. I kiss her shins, her calves with their faint rasp of stubble, her thighs as soft as flesh could ever aspire to be. Sliding my shoulders under them, curling my arms around them, I lower my face to a thick, glossy black patch of secret shadow, from which the strengthened musk in the air emanates deliriously like a smoky incense. It almost has the quality of smoldering autumn leaves.

Above me, my eyes closed, I hear her sleep-heavy breathing, little jags whistling through her nostrils. Maybe the faintest exhalation of a sigh. Lifting my head to pinch a wiry hair off my tongue, I see that these lips are as dark a gray as those of her mouth, both sets enlarged with blood flow. I again press my mouth and tongue into service, my nose pressed into that fragrant lush thatch. But she isn't as moist as Gaby would have been at this point, and I wonder if I'm really exciting her. Perhaps this is very alien to her—I can't imagine that the misogynistic Kalian males administer to their women in this manner.

Her hands find my head, and she draws me further up her body, which again makes me wonder if she's self-conscious or uncomfortable about my technique. I see she has a plastic tube in her hand now. She whispers, "Rub some of this into me, Chris. We don't naturally lubricate like your women do . . . it's the men who lubricate."

"Easier for them to masturbate, huh?" I joke nervously. I squeeze some of the jelly onto my fingers, and ease one of them in and out of her as sensuously as I can make it seem. She's small in that way; I've heard that Kalian men have long but very slender members. I'm hoping we can go through with this after all. I glance up at her face shyly as I stretch her enough to work a second finger inside her. I feel her arch her back a bit, hopefully from pleasure. Her eyes are closed, maybe in enjoyment, though from her compressed mouth I think she's too shy to look at me right now, herself.

"All right?" I whisper.

She nods.

I position myself above her. Lower my full length upon her. I start guiding myself into her opening, and she winces a little, takes hold of me herself and modifies the angle. I press deeper in increments, sliding in and out, but this works in my favor, teasing out my pleasure until at last—thank God—I finally enter her to the hilt, gripped entirely inside the seeming molten heat of her interior. I almost come at once and have to wrestle for control of the urge.

I get it harnessed nicely, though, because it's a good hour straight that we fuck. Me on top, her legs hiking up around me like the hungry jaws of a giant insect. Her sitting atop me, her gray-fleshed bosom hanging into my receiving hands, churning her hips, the sound of it a slickness in the air. Then me behind her, holding onto her waist tightly, her hips flaring out and ass bunched up hard against my belly, cheeks parted. Sweat shines in the groove of the small of her back and our skin is sticky. The atmosphere is dense with earthy aroma, seems fogged. She's giving little husky sobs now, self-conscious little half-stifled moans. For all her shocking modern rebellion, it's as if she can't give herself totally to her pleasure, strains to just barely contain it.

But I cry out loudly, several times, as I speed up and then let myself go inside her with such a burst that I think I might be hitting her in the heart with the ejaculation. I hope I'm not gripping her waist too hard, grinding too deeply in her, but the intensity jolts through me like a current.

We subside to a more relaxed position, me on top again, and I pump very languidly while I wonder if I'm going to die of a heart attack. I reach my right hand between us while I fuck her and rub her clitoris with my fingers. Before today I wasn't sure if Kalian women possessed those fleshy buttons, and if they did, whether they were allowed to keep them.

My wrist is getting cramped but I can feel Saleet building toward a climax at last. She rides the wave just to the crest and then breaks off with a grimace as if in child-birth, pushing my hand away almost frantically.

"No," I whisper, urgent, trying to calm her, "let me finish it for you, baby . . . "

She won't let go of my wrist. "That's enough," she gasps, "I did . . . I came . . . "

"Are you sure? It looked like you could have gone that one more step . . . "

"It's scary. I'm afraid I'll fall off the other side."

"Saleet, no . . . let me finish it for you."

But she won't let go of my hand. "Someday. Not now, Chris. It was great . . . I came. I did. I came enough for now."

"You risk your life in the streets, and you're scared to let . . . "

"Shh," she pleads, and it looks as though a moistness films her obsidian eyes. I realize I've never seen her cry before. "This is harder for me than you might think, Chris. It's hard for me being in love with a man from outside my culture. It's hard for me to fight who I'm expected to be."

I embrace her. Hold her. I push her hair away to nuzzle her ear. "I know," I reassure her. "Please don't be scared. Please don't leave me."

She holds me in return; tightly. But she doesn't say anything.

* * *

I don't know if I should follow a sequence. I don't know which part of Jelena Darloom was deposited first. I can only trust in my intuition, and it has led me to a stone bench in the middle of cobble-stoned Salem Street, where vehicles aren't allowed to pass, in the heart of the old Choom town at the center of Punktown. I sit on the bench where they found the headless, limbless, heartless torso of Jelena. There is no stain, but I can see the ghastly sundered body here in my mind's eye. It helps that I have photos with me, printed out from my computer and folded in my generous coat pocket for reference.

For comforting warmth I have a hot mustard drink I bought from a street vendor. A Choom beverage; not as popular as was the fad a few years ago, but I still like one occasionally. The air is getting a bite to it now that autumn deepens (its progression is a minor shock to me after staying in the moderate climate of the underground for such stretches). The sky is like the inside of a sea shell. I have bought a new coat today, a respectable businessman's overcoat, down to my knees and black with a suede-like feel. It will conceal my shotgun if need be. My money is getting very thin now. I just simply can not go find some prosaic job at this point. I wonder if Saleet can lend me money and I dismiss the thought with a blast of self-directed anger. Bad enough I don't have a job; I want her to respect me. How soon before she starts thinking of me as lazy, unmotivated, a slack-off? As I've considered before (with dread), if worst comes to worst, I'll seek out my father (near here), or my mother in Miniosis. I could take a bus or tube to that nearby city.

I have printed out other sheets as well. They are diagrams, symbols, from *The Veins of the Old Ones*. With a stick of lip balm, I am copying the symbol from the print-out spread in my lap, a gust of wind rustling its edge. I am drawing that symbol on the rough stone surface where Jelena lay disfigured, unrecognizable, just meat. I am counteracting whatever spell was imprinted here by her sacrifice. I am closing one of the windows that my enemies are opening. I don't know who my enemies are. I don't think my enemies even know each other, in some cases. All I know is that there are those whose aims are opposed to my own. Kalian sperm inside Jelena's ruined shell. Hence, some of my enemies are Kalian.

The drawing is just barely visible as a waxy residue. It doesn't matter, apparently, whether it now gets smudged, obliterated, washed away. It isn't the artistic medium that counts, but the form it gives existence to. Apparently that can't be so readily obliterated. It sinks into the very atoms of the stone.

Before I even drew my picture, I laid my hand flat on the spot as if it were a gravestone. Oh Jelena, I thought. I hope it wasn't me who attracted all this to you.

Finished, I cap my makeshift pen. I rise, finish off my welcome hot drink, dispose of its cup. Hands in my new pockets, I walk to the tube station. I have seven more stops to make today.

In the vestibule of a shabby tenement house, where a pretty, slender and disembodied right leg with orange-painted toenails was discovered, I trace a pattern in lip balm on the wall near the floor. I finish and straighten up just as a black woman comes down the stairs, giving me a suspicious look. I smile and apply some balm to my lips because it's in my hands and is an innocuous substance (to the layman, at least—unaware of its more impressive uses). When she heads out onto the street I wipe my sleeve across my lips with a grimace. I never use lip balm.

I render waxen graffiti on the window of a bank. On the window's sill was found a woman's left leg. I wonder how many people passed by it and only gave it a quick glance, like they're giving my act of vandalism now.

A symbol takes form on the shell of a mail box inside which a mail carrier was no doubt incensed to discover a left arm with insufficient postage attached.

A lot of traveling to reach these far points. I've never covered so much of this vast city in one day. It was morning when I started out and it's noon already. Though the smells outside are enticing, I don't venture inside the bakery on whose window box I draw a symbol to exorcize the ghost of a dismembered right arm.

I head back into the thick of town on an old shunt line, sparking along its taut cable. While I wait to pick up another shunt out to yet another of the spots on the printed-out map in my pocket, I decide to kill an hour in the Canberra Mall, buy a cheap lunch in the food court.

From the balcony of the second floor I watch the people pass below me, and it's like watching microscopic organisms swim across a glass slide. In the seething masses, fleeting patterns of different colored clothing and hair interweave with mock meaning. Or is it mock? I look at the patterns in the floor tiles beneath them, and then at my own feet. How was this design of mostly matte white tiles interspersed with smaller powder blue tiles chosen? Consciously? Unconsciously? Like the scales of some great reposing beast on whose back we walk like fleas waiting to be shaken off when it arises.

In the food court I sit down at a greasy and sticky, crumb-strewn table with a tray full of bad Chinese food. As I sip my hot and sour soup, I stare at a giant bubble gum machine against the far wall, near some kiddie rides. Inside this over-sized globe are oversized variously colored gum balls. Toward the lower left side of the sphere, which looms like a planet in space, is an irregular row of six pink gum balls. Six gum balls in a line, touching each other. The law of averages? Chance? Such a minor thing. But it takes on a sinister insinuation in my current state of mind. Six sinister pink gum balls, like a portent in the constellations. Like a statue weeping blood, a plague of locusts. I am either seeing the world with the eyes of a prophet or a madman, but are those designations really so far apart?

At another table close by I see four white boys of about fifteen harassing a young Choom mother who sits at the table next to theirs. She has a toddler in a booster seat and is trying to ignore their sexual comments but I see cowed fear in her face. Her child laughs, crushing a fried dilky root in its fist. One of the youths unseals his fly and fondles himself under the table, cooing in a falsetto to get her attention but he doesn't. I wonder where security is even as I realize I'm floating over to their table and standing above them. I feel like a pillar of black in my new coat.

They could well be armed. Probably are. I am not. One of them looks up at me, and then lightly elbows his neighbor. Now they're all looking up at me. As per one of the latest trends, all four of these unique individuals wears a t-shirt on the front of which is reproduced an enlarged photo of his respective sexual organ in a state of turgidity. Their parents give them the money for such things. They wear sports jackets varying only slightly in their shades of gray. All four are shaved bald except for a monk's ring, another fad. All four are too tall, too skinny, their features too perfectly smugly even. They are a sinister pattern like six pink gum balls. There is a sickness in the cells of this town, a cancer that extends even into insignificant organisms like these.

Peripherally I see the mother look up at me as well. I don't know what I'm going to say, but I prepare myself for the insults and arrogance to be redirected at me. For the boys to stand in unison.

They don't. One mumbles something to another, and they all drop their gaze to what's left of their food. Gather their drinks. They do in fact rise, but not with exclamations of mockery and hostility. They seem wilted within their gangly height, and skulk off away from me and the frightened mother. Without looking at her, a bit embarrassed for some reason, I walk away myself.

They were afraid of me. Because I'm an adult? I've mentioned that there is a squinty meanness in my eyes which—despite my slender build—I believe has protected me from being mugged overly much. But I wonder if it's more than that. Something subtly more, but something those four animals picked up on with jungle intuition. The fact that I've actually killed people now? The fact that I'm willing to kill more? The fact that I'm at war? Even the fact that I am charging myself with knowledge and knowledge is power and I am wielding that power today in something that can only be likened to magic?

I shouldn't let this go to my head, but then again I should. It effects my stride as I cross the food court, return to the mall proper. I *should* allow myself to feel strong. I must believe in my own powers. I must feel I'm potent enough to do whatever things need to be done.

Learning about the vastness of the Outer Gods has hammered home to me the insignificance of humankind in the universe. We are as amoebas to them. And yet, one sperm can spark a life. A microscopic virus can spread a devastating plague . . .

I am the lone killer cell invading the body of Ugghiutu. It is I, now, who is the cancer.

* * *

I locate a men's room in one of the major department stores that bookend the mall; I've found them to be less populated with toughs and dangerous junkies than the general mall rest rooms. Also, I favor stalls over urinals, and I always lock the door. Maybe it's this kind of paranoia already in my nature that is responsible for a flight of fancy, an imaginative delusion . . . this sudden anxiety, as I gaze down at my feet, spread to either side of the toilet's stained base.

Suddenly I have had the impression—no, the *knowledge*—that the number of small colored floor tiles my soles cover up has relevance to my life. Actually, relevance to my death. Their number amounts to something . . . whether it be the month of the year, or day of the month, or the year, in which I will die. Perhaps their number, added, is the age I will be when I die. I don't know the specific message, except that I know there is a message. It isn't a message *sent* to me. It is a message written everywhere, always, that I could just as easily have discovered in the number of veins on one leaf on one tree. But it has surfaced here, through the contact of my feet upon this surface.

I am terrified to move my feet from that spot, as if I stand at a precipice, as if by shifting my soles I will uncover a photograph of myself withered and gray in a hospital bed. Or broken and bloody tomorrow.

Carefully lifting my eyes, and keeping them lifted, I finish my business and hurry from that suddenly terrifyingly empty rest room. I avoid looking directly at the floor as I leave, and I don't even glance at the mirrors ranked over the sinks, for fear of what other secrets and prophecies might become manifested in the number of my eyelashes or the creases in my troubled brow.

* * *

From the shunt car, racing along its elevated cable, I view the melted blur of the city outside, roaring past like a colossal tidal wave of liquified concrete and steel, stone and ceramic. Graffiti covers the interior of the shunt like the garish, ugly thoughts—made tangible—of countless previous passengers. There's a graffiti of stench in the air as well. Sweat, piss, cheap cologne and perfume, dirty hair and dirty clothes, the reek of filth, of decaying teeth, of bodies rotting on the inside from disease and drug use. We are all rotting, though; even me. I am shoulder to shoulder with strangers whose faces I avoid, except to steal glimpses reflected in the windows, where I see them stealing glimpses of me. Despite being pressed up together, inhaling the molecules that make up scent in an actual ingestion of each other, it seems that we only connect through this reflected remove, as we view others on VT and in movies, fascinated with each other but always separated. Disconnected in a convoluted connection.

I hold to an overhead bar and fight not to stumble but give a little lurch when the shunt pulls up to the platform. As I turn to disembark, I see a Kalian man carried ahead of me in the packed mass of passengers. He glances back at me. But his turban is red, not blue; he's one of the moderate Sarikian Kalians, like Saleet's room mate Zoksa.

Still, he looked back over his shoulder, seemed to make direct eye contact with me.

I try to press forward in the crowd but can't wedge myself any deeper. When I step down to the platform and glance about me, I see no Kalians of any kind.

Walking down a narrow side street to my next destination, a few autumn leaves scrabbling out of my way like large insects, collar turned up and hands thrust in my pockets, I think of what Zoksa told me about her people worshiping the Nameless Ones. The Shadow Gods who imprisoned Ugghiutu.

Walking down this narrow side street, two images jostle for my attention on the screen of my brain. Both have their origins in the night before. One image is of Saleet's wondrous nude body, pale gray as if it's sculpted in polished stone. The other image is from the dream I had last night, after Zoksa returned from her movie and I returned to my own apartment. I dreamed I was being led on a tour of Alvine Products, the company for which Saleet's father works. Saleet herself was showing me around, but somehow I got separated, wandered lost until I came to a vast dark hangar-like chamber. In this high-ceilinged room, I approached a long row of genetically engineered animals being grown without superfluous details like heads or limbs. Nutrient tubes snaked into the stumps where heads should have been, and waste tubes ran out of the creatures' other ends. But as I got close to these animals, which stretched off into the darkness there were so many of them, I noted how small and fragile their bodies were. Then I noticed that not only did these animals have no limbs or heads, but each had an open, bloodless wound on its upper surface. On either side of this gaping wound was a small breast. The animals lay on their backs, I realized, and gingerly I leaned over the nearest of them to peek into the hole in its chest.

I thought I saw a crawling blackness inside, like living shadow moving throughout the husk of the undead body. It was as though outer space itself waited behind that portal . . . and outer space was a living thing.

"Jelena," I whispered, even as I woke from my dream.

I emerge from an alley, and ahead is a cemetery dating back to the earliest days of Earth colonization. The fence around it is of black steel, and menacingly spiked as if to ward off grave robbers of old. I near the enclosure, compare it to a picture from my pocket so as to locate the exact section of fence. I'm distracted, however, by an eerie whispering voice and squint at the array of monuments beyond, half-drowned in drifts of browning leaves. At last I settle on a vertical slab upon which I see a woman's face projected, and she is talking. Telling us something about her life in a message she recorded shortly before her death. Either someone passed by her stone a few moments ago, activating the message, or it is malfunctioning and plays its loop endlessly. (Maybe some jokester placed a flower pot in front of its sensor.) On another stone, but this recording silent, I see an ocean, waves rolling in, a sea bird swooping low. A minute later the same bird swoops down in the same way. These images are like ghosts forced to haunt one place for eternity, living out one small fragment of time over and over, condemned to a Prometheus-like punishment.

Returning my attention to the fence, I think I've found the right spike (I've aligned it with a tall obelisk beyond, just as in the crime scene photo). There is no stain on that spike, however, where the girl's right index finger was impaled so as to point heavenward; the clean up crew must have wiped it down. How to draw my picture here? First a look tossed over my shoulder, then I kneel and reproduce the pattern on the sidewalk directly at the foot of the fence. Best I can do.

"Everything all right, sir?" asks a voice behind me. I can tell it's no recording this time. I rise up and spin around sharply.

It's a forcer, in full black uniform and regalia. He even wears a black helmet, though he doesn't carry any assault engine or heavy armament of that sort; this is the suburbs, after all, the outer edge of Paxton, spread to its thinnest point. You can almost get away with not calling it Punktown, here.

"Ah, yeah, thanks," I stammer. "I'm all right." I hold up the object in my hand for him to see. "Dropped my lip balm." Grinning hugely. Heart punching at me impatiently to finish the all-but-invisible drawing at my feet. I only have two lines left to connect. I can't leave it like this.

The forcer inclines his insect-like head to look at my shoes. I wish I could see his face, his eyes. What kind of visual enhancements might he be utilizing inside that helmet? Can he see my waxy drawing as if it stands out in fluorescent color? My throat clicks as I swallow and he lifts his head abruptly; maybe his hearing is enhanced right now, too. "Are you going to move along now, sir?" he drones.

"Oh . . . yeah." I motion over my shoulder. "I was just listening to that message, the woman, when I dropped my lip balm. Trying to listen to what she's saying. I thought it was a spirit at first!" I joke.

"What woman, sir?"

I glance back into the necropolis. There is no more whispering. "Oh," I say. "Well . . . "

"It isn't appropriate to linger at this spot right now, sir," the forcer continues. "You're no doubt aware there was a murder here recently . . . "

The murder was not committed here, I want to protest—the murderer simply left part of his victim here. But I don't want to argue with the officer, despite my irritation with him; in other parts of Punktown more people are being murdered right this moment, and this man is harassing *me* on his cozy suburban beat. Well, I consider . . . I *am* a murderer myself, to be fair. I nod at him obediently. "Really? A murder? Well . . . no . . . it was just that I heard that voice. From one of the stones, when I was passing by. But, ah, yes sir . . . I'll be moving along now. Thank you."

He nods, too. And stands there, watching me. He doesn't move.

"I was just coming this way," I go on, groping, "because I'm a bit of a fan of, ah . . . I mean, I have this interest in gravestones. Epitaphs and such. I've often thought I'd like to write a book about it. This one here, for instance . . . " I turn again to point into the cemetery, and in doing so I drop my lip balm again. "Dung," I say, and kneel down to retrieve it. With my back to the black-garbed law enforcer, I hastily uncap the stick and make two sure strokes, completing the diagram. Rising, I cap the balm as I face the man again. "This cemetery, as I was saying, is probably the oldest one in Paxton to contain the remains of Earth colonists."

"It is, sir," the policeman agrees. He steps to one side to look at my feet again, then back up at my face. Does its flush glow extra bright through his special vision?

"Well, it was nice talking to you, officer. Have a good evening."

"And you, sir."

I walk swiftly away, pocketing my writing instrument, my magic wand. I can't resist one look back at the forcer, and he's standing in that same spot, his featureless face angled to follow me. Did I just hear him speaking softly? As if into a microphone, a transmitter, inside his helmet? I face forward and pick up my pace.

My next stop is a parking lot for a condo complex. Jelena Darloom's heart was found resting on the hood of a hovercar, but the vehicle is not in its spot now; the owner must still be at work. I crouch down to draw my design on the pavement instead.

One last stop. The sun is beginning to set and the chill in the air has doubled as I pass through the automatic sliding doors of the *Clean Machine Laundromat*. Open All Night.

It is warm and yellow inside, smelling pleasantly of detergent. Old style machines that still use a water process, ranked in churning rows, dented and graffiti-defiled. I want the second row, third machine down. It was in that machine that Jelena's disembodied head was discovered.

A homeless man lies asleep across three orange plastic chairs bolted to the floor, like a bundle of filthy clothing waiting to be loaded into one of the machines. Oblivious to him, bachelors pile in or remove their wash. A boy and girl of about twelve neck feverishly in two other chairs. A ponderous and faded mother tends to her chores while her two small children chase each other through the rows noisily. A large vidtank with a graffiti-obscured screen plays above a coffee machine with an OUT OF ORDER message fluttering strobe-like on its front panel.

A story on the VT catches my notice even as I stand with my hands flat on the cool metal hatch atop the machine in which the little prosty's head was found.

The news spot concerns a new office tower being erected in Industrial Square (where Alvine Products resides), in the place of the recently demolished Mangaudis Crystalens building. I don't catch what the new building will house, exactly, but footage is shown of the structure under construction. A framework of metal, a looming skeleton, climbs the sky like a ladder, a scaffolding from which to paint clouds. Stretched across this framework is a mesh, a net, a web . . . charged with a current of low-level energy which stimulates the growth of a synthetic organic material which is likened, in the report, to coral. The reporter explains to us laymen that this semi-alive material will spread across the entire surface of the charged mesh, and thicken to a prescribed and uniform degree, finishing its work within five weeks. It will then be killed by a final week of reversed charge. After that, only its ossified remains will stand . . . a kind of exoskeleton inside which businessmen and women will scuttle like busy termites.

The lower portion of the building is shown, where the organic material has already begun to rise from where it was first applied at the base of the tower. This surface has a pebbly appearance like cured reptile hide. Though the surface is a pale green, not purple, it puts me in mind immediately of that tower I saw from my office window that time. The one that I never noticed consciously before that day. The one that looked a bit like a larger version of the building in which Mr. Dove had his book store, and Jelena had her brothel. Dove and Jelena . . . both of them my acquaintances, both of them now dead.

Living buildings, I think. Ugghiutu, I think.

A black, peripheral movement. A glance out the large front window of the laundromat. I see two forcers crossing the scrap of parking lot, coming in this direction. Both are helmeted. One of them carries a big, two-fisted assault engine that can probably fire half of the projectiles available to firearms.

So, I think, it ends here. This is the last bit of good I can do. Hastily, my guts churning like one of these machines, I start drawing atop the closed metal hatch. It vibrates under my hands.

A woman stands at my elbow. "Ahh," she says in a disgusted tone, "that's my machine, you know. I'm already using that one."

I give her my squinty eyes. She shuts up and backs off.

I hear a little bleep of welcome as the front doors part open.

Drawing half finished. Lucky I know it by heart by now.

Heavy black boots clomping . . .

"Sir?"

I don't look up. My lip balm is worn down to a bare nub.

"Sir?"

"He won't get away from my machine!" the angry woman grumbles to the forcers as they position themselves to either side of me.

One of them reaches to my right elbow. I cap what's left of my lip ointment just a second before my arm is taken in a gloved hand. I'm turned to face them.

"Hello," I say.

"Sir, you've been reported as a suspicious person. Will you accompany us to Precinct 40 for questioning?"

"Questioning? Suspicious . . . "

"Sir, this is the second crime scene you've appeared at within the past hour. You're going to have to come with us to Precinct 40."

The other forcer slings his big weapon out of his way and takes the lip balm from my hand . . . gives it a look, uncaps it, holds it up to a little vent in his helmet; I hear the hiss of artificial inhalation, then the harmless tube of salve is pushed into my coat pocket, dismissed. This forcer looks me up and down, and I hear a soft hum as his viewer scans me for weapons. Good thing I don't have my shotgun on me, good thing my pistol was lost to that bird-faced mugger.

"All right, then, sir," the first officer says. "Shall we go?"

"Might as well," I mutter fatalistically.

* * *

Precinct 40 is a squat building of bronze-colored ceramic, with a bronze-colored dome. A suburban police headquarters, it's fairly small; even has two real trees out front. At first I assume that it's because the staff of P-40 is small and has no specific sex crimes unit that I have to wait for another team to arrive . . . but then it dawns on me that since Jelena's body was found in eight different precincts, her murder transcends the notion of territory.

My wrists are cuffed to the arms of my chair (orange and bolted to the floor like at the laundromat) and again, I numbly watch a VT to pass the time, ignoring the sobbing mutant cuffed into the chair beside me, his (her?) massive lumpen head hanging heavy with its weight and with despair, dangling flaps of raw red flesh obscuring what passes for his face.

"Mr. Ruby?" says Sergeant Gaskin, who briefly questioned me earlier. I look up to see him approaching me with two other forcers—no helmets, not the ones who brought me in. One of them in fact is in plainclothes . . . a burly block-like Choom, his huge mouth turned down in a grim expanse. The other officer, in black uniform, is a Kalian female. Gaskin introduces them. "This is Detective Lardin and Investigator Yekemma-Ur, of Precinct 9-B, Sex Crimes unit. They have some more questions for you . . . "

Saleet shows no emotion. Nor do I. We avoid direct eye contact. I am not surprised to see her. When I was told another team was coming in to talk to me, I think I knew instinctively. At what point did my name come up to her, and how did she feel at that moment? I'm sure she didn't confess to knowing who I am. But it's not only to hide our involvement that I avoid her eyes. It's out of shame, and misery. I know I've lost her.

"Come with us, please, Mr. Ruby," Lardin rasps deeply as my shackles unlatch with a snick. I rise, and walk between him and Saleet into a small interrogation room. My arm lightly, accidentally brushes Saleet's, and I can just barely detect her patchouli-like scent.

I'm seated. I accept a cup of coffee. Still I keep my eyes off my lover.

"Mr. Ruby," Lardin grumbles, "what were you doing this afternoon at two crime scenes related to a single murder investigation?"

"I saw it on the news recently, sir," I reply. "It was on the police netlink site, too."

"Yes." Saleet holds up a bundle of papers. My print-outs, taken from my coat when I was initially booked. Crime scene photos. Maps. And diagrams from *The Veins of the Old Ones*, by the Tikkihotto mystic/mathematician Skretuu. "You seem especially interested in our net site, Mr. Ruby. Especially interested in the unsolved murder of Jelena Darloom."

"Why is that, Mr. Ruby?" Lardin asks.

"I'll be quite honest," I say, dropping my eyes to my oily black coffee. If ever I couldn't face Saleet, it's now. "And I'll even consent to a truth scan. The reason I'm interested in the death of Jelena Darloom is because I was a customer of hers on one occasion . . . "

"I see," says Lardin.

"And when was this, Mr. Ruby?" Saleet asks in a dead dry voice.

I look up at her black eyes, oily and steaming like my coffee. "It was before I met my current girlfriend. I was lonely. It was a mistake. I felt badly for the poor girl—she told me she wanted to get out of the life she was in. So when I heard on the news that she had been killed . . . I guess I became fixated on the case. Here was a person I . . . I . . . it wasn't like I loved her. But I felt horrible about it. I guess . . . I felt guilty for being one of the people who took advantage of her miserable situation. I guess my interest in her became morbid and obsessive."

My gaze does not waver from Saleet now, or hers from mine. "But I swear to you that I did not hurt her. I didn't kill her."

Saleet swivels in her chair to address her partner. "The sperm in the victim was Kalian," she reminds him.

"That doesn't mean anything," he rumbles ominously. "Just because her last customers were a couple of Kalians doesn't mean they're the ones who killed her. The killer may never have ejaculated inside her, or even had intercourse with her."

"He says he'll take a truth scan," Saleet says.

"Will you do that right now, Mr. Ruby?" Lardin asks. "Do you waive your right to have an attorney consulted first?"

"Yes, absolutely," I say. "I have nothing to hide."

Lardin mutters something to Saleet, stands and leaves the room.

"What are these, Christopher?" my girlfriend immediately asks, her voice no less professional, as she pulls the pages from *The Veins of the Old Ones* out of my sheaf of print-outs.

"In case you hadn't guessed, Sal," I whisper, "I have an interest in occult matters. Everything from folk tales to religion. That's why I'm always asking you about Ugghiutu. That's why I was in the Kalian Reading Room. I was just embarrassed to admit to you, before, just how interested I am in these subjects. I didn't want you to think I'm an eccentric."

"That better be all you are," Saleet tells me, narrowing her eyes, which are more terrifying than beautiful suddenly. "Because if you murdered that girl, Chris, I will fucking destroy you."

"The truth scan will prove I'm not lying about this."

"A prostitute, Chris. Very nice . . . "

"It was before you."

"She was practically a child . . . "

"Sal . . . "

"So what were you doing with this occult dung? These pictures?"

"I was saying a kind of prayer at each site where a body part was found. I did all eight of them today, I freely admit. It was a ritual to help her soul find peace. Like I said, Sal . . . I feel so guilty about . . . "

I break off as the hulking, powerful-looking Choom reenters the room, holding a small device. Coming to my side, he presses an adhesive disk to the center of my forehead roughly with his thumb. It sticks there like an Indian's bindi. Then he reseats himself, and activates the truth scan device. Saleet shifts herself closer to him to peer down at it. Her fingers are knotted tightly together atop the table.

"What is your name?" Lardin demands.

"Christopher Ruby."

"Today did you appear at any of the crime scenes related to the death of the prostitute Jelena Darloom?"

"Yes, sir. I appeared at all eight sites."

"To what purpose?" He keeps his eyes on the device's miniature displays.

"I feel guilty about having had sex with the victim," I relate. I can't see or interpret the truth scan, but I know I'm not lying. "I visited each site because I feel connected to the victim. I admit to performing occult rituals at each site. I have an interest in the occult." Again, I knew I wasn't lying. I didn't repeat the part about the rituals being prayers, though, meant to release Jelena's soul . . . that part wasn't quite honest.

"Did you murder Jelena Darloom?"

"No, sir, I did not murder Jelena Darloom."

"Do you have any association with any person who might have killed Jelena Darloom?"

"Not to my knowledge."

"Do you know the identity of the person or persons who killed Jelena Darloom?"

"No sir I do not."

Lardin lifts his heavy skull to scowl at Saleet. She subtly nods, then turns to me. Though her eyes still shine coldly, she says, "Your story checks out, Mr. Ruby."

"Great," I sigh. "Um . . . so am I free to go?"

"Yes, but listen," Lardin says gruffly, stabbing a finger in my face. "Stay the fuck away from crime scenes, active or not. I don't like ghouls . . . not even conscious-stricken ghouls. You just wasted my time coming up here to listen to your weird obsessed dung."

"I'm sorry, Detective Lardin."

"Stay away from unlicensed prosties! I could cuff you for that alone, you know."

"Yes, sir. I will, sir."

Saleet reaches across to me and peels the disk off my forehead. I assume this will be the last time her fingers will ever touch my flesh. Her eyes are still as cold and black as her holstered pistol. "You can collect your belongings and go, Mr. Ruby," she tells me, rising and handing me back my print-outs. "We'll walk you to the check-out station."

My new black overcoat is returned to me, as is my wallet. Lardin has drifted off to talk to Sergeant Gaskin. For a moment Saleet lingers and I whisper to her once more.

"I am truly, truly sorry about this, Saleet. I hope you can give me a chance to explain this to you more, later on."

A beat of hesitation. Then, "We'll see." She turns her back on me, and goes off to join her partner.

I leave the dome-capped Precinct 40, and outside night has fallen as though the depths of space have flooded through the very streets of Punktown.

PART FOUR: UGGHIUTU

For my excursion I wear my black overcoat because it could be cold down there, though I hate to get it dirty where it's new. But it helps to hide my shotgun, which is slung over my shoulder on its strap; I can just swing it up into position from under the coat if need be. I have a box of shells in one pocket. In another, various maps of Punktown's subway network printed out from the official Paxton Transit Authority net site.

I have a new, powerful flashlight. Today I have a can of black spray paint instead of lip balm. I considered acquiring a hard hat so as to masquerade as a maintenance worker, but didn't know where to get one. After yesterday I really don't want any more trouble with the forcers, even though they dismissed me as harmless then. Don't want to push my luck . . . but I still feel compelled to know if there is any significance to the fact that when the great earthquake hit Punktown twenty-one years ago, the Church of the Burning Eye was at its precise epicenter, and sank into the man-made caverns below the city. It's a kind of insistent calling I'm hearing in my head or in my guts, and I've learned to listen closely to that sort of thing these days.

Under my black coat I wear a white T-shirt on which I spray painted a symbol last night. The symbol is a stylized eye inside a star, with a pupil that wavers like flame at its center. It can't hurt. It might even protect me. Though a lot of good it did the Church of the Burning Eye.

Another net site I viewed, this one created by a group of self-avowed "urban explorers", mentioned that the church was "remarkably intact . . . (existing) almost in its entirety" when they encountered it themselves several years ago, in one of the sections of the subway system that were sealed off and have remained disused since the quake. There was a murky, distant photo of it, which made it look like it lay at the bottom of the ocean, but the authors/explorers claimed to have been chased off by a "big white crab thing" which they assumed must have been a renegade robot. After the Union War, a group of rebellious automaton laborers took shelter in the abandoned subway and sewerage tunnels beneath the city, where they now have manufactured more of themselves, sneaking above-ground occasionally to steal or purchase supplies with money earned from various criminal activities (the Nuts gang, all robots, is one of the most dangerous and legendary in town). But the explorers did note that this was not one of the areas normally associated with the robots, and that they encountered no others.

My maps indicate that the closest I can get to this sealed off area is via the Green Line, the closest Green Line station being the Sumner Bridge Terminal. I pick up a tube near my apartment building to enter the first leg of my journey. Most of Punktown's subway tunnels are at the same level as the subtown areas like the one I live in. There is another transit system lower than this system—essentially subway tunnels beneath subway tunnels—but the church didn't drop that far down. I switch to the Green Line, and ride that to the terminal in question.

I pretend to wait on the platform of this smallish station, which has no shops or vending machines like the larger ones. Actually, I'm eying the mouth to the tunnel on my right. The opening is arched, the darkness beyond broken by far-spaced lights for maintenance or emergency, I assume. There is a narrow walkway or catwalk with a railing, again for maintenance or emergency evacuation of tubes, running along the right side of the tunnel, vanishing off into the gloom.

I spot a security camera near the mouth of the tunnel, a couple others in the station, but there are no patrolling forcers, transit guards, security robots. Just a thin scattering of bored people waiting to catch a ride, avoiding each other's empty gaze. The station smells like a high school gym's locker room. Massive riveted girders cross the ceiling and serve as pillars. Along the green-tiled walls, animated ads run across long display screens. Right now, a classy-looking ad for the Solon, a legal brothel, with its large staff of better-paid Jelenas.

A bullet-faced train pulls in almost soundlessly. Most of the people waiting with me board, a few depart the hovering vehicle and trot upstairs (there's not even an escalator on this platform). When the train pulls out there are only two people left with me. Should I make my move now, before more people arrive, or would more people actually be preferable? Is it better to have fewer people to challenge me, or a larger number of people to cover my actions?

While I struggle with my decision, another tube pulls in. On impulse, I make my move now . . . walking quickly to the end of the tunnel, swinging my legs over the low gate that blocks the maintenance pathway, and ducking into the murk of the subway tunnel itself.

I flatten myself to the grimy tiled wall as the train resumes its journey, the damp warm air of its passing rippling over me like dirty waves, and then it is gone, a distant and fading hiss. There is an eerie, thick silence like cobwebs settling over me, muffling me. I turn and begin to follow the slim, raised pathway, grateful for its railing. Because of the regular lighting strips, I don't need my flashlight yet. Despite its weight, the strap biting into my shoulder, I welcome the presence of my sawed-off shotgun. Punktown is scary enough upground and in broad daylight. I hope I'm not throwing my life away today . . . especially on a vague intuition that there might be something to learn at the ruined church of Ugghiutu's enemies.

The tunnel is not yet cold as I'd imagined it might be, still humid instead. A drop of water plops heavily onto my head as I step through a puddle. Here and there, attached to the wall, are locked boxes that must contain machinery, computer consoles. Pipelines and sheathed cables accompany me for a bit before veering away or disappearing, to be replaced by new ones, snaking along the tiles like the roots of great trees.

According to my maps, I'll be encountering another train station soon . . . the old Steam Avenue Station. But this station has not been used since the earthquake, despite the fact that it sees trains streak past it countless times a day. It's on the outer edge of the most heavily damaged section of the subway system. Other ghost stations, deeper in the heart of this abandoned sector, are not nearly as accessible . . . are not visible from the windows of active trains. Some are even flattened, buried under tons of rubble.

Further on, another train comes up on me so suddenly that I crouch down and hold onto the railing as it whooshes past, half to hide myself and half out of instinctive fear of being swept off the ledge. Lifting my head a bit, I see a blur of faces framed in yellow windows. Does a gaunt-faced young woman make eye contact with me? Then, the tube is gone as if it were only a ghost train full of apparitions. A bit shaky, I rise and continue on.

The narrow ledge now opens onto a broad platform, and I step over another gate to reach it. There are enough utility lights on to illuminate this station almost enough for it to pass for an active one. However much graffiti one might find in an active station, however, I've never seen walls so absolutely covered in the stuff. Not a molecule of the tiled walls goes unembellished. Gang insignias, lewd cartoons, avowals of love or lust, some truly fine art and lots of random abstract chaos assail me in explosions of color . . . attesting to the high traffic of "urban explorers". I was worried about the security cameras witnessing my entrance into the labyrinth, but apparently that hasn't hampered many before me. In fact, two young men sit on a bench of this station as if they expect their train to pull up at any moment. I hesitate from walking further across the platform when they turn their heads toward me. One sips casually from a bottle of Zub.

I move forward when I see they are disinclined from taunting or challenging me (or even asking me for change). They return to their quiet conversation and I vault over a turnstile to follow a passageway beyond the station's shadowy automated ticket booths.

Tiles have dropped from the corridor's tessellated walls. I see a small dark animal dart around the corner ahead of me. I walk across a sodden mattress there in the center of the passageway. Empty cans and bottles, used condoms like dead jellyfish. Is it the maintenance crews or the youths and mutants that lurk in these tunnels that keep the utility lights functioning?

The passage opens into a convergence of passages, branching off toward other stations or toward stairways to street level. All of the exits at the tops of these stairs would be sealed up, now (unless youths or homeless people have since broken through them, to better interconnect their haunts). I consult my print-outs again from the urban explorers site, then take a passage on the far side of this intersection. This will lead me toward the old Webster Street Terminal. And that will be the station closest to the spot where the sunken portion of street was deposited when the earth yawned open two decades ago.

The new passage I take has fewer functioning lights spaced along it, and half of these flutter erratically like guttering candles. There is an ad display that still functions, though, remarkably . . . it picks up a current broadcasted loop of advertisements and plays them brightly to no one but me. At least it helps to light my way . . . but by the time I reach the end of this long, glossy corridor, both ads and utility lights have abandoned me. I switch on my flashlight, and a moment later I enter Webster Street Terminal.

There has been a lot of water damage. A puddle that is really more of a pond covers half the platform. The support girders look like stalactites under their crust of corrosion. One might think they're part of a sunken ship, some are so thickly caked; they're almost organic looking. Trash and broken glass litter the floor, and there is graffiti but not a fraction as much as at Steam Avenue Station. My beam is strong, but it can't reach into the tunnel that gapes at the far end of the platform. No lights show in there; it is a tunnel that is disused, and even caved-in at various points under tons of rock, concrete and steel. It is my destination . . . for directly upon its bed will lie the Church of the Burning Eye and its immediate environs.

I venture further along the platform, shining my beam across the faces of vending machines, the candy and sandwiches long since stolen, but there are still newspapers in a dispenser and I bend down close to its dusty window to read the headlines from an issue that came out when I was only eight years old.

"You aren't going in the tunnel, I hope," crackles a voice behind me.

I whirl, pointing the flashlight, fumbling the shotgun up with my other hand. Its stubby thick barrel catches on the flap of my coat; fuck it—I'll shoot through the coat if I have to, no matter how nice and suede-like it is.

Two mutants stand on the platform, facing me, starkly illuminated in my beam. There are mutants and there are mutants. These are really, really mutated mutants.

At first I think it's only these two, until I realize one of them carries a small mutant. This one is having a steady seizure in its friend's arms, and it's wrapped in a ragged blanket like an infant with a head the size and shape of a watermelon that's rotted a slick bluish-black. It has small entirely white eyes that stream gummy tears and reflect my flashlight like the eyes of a hyena. It doesn't seem to have limbs. The thing holding it has mottled blackish-purple skin like a fly-blown corpse swollen with gas. Unlike the infant, it has hair, though wispy as a mummy's. Its face is so bloated and lumpen that I can't tell which of the badly-placed creases are the eye slits and mouth. It wears a stained T-shirt advertizing the band Lust Monkeys. One arm is skeletally thin but at least has a hand, the other arm three times as thick as one of mine and ending in a kind of bony ball. The third mutant by way of contrast has bright pinkish skin but covered in yellowish nodules or tumors, piled upon each other in abundance here and there until they're like an uneven covering of fleshy soap bubbles. This one at least has a more human face, but I can't imagine how it can be alive with that tremendous hole right through the center of its bare chest, as if a huge cannonball was fired through it and the wound's edges healed up.

I retrieve my voice from where it ducked down inside me. "Why shouldn't I go in the tunnel?" I ask warily.

"Some kids went in there to party, fool around," mumbles the larger of the two black-skinned mutants through its swollen face, "about two months ago. They never came out again."

"One of our friends heard them screaming," adds the pink mutant.

"Don't you ever go in there?" I ask, still pointing my gun despite the fact that the trio don't appear to be armed (in one case, literally).

"No," both of the large mutants reply simultaneously.

"Why not?" I ask.

"There's poison in that tunnel," says the pink mutation.

"Poison? Radiation?"

"No, not that. Something else. There's evil in there. The crabs . . . "

"*Crabs?* And what are those?"

"I saw one once," the black mutant manages in a crusty voice through its obscure mouth slit. "Like a crab walking on two long legs, with more legs like arms up front. But no head. Just like a flower where a head should be. A flower or a plant, with the leaves all moving." It wriggles the fingers of its good hand creepily to illustrate. "It came after me but I got away."

"So why do you stay around here? What's to keep them from coming out here after you?"

"They don't leave the tunnel," the black mutant says. "And my father here," at this he lifts the quivering infant a little higher, "can make scary sounds . . . really high sounds that the crabs don't like." I think the black mutant is smiling. "It makes them squeal and run."

No wonder they don't carry spears or makeshift zip guns. I lower my own gun, convinced by now they mean only to warn me. "Are they mutants, too?"

"No," says the bubbly one, his one unobscured eye grave. "They're demons."

I glance in the direction of the tunnel's maw, swallowed up in the blackness around it, like a black hole in black space. "I don't want to go in there," I say, "but I have to. I have to look at the church . . . "

"The church is theirs now. They've changed it," says the black one.

I look at him dubiously. "How do you know, if you never go in?"

"I've been a little ways in the tunnel—that time I saw the crab," he replies. "But my father went all the way in once, with two other men. One of the men didn't make it back, though it wasn't a crab that got him . . . father thought it was a couple of men in robes. Father used his sounds to scare off whatever it was that was chasing him and the man who carried him."

"Don't go in, mister," says the pink mutant earnestly. He nods at the small mutant, who is quaking more violently, his eyes streaming more profoundly; clearly agitated. "Pete's getting upset. He's worried about you. And he thinks you'll stir up the evil."

"I'm sorry. Really," I say. "But I'm not evil. I'm not one of them. I want to fight them. I want to stop the evil from spreading."

For the first time, I hear a gurgle come from . . . Pete, as if he's choking to death on phlegm. The pink one bends his head close to his twisted lips. Several moments later, he straightens again and looks grim.

"Pete says he wants to go with you, then. To protect you. That means we'll be coming, too."

"Well . . . I appreciate that, but . . . I don't want you to be in danger, either . . . "

"Pete insists."

I nod, watching the limbless, swaddled creature's eyes flash at me in my beam. "Well . . . all right," I stammer. "Thank you, Pete."

* * *

I offer to wait until my new companions can go fetch their own flashlights from wherever it is they camp, but the black mutant, Falco, mutters, "We don't need flashlights, Chris."

Hoop, the pink one with the great hole in his middle, leads the way down to the train bed and into the great tunnel itself, wide enough to accommodate two sets of repulsor tracks running in opposite directions. I'm in the middle (and I *do* need a flashlight), and Falco brings up the rear with his father Pete cradled in one arm.

I hear water dripping from the ceiling in places, actually trickling in sheets down the curved wall elsewhere. I hear small living things scuttle off into alarming cracks in the walls, or behind heaps of crumbled concrete, before my beam can touch them. There are places where girders spring up from the middle of the train bed to support a sagging area of ceiling. No way these columns were here when tubes used this chute; they must have been added after the quake to prevent even more buildings from dropping into the underneath. Some of the bigger fissures in the walls look caulked up, as well. Still, I wouldn't want to be here when another big quake hits.

Silently we pass through a spot where the tunnel rumbles, the air vibrates subtly. Can't be a tube in a parallel tunnel; they aren't that noisy. Must be some hulking machinery or other behind the wall. It fades away behind us and the atmosphere is sepulchrally calm once more. No one talks, but once or twice I think I hear Pete gurgle softly.

Hoop comes to a stop and I nearly walk into his back. Aiming my strong cone of light past him, I see why. The tunnel ahead is packed to its high curved ceiling in heaps of shattered concrete, twisted girders, mounds of ceramic tiles popped out of the ceiling and walls like shed dragon scales . . . even a mostly buried hovercar or two. My guide points one of his heavily blistered arms, and whispers, "The maintenance crews just cleared the catwalk after the quake, so survivors could be evacuated from the church. We can get around that way."

"*Were* there any survivors in the church?" I whisper.

"I believe there were only a few people in it at the time, and only one of them died. Come . . . " Hoop stretches on tip-toes for the catwalk's metal railing and slings himself up pretty nimbly.

After hoisting myself up onto the narrow walkway with more difficulty (I won't hand my shotgun ahead of me no matter how friendly my companions might seem), I step back so Falco can pass Pete up into Hoop's waiting hands. Then I lean down to help pull Falco up, his heavy disfigured arm making the act awkward for him. (When he practically stumbles into my arms I get more of a lungful of my new friend than I might have hoped for; he smells as much like a corpse as he looks.) After giving Pete back to his son, Hoop takes point again and we begin squeezing past the mountain of rubble that chokes the old subway's throat. It's a tight corridor; more than once I catch my coat on a metal strut or jag of stone. Water plunks on my head. I cough at the kicked-up dust that settles on my shoulders and on my face. Motes of it swarm in my beam like plankton. I notice there is no more graffiti. No more discarded beer containers.

The corridor goes a long way, like a mine shaft or a cramped tunnel inside a pyramid. Along the way I see a few more vehicles pinned in the debris, and when I shine my torch into one that's crumpled up close to the catwalk I wish I hadn't: the mummy-like cadaver crushed against the control panel has all of his teeth and none of his eyes.

But at last, the mountain starts to slope down at an angle away from the ceiling. Here, it's more apparent than it was in the packed section of tunnel that the ceiling has been replaced since its collapse two decades ago, so the street could be rebuilt over our heads. But the sunken remains of the old street, for financial considerations, have not been cleared off these old repulsor tracks. Ahead of us is a chunk of the Punktown of twenty years ago, secreted away nearly intact, preserved in the amber of darkness.

The old street rests on a thick jagged base or platform of underlying concrete, dirt and rock, so that the few structures resting atop it all but brush their roofs against the replaced ceiling. We scramble our way up onto this level plateau. The pavement is mostly unbroken, except at the sides where it snapped off against the curved tunnel walls. There's a small Tikkihotto bakery that is pretty much just a shell, its flat roof fallen in and a big ruptured sewer pipe jutting up through its guts, but I can still see ads posted on its buckled but unbroken plastic front window. There's a mail box standing beside it, bolted to a surviving strip of sidewalk. I wonder if there are still letters inside waiting to reach the hands of lovers and bill collectors.

Beyond the bakery there's a brick tenement building shorn off at the second story (probably by repair teams so as to reseal the ceiling, rather than in the quake), the bottom floor housing a Tikkihotto apothecary (more signs, some in English and some not, in its display window) . . . and there are apparently a few more structures in various states of ruin beyond the largest of these derelict edifices, but that's the one we want; our destination. We've reached the Church of the Burning Eye.

Actually, this temple is only one story high, with a flat roof that's mostly held up, though I can tell it's caved in here and there, and mounds of rubble on the roof threaten to flatten other sections. There are few windows, and there's no ornamentation; unprepossessing for a church. It looks like it might have once been a small school or day care center. I notice something right away. Nowhere is there any representation of the symbol of the church, like the one I painted on my shirt front—the sign of the Elders, the gods this obscure sect worships: nowhere do I see the eye inside a five-pointed star, with its wavering flame for a pupil.

"They took the eyes down, didn't they?" I whisper to Falco.

"Yes. The demons. Or the robed men."

Ice picks are punched through my ear drums. I drop my flashlight and clamp my palms over them, crunching my face in agony. My brain is liquefying, turning to steaming blood that will soon be leaking between my fingers. I'm going to cry as I sag to my knees. And then the ice picks are slipped out again and I gasp and sob at once and pitch forward onto all fours.

Hoop crouches beside me, a hand on my back. "Are you all right?" he hisses.

"What was that?" I pant, dragging my flashlight to me.

"That was Pete. He saw one of the demons, behind us." He supports me as I stand. "It's gone, now."

"He'll bring the ceiling down on us again, doing that," I say, glancing at the teary-eyed, quivering little mutant. Pete seems to be looking at me.

"Let's get out of the open," Falco suggests, leading the way to the church's open threshold, its doors hanging half off their hinges. "We'd better let Pete go first."

"Yeah," I agree, nervously looking all around me as I follow. Hoop sticks close behind me.

The vestibule and room beyond it are barren. Was the furniture removed or was there never any in the first place? No paintings, tapestries, plaques, idols, candle or incense holders, anything that might prove this to have been a place or worship. Though I do notice that the ceilings are all painted black, whereas the walls and floors are white. We pass through a hallway into a large central chamber like a classroom without desks, but this time there *is* something which suggests worship.

There's a bed in the middle of the floor, with a nice brass headboard and sheets that look like they might be white satin under the thick, crusted tar of black blood like one huge scab. There is a young man's naked torso on the bed, with a hole yawning in the chest. A thick white candle, unlit, pokes out of the wound now. I spoke too soon about there not being candle holders. Strands of web seem to radiate out from the body and I follow one with my beam. It extends from where it's pinned to the candle to the wall at my right. There, a human heart is nailed to the plaster. I follow another of these cords, which look like white plastic twine, and it is pinned to the forehead of a human head spiked to the wall through the ears and eyes. I know what else I'll see these cords connected to, ringing the room. An arm. Another arm. A leg. Another leg. A single finger pointing toward the black ceiling that looks like gaping night sky. Blood streaks down the walls from where they are mounted like terrible artifacts on display in some museum. What spider wove this nightmare web?

"We're not alone," Falco whispers.

I begin to turn. I expect to hear Pete's terrible, inaudible attack again. Instead, a voice I know.

"Is this where you killed Jelena, too, Christopher?"

A figure in a black uniform stands in the doorway behind us, pointing an ominous, two-handled assault engine that can fire just about any projectile or beam you might think of; simultaneously, too. The figure's head is hidden inside a glossy ant-like helmet, and I know this provides the wearer with night vision so they can see in total darkness. Despite this and the distorted voice, I recognize . . .

" . . . Saleet," I say, holding up a hand to Pete to indicate that he should refrain from his shriek. As I turn more fully to face her, I make sure to keep my hands out away from my sides, away from the shotgun slung over my shoulder.

"Are these your accomplices, Chris, or were you going to murder them, too?"

"*Murder us?*" Falco says, stepping away from me. Hoop starts backing up, too. They see this forcer pointing a gun at me and I can't blame them for their doubts.

"I wasn't going to murder you!" I protest as they start edging toward another doorway on the far side of the room, ducking under the strands of the plastic web.

"Hey!" Saleet jerks her gun at them. "I'm not done with you!"

"They're harmless, Sal." I block her and I hear Falco and Hoop dart through the doorway, in search of a back way out. I hope they make it home safely. "They don't know anything; I ran into them and they helped me find this place." I look over her shoulder. "Is Lardin here with you?"

"No. This was a personal investigation, Christopher. I've been following you."

"You know I didn't kill that prosty."

"Maybe not . . . but coincidentally you fucked her. And you visited the crime scenes where her parts were found. And now, conveniently, here you are with another person dismembered in the same way."

I take one involuntary step closer to her. "The truth scan proved I didn't kill her, that I don't have anything to do with the killers or even know who they are."

Saleet takes one hand off her gun to unlatch and remove her tough but lightweight ceramic helmet. She steps closer to me to see me in the light of my torch. "Then how do you explain *this*, Chris? What *is* this?

And how did you know about it?"

"I didn't know about the body. I only knew that this church was significant in some way. I felt it. I *am* connected to all this, but not in the way you think . . . or in a way I can easily explain."

"Well you'd better do your best, Chris, because I'm inclined to arrest you right now."

I gesture helplessly. "Saleet . . . there's a cult that's doing this. This and other terrible things. Probably a number of cults, maybe only loosely connected, but united in one goal. They want to awaken and release Ugghiutu, Saleet. Him and the rest of the Outsiders. They worship the god of your people but in another way than you're accustomed to. Not to pay him tribute, not to pray to, but to actively become his servants, his living hands."

"Chris . . . "

"Look around you. This is obviously ritualistic."

"Serial killers tend to be."

"I thought you were agnostic, Saleet. If you can possibly believe in Ugghiutu yourself, why not that there are fanatics doing things like this to summon him? Ugghiutu permeates Paxton, Sal . . . he's all around us, in everything . . . "

"Your brain is *zapped*, Christopher. Listen to you."

"This city is *evil* . . . "

"A city doesn't need the Devil to be evil. That's the job of the people who live in it." She shifts her weight and the weight of her weapon. "How did you know about this place, Chris?"

"Off the damn net!"

"You expect me to believe that you just stumbled on this body, cut up exactly, *precisely* like that prosty you . . . "

"There is no coincidence. There are only patterns. I'm in the weave. Look . . . I knew someone, all right? This person was dabbling in occult stuff. Very lightly, playfully at first. But she performed a ritual from a very, very rare and powerful book. She left a door open and forces have leaked through. Things have been getting worse since. I think they're going to continue to get worse, until they come to a head."

"How is it that a playful dabbler could open this portal or whatever but these organized cults haven't already done so?"

"I'm sure they are doing so, but she did more damage because she had this book, and now they feel the power that surged through and they're stepping up their activities."

"Why don't they have this book?"

"It's unbelievably rare, and suppressed . . . "

"So where did this friend of your gets it?"

"From another friend, who was murdered. Beheaded. By who knows who—either these cultists, or other secret groups that are trying to thwart these cultists. Like I'm trying to do. Either way, they obviously didn't find the disk the girl had the book on. Maybe they were mistakenly looking for an actual book."

"Where is your friend, this dabbler? You said it's a 'she'." Saleet sounds not only dubious, but jealous.

I look at the gun in Saleet's fists, still pointing its array of barrels and nozzles at my mid-section. I hope she realizes she could cave in this whole tunnel for good with that thing. Looking back up at her face, I confess, "I killed her."

"You . . . killed her."

"She was my ex-girlfriend, Saleet. I didn't kill Jelena. I didn't kill this guy, whoever he is. But . . . yes . . . I . . . "

White blur, a skeleton swinging into the frame of the doorway behind Saleet, and suddenly I'm reaching under my coat, sweeping the shotgun up, yelling at Saleet to get out of the way, and she does—I think she thinks I'm going to shoot her—and I blast the crab-thing through its middle just as its four upper limbs are reaching out for Saleet's back. In the muzzle flash I glimpse segmented arms, barbed pinchers at their ends, and a translucent sea anemone instead of a head. Violently jerked back out of the doorway by the impact of my tight swarm of projectiles, piercing its bony armor.

Saleet has rolled on her shoulder and come up into a crouch, and peripherally I see her gun trained on me, hearing the squeal as it becomes instantly charged for heavy fire, but she whips her head around and perhaps gets a quick look of the demon as it's launched back into darkness. Instead of shooting me, she scoops her helmet back onto her head, and I point my flashlight into the doorway. Dust motes churn, but no sign of the crab thing, living or dead.

Coming to my side, but facing in the other direction, gun on the far doorway, Saleet whispers harshly, "What the dung was that?"

"A demon, the mutants call them. I think it's something from the other side. A servitor . . . "

My ears ring from the thunder of the shotgun. Everyone and everything in these tunnels knows we're here, now.

"It was Kalian semen in Jelena," Saleet muses under her breath.

"But it's not just Kalians," I tell her. "Earthers. Chooms. Tikkihottos. Coleopteroids. The worship is universal. Just that Kalians might be more in tune with Ugghiutu in particular. But he's not the only Outsider . . . "

"No . . . no . . . listen . . . that thing you shot might just be a mutant . . . "

"You know it wasn't. And I've seen these demons before . . . in an old tapestry in a bookstore run by one of these cultists. It showed Tikkihotto warriors fighting these crab things . . . "

"We need to get out of here, Christopher, and get a forensic team in here. You can't be in this place, whatever it is you think you're doing to help. You're a civilian . . . "

"You can help me fight these people, Saleet . . . "

"Do you want me to kill any more ex-girlfriends of yours?"

"We need to talk about that . . . "

"Uh, *yeah* . . . "

"Dung!" I hiss, as I see a white shadow flash left to right past the threshold of the door I'm covering.

"Did you see it?" Saleet whispers.

"I don't know if it was the same one . . . "

"Let's try the door your friends went through. Come on."

Saleet ducks under one of the plastic strands and starts across the room, but I say, "Wait," and I bring my shotgun down on the string like a club. The blow pops out whatever nail or fastening attaches the end of the strand to one of the legs crucified to the wall, and the string floats to the floor, trailing limply from the central torso like an errant vein.

"You can't do that!" my girlfriend snarls. "This is a crime scene! Leave it intact!"

"I can't. This is like a battery, maybe even a portal; it's what these demons are protecting. We have to destroy it." And I swing my heavy gun down on another of the white threads. I have to hit it twice to dislodge the pin that fixes it to a grayish-skinned limb nailed to the white wall. "Help me!" I say.

"I can't," Saleet replies, but she doesn't try to stop me as I move around the room, severing each link to the torso in turn. I try not to look at that terrible head with its slack mouth and hair spiky and stiff with dried gore, pierced through the ears and its blood-caked sockets. When I've disconnected each satellite body part from the nucleus, I gingerly reach into the cavity where the heart was removed and extract the thick white candle plugged in there. I hurl it at the wall.

The air seems to slither, suddenly. Reality is a spinning plate wobbling on a magician's finger, and it takes a stomach-churning dip. Are those cicadas?

"You hear that?" whispers Saleet.

"Let's go!" I yell, as the first of the white things plunges through the door I blasted one of them out of just minutes before. It's like a huge bipedal insect, skittering at us, thrashing four articulated upper limbs, making an angry chittering noise though it has no mouth parts. All around us now there is a distant susurration like grasshoppers in summer grass.

"Move!" growls Saleet, and wheeling around with her monster gun at waist level, she lets loose an intensely green ray bolt which lights up the whole room for a second. I see the bolt disappear into the being's segmented chest area like a javelin, and emerge out the back of its shell-like carapace in an explosion of translucent fluid. Their blood is greenish and looks and smells like aloe juice. Are they more plant than animal?

I race past her toward the other door, and a second demon leaps through it to block my escape, spinning its arms like four whooshing scimitars. I hold the flashlight against the pumping arm of my shotgun, and I aim both at the creature simultaneously. The shotgun bellows, and just as I feel the wind of a missed blow across my nose the demon goes stumbling backwards, that plant-like juice sloshing out of a jagged wound in its albino chitin.

Skirting the dying thing's kicking hind legs, I jump through the door and jerk my gun/light to the left and right. Two corridors forming a T. One ends in a heap of caved-in roof. Down the other, a third demon comes racing toward me out of the gloom. The close walls shake with the rumble of my gun and my ears are stunned from the enclosed concussion. Forging ahead, I hear Saleet following behind me. I also hear her curse and fire another ray bolt. I hope she hit what she aimed at but I don't look back. There are several doorways along this dark hallway and I expect slicing/crushing pinchered claws to lunge out at me from any one of them.

Saleet braces herself in front of one doorway and lets loose three jarring shotgun blasts in quick succession from her own weapon; I don't know what she saw but I'll bet it's sorry now.

"My sign is supposed to ward them off . . . the symbol on my shirt," I hiss. "I don't know why it isn't working . . . how they could tear down the signs in this church . . . "

"They must be blind," Saleet says. "They're going on vibration, maybe. It's how they move in the dark"

"Or maybe this eye thing is just symbolic. Worthless . . . "

We've reached the end of the corridor, and I wrench open its door. The room beyond is filled almost solid with debris, the roof fallen in so that I can see the tunnel's ceiling just a bit beyond. Did my mutant friends clamber up this precarious mound and escape that way? I'm not sure I can even squeeze through the doorway . . .

"In here!" Saleet commands, heading through one of the other doors in the hallway.

"Holy dung," I say after I've stepped through the threshold to join her. When I passed this room a second ago I didn't notice the soft greenish glow on the walls, or hear the soft liquid burbling.

Would the church have had a computer center like this? And even if they had, would it have survived the quake and the intervening two decades intact? Specifically, would these encephalons still be alive in their gurgling tanks of greenish amniotic solution? The artificial brains—three of them—are flattened into vertical frames about the size of the one at my old company: about four feet by two feet by six inches thick. But my company's mainframe got by on one artificially-generated brain . . . why would a church or anybody need three?

Tables, chairs and two old desks have been dragged in here, and numerous components of computers and machinery rest on them, hard-wired into the brainframes. Some components look store-bought, others cobbled together. Static fizzes on one monitor, but three smaller monitors show the flowing blips of the brains' health status. Thick bundles of wires and power cables snake across the floor and through holes drilled in the wall; do they connect to a private generator? I doubt it. Somehow I know those cords connect somewhere into the energy sources and major cable lines of the city itself. Drawing from its power. And feeding God knows what data and poisons back into the entire city system.

We are at the very center of Punktown. The heart of the web.

There's a second door into this room, and I think that's more what is on Saleet's mind, but I have got something to do first . . .

Raising my shotgun and spreading my legs wide, I avert my face to protect it from flying splinters and splashing solution as I discharge my shotgun point blank into one of those dreaming grayish brains.

Through the ragged hole in its plastic case, a flood of nutrient bath washes out, puddling around my feet. Lacerated brain matter comes sliding thickly after it, through the hole, oozing out into the air and smacking to the floor. About a third of it drools out, glistening, until the rest of its bulk clogs the blasted opening.

Instead of berating me for damaging a crime scene, for obliterating important data we might be able to download from these brains, Saleet turns to a second one of them and fires a blast of heavy OO buckshot through the transparent casing. Then she follows that up by launching a plasma capsule through the opening. The brain catches fire with the green, corrosive plasma immediately, burning up like toilet paper in a flame. It blackens, liquefies, and the air stinks with its dissolution. She nudges past me to melt the brain that I've just killed, while I move on to the third encephalon, but then a demon lurches into the room from one doorway. And another, from the other.

A wild blow from one of those serrated claws collides with Saleet's head and I see her spin to the floor as if hit by a hovertruck. Her black helmet may have protected her skull from being split but I hope she hasn't been jarred into unconsciousness or, worse, had her neck broken.

BOOM! I let loose a load of pellets into the swimming head tentacles of the extradimensional entity directly in front of me. It bounces back against a chair laden with machinery and both crash to the floor, limbs flailing in convulsion and arcs of electricity fluttering. I begin to spin toward the one that downed Saleet—I can see it hovering over her, reaching down to her, it's going to remove her helmet—when BOOM, Saleet lifts her gun and fires a shotgun blast into its belly with the muzzle nearly touching its shell. The thing practically hits the ceiling before it crumples to the floor.

On my way to help Saleet to her feet I have to stop and spin and aim my shotgun at yet another demon whisking into the room behind me.

My shotgun clicks empty.

From a kneeling position, Saleet leans around me and streaks three green ray bolts at the demon. It goes down fast and hard and writhes in its last agonies. Saleet gets up on her own, apparently not even dazed. But as if to take her revenge, she kills the third and final encephalon with a load of OO followed up by a gel cap of that hungry plasma.

"Can we go now?" she says.

"Yeah." Having fed more shells into the underside of my shotgun and pumped in the first round, I lead the way out the second doorway and into another narrow corridor in this dark maze.

Swimming at me out of the murk and into my light beam are three more demons.

Behind Saleet, I hear the cicada chirping of even more demons entering the brain center. I get the impression that they're not so much coming from elsewhere in this church or even the subway tunnel, but that they're pouring into our dimension from another as fast as we can kill them.

Then, sharp awls are driven into my ear drums. I hear Saleet cry out inside her helmet. The pain is so intense that I even involuntarily drop my shotgun so as to slap my palms over my ears, dropping to the floor and curling like a fetus. Saleet collapses across my back, beginning to add her own wail to the inaudible shriek that burns up my brain the way the plasma ate the encephalons.

And suddenly, it's gone.

Looking up from the floor, scrabbling in a panic for my flashlight, I see that the demons have vanished. Instead, out of the darkness a hideous black face leans down into mine. That familiar stink, but I'm hardly resentful as Falco says, "Come with us . . . we know the way."

Hoop helps Saleet back to her feet and we gather our fallen weapons. With Falco and the cradled Pete leading us, we wind our way out of the Church of the Burning Eye.

* * *

Silver eyes under grayish cataracts of encroaching decomposition gawk up at me no more mindlessly in death than in life. Gaping mouths bare combs of brittle razored fangs. Pewter-colored scales and jagged fins against dirty beds of crushed ice. I'm reminded unpleasantly of Mr. Dove. I like my fish without heads and fins (and battered), and this thought puts me in mind of the engineered animals farmed at Saleet's father's place of business. Do they grow schools of headless fish in aquariums of greenish solution, I wonder, tethered by wires to a bubbling life support system? The image is too uneasily like that of those three huge encephalons squished into their transparent frames, which I administered crude lobotomies to only hours earlier.

As unappetizing as these whole, scaly fish are, at least I know *what* they are. But what about those pallid, slick bundles of flesh, their formless, boneless limbs covered in huge suckers? Their squashed and deflated faces, like discarded rubber masks, disconcertingly resemble those of obese human infants. A price is given, but there is no label. I point them out to the young man behind the seafood counter. "What are these?" I ask him.

He only shrugs, but blandly reiterates their cost. I'd rather fry up those encephalons . . .

Saleet drifts up to my elbow, and indicates that I should follow her over to the supermarket's deli counter. She has locked her helmet, jacket, long-sleeved shirt and equipment belt in the trunk of her hovercar, and just wears a black t-shirt tucked into her dirty black uniform pants, her glossy boots almost white with caked mud and dust. I'm sure I'm just as disheveled if not more so. Neither of us cares.

On the ride here, I asked her if she's afraid or ashamed to be seen in public—perhaps by a colleague—with a man who has recently been questioned in connection to a murder. She told me she isn't. But she did say she wanted to know why I killed my girlfriend. After all: (A) she's a forcer, and (B) she's my new girlfriend.

Wait 'til we get to my apartment, I told her. She said, "Let's pick up some dinner, then."

So, here I am. Two hours ago I was fighting extradimensional crustacean demons beneath the city, and now I'm picking out a frozen pizza at the supermarket. Well, it's a freshly made Mediterranean pizza, black olives and all, so it's not like I'm complaining about that. But this prosaic activity seems more surreal to me now than the time I spent in the underworld.

While we're perusing some of the other deli selections I glance up at a bulky human with greasy hair and greasier mustache who is glowering at me sideways. Suspiciously, and with open hostility, from the corners of his eyes. Immediately I drop my own eyes, but when I look back up, he is still openly glaring at me, so I avert my eyes again out of instinctive meek politeness, animal submissiveness to a beefier animal. But I'm forgetting what he doesn't know—that I'm a murderer now, a killer of one human, one fish-faced mutation and I don't know how many servitors of the Outsiders, and I sort of wish I could convince myself that this beer-bellied plumber-looking fuck is Dove's second cousin twice removed so I could heft a frozen (headless) turkey out of the nearby poultry section and cave in that low forehead of his with it.

He's gone now. What was his problem? The dirt on my coat and shoes? That I'm with a Kalian woman? Maybe he saw a hardened wariness, a too-easy capacity for violence, unconsciously made manifest in my owns eyes, and was merely alerted by it on an animal level. But I don't care. It was a poisonous touch and it's soured me.

In another aisle, I watch Saleet reach for a box of cookies on an upper shelf. She knocks it to the floor with a loud slap. A woman with a carriage behind Saleet stops short and gives an audible sigh of disgust, because Saleet has startled her with this unforgivable act of clumsiness, and most importantly, Saleet has obstructed and delayed the woman's shopping by as much as three seconds. The woman seems to realize that I'm with Saleet, and glances at me, and I give her a look that says, "I want to slam you with that frozen turkey, too." She looks away quickly and resumes her intense carriage-pushing.

Saleet has turned and seen my face. "What's wrong?"

In a bitter whisper, I tell her about the sighing woman and the glowering man. "What am I doing this, for?" I ask her. "Why are you and I risking our lives trying to help these people, to save this whole stinking city?"

Pointing past me, my girlfriend says, "For him." I follow her gesture and see a Choom infant riding in another shopping cart, his huge smiling mouth as yet devoid of its multiple rows of molars, chin slick with drool.

Grumpily I mutter, "He'll grow up to be like the rest. I just feel sick at how fouled and diseased everything is . . . straight to the core."

"We're fouled, too, aren't we? It's all yin and yang. This city can be as beautiful as it is ugly."

I give her a raised eyebrow.

She amends, "Well, it can be beautiful sometimes. In places. That little baby is beautiful, and he could grow up to be like us instead of those two dungholes."

"Beautiful like me? The girlfriend killer?"

Saleet just appraises me silently for a moment, then nods solemnly at our cart. "Let's cash this out and get home, so you can tell me all about this."

"So you can interrogate me?" I joke humorlessly.

"So you can confess," she corrects me.

* * *

We leave the VT on a news station while we have our dinner and talk, the volume set low, though we don't really expect to hear anything regarding our frantic life and death battle in the bowels of the city today; even if anyone had heard all the gunfire, odds are they wouldn't have reported it.

On the way here from the supermarket we made a quick stop for some beer, which Saleet paid for like the groceries because I'm on my last munits. Knowing this, earlier tonight Saleet offered, "Let me pull some strings with my father and get you into Alvine Products."

"Feeding the cows?"

"Hey—I'm serious. They have a customer service department, if that's what you do."

"It would be pretty weird going back to a life like that now . . . "

"What are the alternatives? Full time nemesis of the Outsiders? The pay isn't great. You have to eat and have a roof over your head, right? And much as I might like to, I can't support you . . . "

Embarrassed, I lowered my eyes. "All right," I conceded. "Do what you can. I'll make up a new resume to show them."

But that was earlier; right now, Saleet is digesting not only our pizza, but my confession.

"It was self-defense," she mumbles, subdued, "like you said . . . "

"Are you convincing yourself, or do you really believe it?"

Her black eyes leap up to my face, glinting in abrupt anger. "I believe you!"

"You can give me a truth scan, if you ever doubt anything I'm telling you . . . "

"I didn't say I doubted you, Chris, did I?" She sips the beer she's nursing. I'm into my second. After a moment she resumes, calmer: "Gabrielle was self-defense . . . but Mr. Dove . . . that was cold-blooded, premeditated murder, Christopher . . . "

Pacing the room already, beer in hand, I whirl on her and lean toward her face, practically snarling. "What was I supposed to do? Let him go on with being a puppet for these beings? Was I supposed to report him to the forcers? What would *you* have thought if I came to you with my concerns about him?"

"I'd have thought you were insane," Saleet admits. "Though, in a way, you are."

"Be that as it may, I did what I could to stop all this . . . or at least to hamper it, make it harder for Ugghiutu to enact his will. I'm not some sorcerer, Saleet . . . but I can pull a trigger."

"Well you told me you've since learned a few things from those two books that you got from Dove. You did those spells at the sites where Jelena's body parts were found, and you drew protective symbols here in your flat. I suggest we go to the building where Dove Books was and do a spell there, just in case some portal or such is open at that spot. And we should try to get into your old apartment, and do one there."

"I'm sure it's rented out already."

"I'll go in uniform, with some excuse or other; I'll get us inside. Then you do your part."

I nod sullenly; I'm tired and that makes me pessimistic. "Can't hurt."

"And we'll do the bookstore in the morning. Would you need to perform your magic inside, or will outside do?"

"There's one formula where you can encircle a house or temple or such with a kind of protective moat, supposedly to keep things from getting beyond its parameters."

"You should have done that to the Church of the Burning Eye."

"Admittedly. Too intent on guns, still."

"You realize, Chris, that this is a war we can never win by ourselves. Not that we shouldn't do all we can . . . but we'll only ever be able to do so much. We have to hope others are fighting them. Trying to maintain the cosmic balance."

I nod again, in slow motion, and muse aloud, "I think we did some major damage to them today. Not just disrupting that ritual site, which I'm certain was a portal, but more importantly, destroying the brains. I don't even want to imagine what they've been doing, plugged into the city's veins . . . but we destroyed them."

"We can only hope they don't sacrifice a new victim to reopen that doorway. And hook some new brains up at that site. But chances are good they'll be afraid to use that place again, now that we know it's there and that we could always mount another attack. And in fact, we should check it out again in the near future . . . and this time draw that moat of power around the temple like you say."

"I wish the priests themselves had been there."

"Me, too," Saleet says. She lifts her eyes to me. "I think I'd have killed them like you killed Dove, Chris."

I smile at her wearily. "That's my good girl."

She's going to pour half of her beer down the drain but I take it to finish off for her (I'm frugal now that I'm poor). Though neither of us have discussed it, I can see she's going to stay the night. While I shower, she calls her roommate to let her know she won't be home, and then she showers while I stand watching VT with a towel wrapped around my waist and that half a beer in my hand.

Then on VT I'm seeing various camera shots both long and close of encephalons in rows of brainframes, dreaming in gurgling nutrient solutions of light green or pale violet or rusty orange. I see a news reporter talking to some business executive in an immaculate gray silk suit and I'm suddenly yelling at the VT (set to vocal command) to increase the volume . . .

Now facing the camera and walking toward it through a long corridor of burbling brainframes, the reporter is saying " . . . deny that there is any problem or defect with their products, and will not confirm these reports that an incredibly fast-acting and potent virus swept through their facility today, all but destroying their entire stock. Cephalon further denies that this alleged virus has also damaged their encephalons that have been installed in a great many businesses in Paxton. But despite Cephalon Corporation's denials, tonight a lot of business owners want some answers as to why the products they purchased from Cephalon have suffered severe malfunction and even outright decomposition. This is Martin Brightlingsea, reporting for . . . "

"VT," I command, "search all local new stations, key word: Cephalon."

Attracted by the urgent tone of my voice, Saleet pads barefoot and feline into the room, wrapped in a towel herself, her long black hair in matted wet tangles. "What is it?" she says. I can't believe I'm not even glancing at the bared gray skin of her upper chest, arms and legs, so intent am I on the huge vidtank.

The VT has diligently switched to another station, in the middle of a similar story about this company I've never heard of called the Cephalon Corporation. But I can fill in the blanks myself: Cephalon obviously designs, mass-produces and sells the artificially-generated brain masses that are used in mainframes, servers, sometimes even in individual computers by many large companies such as my own past employers. Again, a reporter (this time apparently in the vast, impressive lobby of the company) relates that Cephalon denies a devastating virus has raged through their stock today, and through a good many encephalons they've already sold, as well (which must be linked in one way or another—probably for the ease of maintenance or upgrades—to the company which created them).

"Chris . . . " Saleet hisses beside me. And I know she's beginning think what I'm thinking. I shush her impatiently.

The reporter goes on: "Cephalon dismisses rumors that the virus continues to spread, communicated from the parent company to more and more of those companies in possession of their product. In fact, Cepahalon spokesmen continue to insist that there isn't even a virus at all . . . or if there is, that it did not originate with their systems . . . "

"Chris," Saleet persists, "is this a coincidence? Or do you think we did this, when we destroyed those computers today?"

"I don't know . . . " I breathe.

And then I do know, when the report cuts to an external view of the building which houses the Cephalon Corporation.

It is the pale violet colored building I discovered one day from the window of my office at work. The one that looks like a much larger version of the building that housed Dove Books. It tapers at the top like a ziggurat, culminating in a silvery spike. Its surface looks like a cracked, dried-out mud bed, or the hide of a crocodile, and I remember that other news story I saw recently where they showed how some buildings are formed from an organic material like coral, stimulated to grow along metal understructures by introduction of current.

Our human and humanoid enemies are powerful. Very nearly like gods themselves. They've been spreading their corruptions . . .

. . . but today, Saleet and I spread some corruption of our own.

"Yeah," I say, sliding my arm around her shoulders. "We did good today, didn't we? Better than we could have known . . . "

* * *

Over the next two weeks, encouraged by our major victory—which had to be a crippling blow to our enemies—Saleet and I inspired each other to a great deal of further activity (the first project being to mount a security system to my door and windows like she has in her own apartment, in case our enemies ever trace our identities to the places where we live, and in the event that my formulae aren't sufficient to keep out every sort of their many pawns and servitors).

As she had suggested, and in her presence, I walked around the building on Morpha Street B which had housed Dove Books (that shop now vacant and not yet rented to a new tenant), tracing an invisible pattern with a cane she'd bought me for the purpose and simultaneously reading from a print-out of a chant from Skretuu's *The Veins of the Old Ones*.

I performed the same ritual around the much wider base of the Cephalon Corporation. While in the process, a security officer in a gray uniform and holstered gun emerged from the front doors to approach me, but Saleet came forward in her own more impressive uniform to intercept him, telling him that everything was under control and that he should return inside. Later she informed me that the security man had glanced at her badge as if to take her number, but so far nothing has come of it: no calls from her superiors, and of more concern, no visits from vindictive Cephalon agents.

As promised, she got me inside my old apartment when the landlord wasn't around to recognize me; she told the current tenants, a young Choom couple, that there had been complaints of loud music and fighting. While they protested in one room, I was doing my formulas in another, and when they switched rooms, I did the same. I felt a deep stab of sadness which actually caused my throat to tighten when I stood in the bedroom where Gabrielle and I had made love. And where she had burned eight candles in the corners . . . eight corners where I now hastily traced a design with my trusty lip balm.

During this time Saleet also spoke to her father, an executive at Alvine Products in Industrial Square, about getting a job for a friend of hers. I imagine she downplayed our "friendship" so as not to alert him, just yet, to anything romantic in nature. Her father assured her he'd put in a good word with the customer service department, and over my computer I was invited personally by the department head to submit my resume. I did so, again over my computer. I have an interview with them tomorrow, in fact.

I feel a little better about going back to work now. Cephalon can no longer deny the disastrous extent of the damage Saleet and I inflicted . . . *every* one of their encephalons, both in their home building and in *every* company that has purchased one, have now blackened and decayed. Even Cephalon Corp. encephalons as far away as on Earth have rotted to black slime. Word is that the company can not support these catastrophic losses and will declare bankruptcy. So I have a sense of climax, of fulfillment. Of revenge . . . for Gabrielle, for Jelena, for God knows who else have lost their lives to the Outsiders and their heterogeneous flock. I feel like I can now return to a more conventional lifestyle without guilt, that obsessive sense of personal responsibility.

Later on we still plan on revisiting the Church of the Burning Eye, to perform another of my rituals, but right now we both feel like we've done a lot. All we really can, realistically. Yes . . . we could hunt down and kill every executive who works for Cephalon. How widespread is the poison within its walls? Does it extend even to that guard who began to accost me? We've taken note of the names of the top Cephalon people, but we're not eager to become outright assassins unless desperate situations should arise. We will remain alert, watchful, we are sentinels and guardians. But we are only the two of us, two tiny hermit crabs facing a vast rolling ocean, and it's remarkable that we've done as much good as we have.

We've been sure to make time, despite all our activity, to further our love life, and I'm happy to report that Saleet is more comfortable with her passion now. Every third night or so, she sleeps over my place (though I never sleep over hers).

We have woken from the nightmare, and the cold sweat dissipates from our skin, to be replaced by a hot sweat which I find much more to my liking.

She's coming over to stay again tonight, though she won't be driving me to Alvine Products tomorrow afternoon; I imagine she doesn't want to risk having her father see me in her vehicle. I'll be taking the subway to Industrial Square. Yeah, I'm nervous . . . but I feel like I'm beginning a new life.

Well, this is pretty much it now, isn't it? Better get myself ready for my woman.

* * *

I wake up in a world of screams.

I'm lying on my side, my cheek painfully pressed to a floor littered with crushed glass and pebbles of decimated ceiling tile. Convulsively, at the shock of awakening, I gasp in a chest full of dust, and begin to hack violently, which sets off a chain reaction of aches and pains throughout my body . . . but in my skull it detonates a nova burst of molten agony. Any wound above the neck bleeds like a bastard and my face is caked and crusted in blood; I feel for its origins timidly and wince when I connect with a gummy and gritty laceration at my hairline. I'm afraid to sit up, lest I set off another nuclear blast in my head, so I lie here and listen to the shrieks and wails of the damned.

I don't know why I'm lying on the floor, or even where I am, or what caused this demolition. But I think I can guess, as terrified as I am to do so . . .

The stars have cranked slowly, like the clockwork gears of a cosmic time piece, into position at last, and the gong of doom has rung. The Old Ones, the Outsiders, have been summoned back from the dead, their suspended animation, through the necromancy of their cults and cronies. And they have reasserted their domination of our galaxy, perhaps of the entire universe and all time and dimension. Out of wrath or out of pure mindless force, they have leveled Punktown as a man might trample an ant mound. What I'm hearing are the other survivors like myself, wounded and mad, the half-crushed ants that will be lucky to scavenge an existence in the terrible New World, forever scurrying and lurking and hiding from the vast eclipsing shadows of Ugghiutu and his brethren. Punktown, which once embodied that slumbering god-like entity, is now no more than the cicada husk he has sloughed off, the remnants of his cocoon.

A shattered coffee mug close to my face puts reality into perspective for me; its exploded chunks help fit back the shards of my fragmented memory. The mug belongs to me. Saleet bought it for me as a good luck present the first day I began work at Alvine Products. Now I recall where I am.

The Old Ones have not returned. As far as I know. But I do know there has been an earthquake.

I roll onto my back and gasp again at the blaze of pain. When it clears a bit, I see the ceiling is half caved in. A few emergency lights are on in the office here and there. Distantly, beyond this building's walls, I hear the further shrieks and wails of police and emergency vehicle sirens.

After gathering my strength and my courage for several minutes, I creak myself up into a sitting position, and nearly pass out for my troubles. But sitting up, I can see more clearly around me the shambles of the large office area, its half-demolished honeycomb of padded cubicles, the idiot gaze of computer monitors. Here and there, vidphones are ringing unanswered, something that would be severely frowned upon in the customer service department under normal circumstances.

Yes, now I remember everything . . .

I've been working at Alvine Products for about a month now; winter is falling over Punktown like a misty gray burial shroud.

After my interview, after I was hired, I was given a tour of the offices and the sprawling plant itself by the head of the personnel department, Dawn Andrews, who had only started at Alvine recently herself. She was sincerely amicable for a personnel director, and I liked her cheery British accent. She even made some funny jokes about the pitiful undead animals that I saw along my tour, which made me want to become a vegetarian if only my will were stronger.

Pseudo-chickens without heads, feet or feathers were heaped upon each other inside long aquariums filled with greenish nutrient solution, each chickenish organism with a tube snaking into the rounded stump of its neck; they reminded me more of lobsters piled up in a tank at a supermarket. They also looked grotesquely like dismembered human infants preserved in formaldehyde. There were row upon row of these tanks set into the walls, said tanks being able to be slid out on runners so the chickens could be harvested or new ones added.

As I strolled with Dawn, I said, "When I was in school we toured a plant in Miniosis where they grow generic human clones for body parts and organs. I was only seven. I got so scared just looking through the door into the first farm chamber that I wouldn't go in, so I never saw the things up close. Just seeing all those pale bodies floating in yellow fluid from a distance was enough to give me nightmares for years."

"It offends something in us on a very primal level," Dawn admitted, "our biological programming rebels against it. At first, anyway. But it's all done for good. Those clones don't suffer any more than our little menagerie does."

There were high-ceilinged warehouse-like chambers where big headless hogs were grown from little headless piglets. In stalls lining the walls of the largest farming room, cows stood upon rudimentary half-formed legs like flippers. Without their massive placid heads they looked already slaughtered, though they shifted their weight subtly and you could see their sides pulsing (did those cables inserted into their neck stumps breathe air into their lungs, or did they even have lungs?).

There were Kalian glebbi, in lesser numbers. "They normally have scales," Dawn supplied, "but our customers don't need to bother with that." Each flayed, glistening living carcass had its own bar code identification stamped on its haunch in nontoxic ink, like a brand.

It put me in mind of the glebbis shepherded by Zul, the overly-curious Kalian folk heroine who was lured into the web of the dreaming but still deadly god Ugghiutu.

I liked the people at Alvine; my immediate boss and all my coworkers in customer service, except for one Dacvibese, an alien species I'd never worked with before, who put me in mind of an albino greyhound walking on its hind legs, his pink eyes with unnerving goat-like irises (and his naked body had an unnerving goat-like smell, appropriately). He'd been hired through some kind of government-run interplanetary relations program, and whenever he imagined he'd been slighted made known his disapproval in a high screeching barely coherent voice. He would also express his displeasure by deliberately squirting mucus from glands at the corners of his mouth, this mucus smelling like rotting teeth. Once I saw him squirt my boss in the midst of a pointless dispute, and my boss mildly responded with, "Fedadar, I recognize your right to express your unhappiness to me in the manner of your culture, and we want to accommodate you in every way we can here at Alvine. I'm sure we can find a way to take a little of the pressure off you, etcetera, etcetera." All I can say is Fedadar was lucky he never found out the manner in which I might choose to express my unhappiness if he spit on me. I was hoping to leave my murdering days behind me.

(I can see Fedadar now, in fact. He's sitting upright like me, except that a fallen ceiling support has cut through his shoulder all the way down to his groin, so that his two halves yawn away from each other. A string of rubbery drying drool dangles from the corner of his muzzle.)

A week after I started at Alvine, I met Saleet's father. He seemed surprisingly open and friendly, too.

He purposely sought me out and introduced himself to me. I had seen him around before and already knew who he was, but I had been too nervous to approach him. He was handsome and dignified in his nonKalian black business suit, though he still wore a blue turban. Shaking my hand, Petar Yekemma-Ur smiled and said, "Nice to meet you, Christopher . . . so you're Saleet's friend. How are you getting along so far?"

"Fine, sir, fine, thanks. I think I'm fitting right in."

"I hear you're doing well. You came highly recommended by my daughter. Where did you guys meet?"

Despite his bright smile and his casual slang, his question obviously had sharp probes sheathed inside it. "At the Kalian Reading

Room, in the Subtown Library. I, ah, have an interest in your very fascinating culture, sir, so it was nice to meet Saleet and hear her talk about Kali and your people."

"She's a bright girl, my Saleet. A very willful child." Did I detect the slightest twinge of regret or disapproval at his daughter's stubbornness, rebelliousness? "I'm very proud of how well she's doing in her job, though of course I worry about her safety on the streets. This is a very dangerous city . . . "

"Yes, sir, but she's very tough, Saleet."

"Yes she is. She certainly is." He chuckled with mock weariness and wagged his head. "So Christopher, do you have any children yourself?"

Another probe. He wanted to know if I were married or involved with someone other than his daughter. "Not yet. Someday, I hope." I tried on a quivery grin. I was terrified of incurring the anger of my girlfriend's father, however untraditional he might appear. How long would we have to mask our relationship from him . . . forever? I knew Saleet wasn't ashamed that I was her boyfriend, and it was encouraging that she was willing to risk being found out by getting me hired at Alvine, but I still hated to be sneaking around behind her parents' backs as if we were doing something criminal.

"Well, I'm glad to have you as part of our team, Christopher. Best of luck with it." Saleet's father offered me his hand again; his grip was strong.

"Thank you, Mr. Yekemma-Ur."

"Chris, oh my God, are you all right?" I turn toward a voice and return to the present. The voice belongs to Tammy, a young customer service rep, and with her is Moira, an older rep, both looking dusty but unscathed. Behind them, at the end of the room, I can see several narrow windows spaced along the wall before cubicles and debris blot the others out. Outside the windows, I see scattered flames rising from the skyline of Punktown. With the leaden late afternoon sky full of firelight and smoke, it's like a view of the capital of Hell.

Shakily I pull myself to my feet, and the two women move forward to help me. They're alarmed at the blood drying on my face but I wave them off. "I'll be all right," I assure them.

"You'd better get out of here," Moira says, between sobs, "parts of the company are on fire."

"I will. Go on . . . go . . . "

They pick their way toward an unobstructed exit from the offices, which will take them into the plant proper. I turn stiffly toward my cubicle and see my computer still running serenely. While it waits in blissful mindlessness for my return it runs a decorative slide-show I've programmed into it: alternating diagrams of chromosomes that look like complex circuit boards, and mapped views of the human genome looking like intricate blueprints of an immense city. The personnel director, Dawn, once casually inquired why I had this decorative pattern, and I told her I'm a bit of an amateur scientist, though amateur sorcerer might be more like it.

I take my suit jacket off the back of my chair, slap some dust off it half-heartedly, slip my arms into it and begin to work my own way out of Alvine Products.

The exit from the office into the cafeteria is blocked by collapsed ceiling, and from here the exit to the reception area doesn't look promising either, so I decide to follow Tammy and Moira out into the plant itself, and pursue other exits from the building there.

In the plant, with its high ceiling crossed with naked metal beams, struts and girders, there's a mist of smoke through which emergency exit lights strobe, and somewhere ahead of me over the whooping klaxons I hear a man calling to other workers, "This way! Over here!" I also smell a barbecue. It isn't hard to imagine the origins of that; throughout the plant, rows of pseudo-pigs and quasi-cattle are no doubt blackening right now, with no voices to give expression to pain (I can only hope that pain is beyond them) and no legs to escape with.

My curiosity gets the better of me; I trudge over to a nearby door that would be closed and perhaps security-locked under usual circumstances but which, like the rest of the doors in the plant I'm sure, was automatically opened when fire broke out, so that employees would not become trapped. From this threshold I peer into a smoke-hazed hellish gloom illuminated inadequately by emergency lights and here and there by small fires. A burst pipe near the ceiling hisses out billows of steam, and on the floor writhes a crackling, sparking power cable. Another severed power line has dropped into a shallow nutrient pool in which rests the globular torso of an hetreki, a domesticated Tikkihotto animal much like a prehistoric sloth with tendriled eyes like the Tikkihotto themselves (though you wouldn't know that from this headless specimen); as a result, the poor blob twitches and spasms, a web of greenish electricity dancing across its hide, which is seared from its usual white-with-black- blotches to a crispy leathery brown. The nutrient bath is bubbling, boiling.

Other of these spherical hulks are undamaged; one close to me looms almost to my shoulder, and I can even see the fat squiggles of veins pulsing beneath its skin (which would have hair if this were an unadulterated hetreki). But another of these animals a bit ahead of me is crushed under slabs of ceiling and a conduit of some kind has harpooned it deeply, so that a dark red blood has poured down its flank in a thick sheet, dyeing its shallow pool and overflowing onto the floor. That very natural, very vital blood against this pitiful half-animal's cadaverous flesh is so anomalous in contrast that I'm almost made nauseous by the sight.

I wander down the corridor of zombie hetreki, careful to avoid that wriggling power line, ducking under a propped section of the partially fallen ceiling. *What am I doing?* This is no time for a zoo tour. What if the fire spreads behind me and I can't retrace my path? What if I become lost, trapped, asphyxiated, crushed under another cave in? But I am compelled to go on, and I catch myself listening for something . . . perhaps not so much audibly, however, as mentally. I'm drawn to the end of the hallway of meat, through another door and into a larger chamber containing the blocky bodies of earthly cattle, their hip bones jutting like the ends of poles that support the leathery tents of their hides, looking like cows with their heads lowered out of sight as they graze. These creatures rest on their short, broad, flipper-like appendages rather than loll in solution. But here, too, some burn while others bleed, and the dying ones are just as placid as the uninjured ones. None try to break free of the yokes and reins of their life support. There is no lowing, no groaning; the most I hear from a few is a kind of gurgling when their nutrient hoses have been damaged. There is a disturbing wheeze, though, from one animal with a deep wound in its upper chest, perhaps where its lungs are (or should be) situated.

I look up from the wheezing bulk with a start as a man races toward me, his hand clamped over a bleeding wound in his cheek. His eyes are on mine and without breaking stride he hisses at me, "Get out of here!" It seems partially a warning of concern, and partly a stern order. But he doesn't linger to see how I'll react to either; he is gone out the end of the hallway in a flash.

At the other, far end of the hall, I hear a terrible scream through another opened doorway. It sounds like an animal, though I know that's impossible. Horribly, it's the cry of a terrified or dying man. Or both.

Without thought or hesitation, I start running down the hall in the opposite direction of the man who just bolted past me.

Just as I am about to reach that doorway, I stumble to a halt, because there is gunfire in the room beyond. There are bursts of muzzle flash that cut through the smoky mist like lightning inside thunderheads.

Two more men come tearing toward me out of that fog, startling me so that I fall back a few steps. Both wear white jumpsuits, as do most of the workers in the plant from those who nurture this meat to those who slaughter it. But I've never seen an employee with guns like these two have. One has a pistol, but the other cradles a bulky black assault engine on par with the one Saleet used when we were in the subway.

And both men lift their weapons to point in my face. I can smell the burnt exhalations from their muzzles.

"Where do you think you're going?" the one with the assault engine barks at me, his eyes bulging feverishly. "Turn your ass around and get the fuck out of here!"

"I heard a scream," I stammer, backing away a few steps more.

"*You're* going to be screaming in a minute if you don't do as I say! This area is off limits! Now *go*!" He motions with his firearm.

The one with the handgun glances over his shoulder back into the murky room they've just left, and I don't know what he sees, but suddenly he's aiming his gun that way instead of at me. "Garry!" he yelps.

The one named Garry whirls around with his assault engine at waist level and then the doorway is filled with something large and the glossy purple color of eggplant. Garry's head is suddenly transformed into that same dark purple color. That is because a thick, boneless limb has lashed out from the mass in the doorway, and coiled around his skull.

The tentacle lifts him and his legs kick and dance like a marionette's. Either his finger spasms or he fires on purpose, but his assault engine sputters, set to automatic solid projectile mode. The one with the pistol fires as well. The combined fusillade causes the purple mass to release its grip on Garry, but when he drops into a heap his already bulging eyes have bulged grotesquely almost completely from their sockets, his skull crushed and blood pouring thickly out of his ears.

The one with the pistol keeps blasting the mass, which lashes its punctured tentacle angrily. A second and then a third tentacle squeeze past its own bulk through the threshold to whip at us. One of these thrashing arms inadvertently sends Garry's assault engine skittering across the floor, and I dash to it, scoop it up . . .

I look up to see that the man with the pistol has run dry, but into the handle of the gun he slaps a fresh magazine. Before I can figure out which of the multiple triggers I should use on my weapon, and what sort of beam or projectile they'll loose, the man with the pistol has already taken aim at the creature again—just as it has pressed half its body through the doorway. It seems to me now that there are eight of those smooth tentacles at the fore of the creature, set in a ring, and in the center of them there is a much smaller nest of tentacles, many more in number, and these writhing tendrils are a contrasting bright white in color. There are two paddle-like forward limbs that drag the hulk along, that look like they might have finger bones encased inside them, like the hands of a still-forming fetus. Along either side the monster has pulsing gill slits like those of a shark, showing starkly white meat beneath the purple outer skin.

The man with the pistol is firing into the faceless face of the animal or being, and I can tell instantly that he's using plasma rounds this time.

I have to back off even more from the smell, as black clouds mushroom out of the behemoth like squid ink under water. It's melting, sizzling, and the arms flail even more maniacally, slapping the walls, ceiling and floor. One limb goes flying away from the body, melted off at the base. The stink reminds me exactly of the smell when I dissolved Gabrielle's mutated corpse.

At last, the arms merely slither back and forth across the floor, and then even that stops. The man quits firing and for a moment we both watch the creature crumple in upon itself like a ball of newspapers set to light. Then, before the animal has fully vanished, the man with the pistol turns to me and says, "I'm sorry you had to see that, friend." He lifts his handgun to point at my face again.

"No!" I cry, trying to bring up the perplexing assault engine.

A loud crack, and the top of the pistol-man's head is sheared off. A uniform curtain of blood flows over the crater's rim like lava from a volcano. His eyes flutter and he makes a sputtering noise, blowing the running blood out of his mouth and snorting a gout of it out of his nose. Teetering a bit, he turns to look at the person behind me who shot him. I look, too.

I see the personnel director, Dawn Andrews, standing there. She's holding a pistol of her own, and she squeezes off a few more rounds on it.

I whip my head back around in time to see my would-be

executioner collapse not far from his friend Garry. I then turn to Dawn again, and I see that she has pointed her gun at me, now. That makes things fair, because I have swivelled the assault engine to point at her. She doesn't need to know that I'm not quite sure how to use it.

"Hello, Christopher," Dawn says in her pleasant British accent, as if greeting me for the beginning of the work day.

"Thanks," I tell her. "Why did he want to shoot me?"

"You saw one of our precious little babies, from the nursery in there." She gives a tilt of her pretty chin. "The first hatchling, so to speak."

"What are you people making in this place, Dawn?" I ask in a tremulous voice.

"You really don't know, then?"

"Why would I know?"

"I saw those weird patterns on your computer screen. Geometric designs, of various sorts. I looked into your file after I saw that, to see what your background was, but it seemed innocent enough. Then again, you were recommended by Mr. Yekemma-Ur's daughter . . . so I assumed . . . "

"I don't know what you're saying, Dawn . . . "

"You aren't one of them, then? One of the followers of the Outsiders?"

"Me? One of them? If I was, why would that guy have been seconds away from killing me?" I nod at the man she just murdered.

"That's the reason why I haven't killed you yet, Christopher. But you seem to know what I'm talking about, when I mention the Outsiders."

"Yes, I do know about them. But I had no idea there was anything going on in *this* place. What about you, Dawn? You mean to tell me that you don't have something to do with that animal I just saw?"

The personnel director smiles tightly, proudly, flicks her hair out of her eyes with her free hand. She still looks very much the sharp businesswoman despite the dust and grit on her. "Would I have killed that man if I was on his side? I've infiltrated them, Christopher. So as to destroy them from the inside . . . "

I lower my gun muzzles at last, as if out of respect and awe. I realize what Dawn Andrews is. "You're one of the Children of the Elders . . . who've suppressed the *Necronomicon* . . . who fight against these cults . . . "

Her smug smile falters a bit. "How do you know so much, Christopher? Who are you, really?"

Now it's my turn to smile. "I'm like you, Dawn. We're on the same team."

"Prove it," she says.

"While you were infiltrating this place, I brought down Cephalon Corp."

"Cephalon. Then it's true about them. We wondered." She nods slowly, and at last she lowers her gun, too. She tips her head toward the doorway that monster tried squeezing through. "We'd better stop squabbling, then, and get in there and stop the rest of them from waking up."

"Rest of them?"

"This is a factory, Christopher, isn't it?" And then she leads the way into the haze.

* * *

Even through the mist, I can see it's like any of the other farm chambers. High ceiling. The gargling of nutrient solution being circulated. And a living corridor of large, insensate bodies hooked up to life support, monitors silently scrolling figures and statistics. As in the other chambers, some bodies are crushed under girders and sections of fallen ceiling, though the blood that flows in here is translucent and syrupy, like the sap from a plant.

In facing rows are more of that dark purple creature, perhaps a hundred of them, stretching off until they're lost in the haze, as if their ranks have no end.

They seem to dream, patiently, waiting for the right time to be awakened. Their tentacles are tightly coiled inward, hiding the inner nest of white tendrils, as spiders will clench their bodies in death, but I can see their gill slits rhythmically opening and closing. I see one of them shift its half-formed paw slightly, like a fetus moving in its womb. A nursery, Dawn called this . . .

How big will these things grow?

Not far from the door, one of the creatures holds a dead man in its furled limbs, like a child clutching a teddy bear to its sleeping breast. It must have woken, seized this lab worker, then returned to its slumber. This must have been the man whose shrieks drew me toward this room. He is flattened horribly in some places and bulging even more horribly in others.

"They're not the Outsiders themselves," Dawn informs me, watching my face as I take it all in. "They're spawn. They're an army . . . "

Drawing closer to another of the animal-like beings, I see that its life support monitor shows a flat line. I hear another monitor buzzing an alert, nearby; another creature is flat-lining. The earthquake has taken its toll on them. Just as it seems the followers of Ugghiutu brought about the first great earthquake in Paxton, two decades ago, I wonder if the enemies of Ugghiutu have brought about this one. To tear his massive, dreaming form. To break his body and break his hold on this city.

Or was this earthquake simply the work of the blind god of Nature?

Suddenly I think of Falco, Pete and Hoop down in the underworld. I hope they're all right, that they survived this. This time has the Church of the Burning Eye been totally buried, flattened?

I think about Saleet. Is she safe, wherever she is out there in the city? How extensive is the damage? Is this, then, the Apocalypse?

"Help me kill the rest of them," Dawn says, "before anyone sees us, or more of these things wake up." And she doesn't point her gun at the first of the spawn, doesn't need plasma. She simply goes to its life support unit, touches a few keys, and flips a single switch. I lean over her shoulder to watch what she does. I follow her to the next unit, just to watch her again. It looks simple enough, so I cross to the opposite wall of monsters. We work our way down the line. There are no visible reactions in the sleeping infant monsters that have been grown in this factory . . . but yes, I do notice something. The gills are starting to pulse more erratically, more slowly, and then they are becoming still. Several beasts quietly snort a few mucus bubbles from these gills, which burst and trail fluid down their flanks. But there is no heaving, no convulsions, the tentacles do not come uncoiled. Peaceful euthanasia. Or, more properly, infanticide.

"When we're done," Dawn calls over to me, "give me that gun. It has rockets in it. I'm going to set fire to this room. There are some other rooms, too, we need to destroy."

I glance at the gun slung over my shoulder, even more afraid of it than before. Rockets? I ask, "Why didn't you shut these things down earlier, Dawn, if you were trying to destroy this place from the inside?"

"I've been sabotaging their efforts all along, since I started with them four months ago. They didn't know it was me. These things would all be bigger than houses and roaming the streets now if I hadn't been mucking with the works. I did everything I could without giving myself away. I was waiting to get closer . . . they were starting to trust me . . . "

"The one that came awake—is it because they're ready to go on their own, now?"

"No, they aren't ready. But it was awakened prematurely by the quake; it must have disrupted its life support in such a way as to give it a jolt, I suppose."

We are nearing the end of the hall, at last. We've had to clamber over a small mountain of debris to reach the last of the spawn, and I take Dawn by the waist to help her hop down off a fallen girder. Monster-killing is a bit awkward for her with those high-heeled shoes of hers. When I've lowered her down, she smiles up at me. "I'm glad I'm not alone in this, Chris."

"Where are the rest of your people, Dawn? Why *were* you alone here?"

"There aren't many of us left. They've killed most of us. Not that there ever were many of us. But the others have other battles to fight. On Earth. On other colonized worlds. We have to spread ourselves thin . . . "

"I'm glad I'm not alone, too," I tell her.

"You need to join us, Chris."

"I don't know . . . I know I should . . . but I never wanted to make a career of this. All I ever wanted to do was avenge my girlfriend." I sigh, "I lost her to them."

"If you really did bring Cephalon down on your own, then we need you, Chris. You can't be selfish, when you know what we're facing here . . . "

"It isn't that I'm selfish. It's just . . . just that I do what I can. And I'd rather do it alone. Well, alone except for my new girlfriend. She helped me against Cephalon . . . "

"Where is she now? Who is she?"

"She's Saleet Yekeema-Ur. Petar Yekemma-Ur's daughter."

"Petar Yekemma-Ur?" Dawn looks suddenly horrified. "Chris, don't you realize?"

"About what?"

"About Yekemma-Ur? For God's sake—he's *one* of them!"

I stammer, "One of them . . . Saleet's father . . . "

"He isn't just one of them, in fact . . . I think he's their leader, here in Punktown."

"It can't be . . . "

"Why can't it be?"

"His daughter's a police officer!"

Dawn throws up her hands. "*And?* How much do you really know about *her*, Christopher?"

"I told you!" I snap. "She helped me ruin Cephalon!"

"Saleet did that?" a voice behind me says.

I begin to spin, but halfway through my spin it turns into a duck. Shots are cracking, first from one direction and then the other. But Dawn's shots come second. And they come too late. I see her stumble backwards and fall, with blood spattered across her crisp white blouse.

Springing back to my feet, I raise the assault engine to find that Petar Yekemma-Ur is sheltered underneath the debris Dawn and I climbed over, and pointing a pistol at me over the top of a slanting girder. He could have already killed me, too, if he'd wanted.

"Fucker," I hiss, my fingers aching to press every trigger on my killing machine. But that cold cyclops eye is staring me right in the face. And behind it, in shadow, floats the gray handsome face of my lover's father.

"Just what have you gotten my daughter into, Mr. Ruby?" he asks sternly, as a father would do when confronting the boy who's impregnated his princess.

"Tell me she isn't in this with you!" I blurt.

"You know she isn't. But I only wish she wasn't in this with *you*, Mr. Ruby. I had no idea I was hiring such trouble makers." He jerks his chin past me, in Dawn's direction. "Then again, look who's been doing my hiring."

"I don't want to have to kill you," I bluff.

"You'd never get a shot off before I'd cleaned out your skull, little boy."

"These things you're making . . . you think they'll spare Saleet? And spare you?"

"When the Great Old Ones arise again, we who were their chosen servants will be at their sides."

"You'll be under their feet, like bugs. They won't need you any more."

"My daughter . . . " Yekemma-Ur changes the subject " . . . you're romantically involved with her, aren't you?"

"Yes," I reply defiantly, but I hear my voice crack. I know he'll want to kill me more for this fact, than the fact that I've just helped exterminate the brood of his gods. I expect to be shot right this very second . . .

"Have you . . . have you slept with her?"

A beat of hesitation. My finger ever so lightly caresses a smooth trigger. I have no idea what it might unleash from the weapon's combined arsenal. Would I even hit the Kalian, set back amongst the debris as he is, that metal girder angled in front of him? But he has a clear shot. I can feel that gun muzzle as if it presses against the skin of my forehead.

"Yes," I answer quietly.

Another beat. He nods resignedly. "Then I've lost her. I've lost my daughter as surely as if you had raped and murdered her, Mr. Ruby." He says this so calmly. That's the scariest part of all. "You dirtied her. You stained her very soul. She is irredeemable now. Lost to me."

"I'm sorry you feel that way."

"She must die with all the rest, now. In fact . . . in fact, Mr. Ruby, I want you to know this. That I am now going to have to kill Saleet myself."

"You don't love her."

"*How dare you!*" he bellows. I flinch. It's as if he just fired his gun over my head. "How dare you suggest I don't love my child! It is because I love her that I must kill her! Destroy the blasphemy you have made of her!"

"You can't kill her if you love her. And you can't kill me, because she loves me. If you killed me she'd hate you. She'd hate you, Petar . . . "

"That is because you have poisoned her mind!" Yekemma-Ur roars, spittle flying from his fanatic's lips. "You've defiled her! My beautiful child!"

"Please . . . " I whimper, my appeals to his reason and his emotions having failed. Now panic and despair are rushing in. Terror.

"Please *spare* you? Spare you, is that it? After you murdered my daughter? The only reason you are still alive is because I can not conceive of a death that befits . . . "

To my left, something huge and dark rears up, tearing cables out of its life support system, snapping a tube that sprays a life-giving solution. I look up to see a rubbery purple tree looming above me, a swarm of serpentine limbs waving at its summit. It's as if

Yekemma-Ur's shouting voice has woken this entity from its sleep . . .

I hurl myself away from it, ducking between two of its sleeping brothers. The last of the brood, which Dawn and I didn't have the chance to kill yet . . .

Distracted by the awakened monster, Saleet's father fires after me, but too late. I hear a bullet thunk into the hide of the slumbering creature I throw myself behind.

The roused monster falls forward onto its belly, its tentacles still snaking in the air. It drags itself a few uncertain steps forward.

In my direction . . .

"See, Ruby!" I hear Yekemma-Ur cry out, with the fervor of an evangelist. "Ugghiutu's children rise to avenge me!"

From the floor between the two sleeping spawn, I watch the one that crawls toward me. The white tendrils move as if tasting vibrations, fingering the trail of air molecules I have displaced in my wake. Lying on my back, I lift the assault engine up and point it at the encroaching nightmare. I want to scream, but the scream turns to stone in my constricted throat. Those snakes . . . Medusa . . .

I squeeze one of the triggers.

A whoosh, a streak, and an apparently largish projectile disappears inside the creature's front, just below the ring of its tentacles.

A single beat . . .

And then it explodes from within.

Rockets, Dawn said.

Meat flies in all directions, in all cuts from steak to hamburger, and all of it vile. It splatters around me and across me, slides wetly down the sides of its dozing brothers. A great waterfall of sap is disgorged out of the huge, ragged pit in the beast's chest. It slumps forward and the tentacles smack the floor, lie inert, without so much as a tremor or nervous convulsion. Now I can see that the back and sides of the thing have long splits, like cracks that show the white meat under the purple.

I spring to my feet, slabs of flesh dropping off me, jump out from between the sheltering monsters, and—without aiming—launch a second missile into that mountain of debris. Then I'm diving for cover again . . .

There seems to be yet another earthquake behind me.

Fragments of rubble rain, clatter, then the rain subsides. There is relative stillness, though klaxons still wail beyond this room. Fire crackles. Aching, covered in the blood of a god's offspring, I hoist myself to my feet, stumble warily out into the center of the hallway . . .

I don't see Yekemma-Ur inside the now even more twisted heap of ruin. But through the smoke I've added to the mist already in the air, I hear one long, drawn-out, utterly pitiful moan of agony.

I go to him, stepping over this hunk of ceiling, stepping over that wrenched support arm. And there he is, lying on his back, half under the wreckage. Crouching down next to him, keeping the gun trained on him (though I won't use *that* trigger again), I ascertain that he doesn't have his pistol any more. After all, one arm and half his chest are pinned under that big girder he was hiding behind, and the other hand hangs off its wrist by just a scrap of tissue.

His eyes slowly open, black and deep as space, but they don't appear to be seeing me.

"I'm sorry," I whisper to him.

"Why?" he gurgles, through the blood in his throat.

"Because I love your daughter," I tell him.

"She'll hate you now," he croaks. I expect him to smile, triumphant, gloating, a small sadistic vengeance. Instead, after a moment, blindly staring, he says, "Save her from them, if they come. If they come . . . protect her."

I nod. "I will."

"I do love her, you know," he rasps. "I'm . . . proud of her."

"I'll tell her."

And I watch his eyes close.

* * *

On the VT news, they show the fires. Alvine Products is just another of these fires, and I'm certain no one will look closely into it. No one will know how the fires were aided by rockets and beams. How a lab filled with tank after tank of aquariums—in which were piled thousands of small tentacled creatures in amniotic baths—was riddled with bullets and voracious plasma capsules before it, too, burned. I hope no innocents, trapped in rubble, lost in the building's maze, were killed as a result of my actions. It is a war. It is very ugly, and very sad . . .

There is a huge crack that runs diagonally across the wall of my flat, and it caused dozens of shiny banana-colored tiles to drop off like autumn leaves. I gather them up. I try calling Saleet again on her remote comlink. She isn't answering. I look out my window and see it's raining below ground, and there's lightning too, but that's only burst water pipes and sparking cables overhead. I have power, but I can see there's a blackout on the next block over. Sirens still ululate.

My computer beeps, and I rush to it. On the screen, her gray face shiny with sweat and her hair coming frizzily out of the thick braid that tries to contain it, is Saleet, calling from a payphone. Someone is sobbing in the background.

"Thank God!" I cry. "I thought you were dead!"

"I thought *you* were dead!" she snaps. "Didn't they teach you the fire drill at Alvine? All personnel were supposed to gather for a head count in the parking lot, not go home."

"Come on, Sal, I'm sure not many people stuck around for that . . . "

"Chris," she says, and suffering flows suddenly and fully into her weary face, her ritual scars making it looked crudely patched together from cadavers' flesh, heavy unified brows contracted in intense misery, "my father isn't accounted for. And he didn't go home to my mother . . . "

"Saleet . . . "

"The place is on fire very badly . . . " Her voice breaks.

"Saleet. I know what happened to him . . . "

"You know . . . "

"Come here and talk to me," I say quietly. I can barely stand looking into her black, anguished eyes. "I need to see you in person."

"Is he dead, Chris? Just tell me if . . . "

"Saleet. Please. Come see me." And I break the connection.

* * *

Her black uniform is white with plaster, and someone's blood is caked on her boots. Her sidearm's holster is unsnapped. I point to it. She glances at it and snaps it, saying, "I had to shoot over the heads of some looters. It's absolute chaos out there." Her eyes lift. "Tell me, Chris."

"Please . . . sit down."

"Fucking tell me!" she shrieks, stepping toward me, and I flinch hard.

So I tell her. Tell her everything. The two of us standing there facing each other in the center of my flat that has been riven as I know my life is now to be riven.

When I tell my girlfriend that I murdered her father she blinks hard, there's an almost invisible spasm in the muscles of her face and the clench of her jaw, but she does not scream, does not lunge at me, does not unsnap her holster again. With dark lips pressed firmly together, she silently listens to the rest of the story . . . the tanks I found, the fires I set. But though she doesn't interrupt me, fat tears begin to drop from her eyes to tumble down her cheeks, tears like those of a little girl.

The story is over. Now it's my turn to be silent. She nods at me, as if I'm still talking and she's listening, absorbing it.

"I'm sorry," I whisper. I want to put my hand on the back of her head and draw her face against my shoulder, but I'm afraid. And that would be too mockingly paternal a gesture.

Saleet nods again, her expression frighteningly blank. She takes a step back from me. Her eyes still on me. Then she turns, walks to the door, and leaves my apartment.

I'm still standing in the same spot. I stand here a long time, staring at the closed door. Then I look again to the jagged crack that splits my wall from ceiling to floor like a suture in the skull of a giant.

* * *

A pattern, a network, a latticework, a nervous system, a web . . . and Saleet was drawn toward me along one strand, only to slide away from me down another. Gabrielle and Saleet's father drawn toward me, as if I am the spider at the center of that web, only to die at my hands. All the strands converge at me. Yes. I feel like it's *me* who is Ugghiutu.

All these interlacing secret maneuverings, this intricate synchronicity, only to weave a tapestry of desolation. Well, we're all a little safer—for now. I mustn't be selfish. But I feel like I've been sacrificed to a greater end. I was a pawn, in a way, in a larger conflict I can't encompass with my limited human mind.

I mustn't be selfish, Dawn Andrews told me . . . I must join the ranks of the Children of the Elders. But Dawn is dead now, and I don't know who the other members are, how to contact them.

Perhaps they'll find their way to me along the strands of the weave.

On the news, I see that most fires have been beaten while some still rage three days after the earthquake (mostly in rough parts of town where the firefighting teams are reluctant to go, and shot at when they do). Little Manila is almost entirely gutted. Several sections of the subway system have caved in, and a train full of passengers remains buried; they think the people aboard might still be alive. Maybe injured, maybe starving. When I hear a story like that I always hope there are no children involved.

Looters in packs are dragging people out of their hovercars at intersections, stoning them with big chunks of fallen stone and clubbing them to death and driving off in their vehicles. I watch aerial footage of this taken from helicars and police hoverobots, called into service to contain the rioting. I see a man in the civilized emblem of a business suit crawling on all fours, his face lost in blood, while several youths run at him when not slamming him with cinder blocks, leaping on his back and springing off it jubilantly, frolicking like kids dashing through an open fire hydrant. These are the people I've saved from the snaking arms of Ugghiutu's children.

I had hoped to see the opposite. A decrease in crime, in mental illness, in murder and rape. I had hoped the disruption in Ugghiutu's plan would lessen his influence. That he might fall deeper into slumber, and the poisonous tendrils he inserts into our minds would withdraw. Either he is too powerful to be greatly inconvenienced by my efforts, or else I have overestimated his strength and the hold he has over our city. Perhaps even if I had killed that powerful being, dreaming in some overlapping dimension, the people here would be just as hateful, just as dangerous, just as poisoned. Maybe a god can't be blamed for their actions. Maybe all together, they dwarf the corruption of all of the Old Ones combined.

Maybe it isn't Ugghiutu who makes Punktown more evil, but Punktown that makes Ugghiutu more evil.

There is a news story that makes me stop munching my junk food dinner so as to listen more closely. The three surviving top executives of Alvine Products and the driver of their hoverlimo have been shot and killed, apparently by a looter, when the limousine stopped at a traffic light. Witnesses say that the assailant, however, did not steal the limo or even enter it so as to rob the victims. Perhaps just a thrill killing; a lot of that is going on as well in the current climate.

Witnesses describe the killer as a young Kalian woman with a military-style assault engine.

* * *

After five days of letting the VT run constantly, even when I slept, I shut it off, and the silence inside my apartment is like standing at the bottom of the sea. I've heard no further mention of the destruction of Alvine or the murders of its executives since yesterday.

I'm out of work again so I need to conserve my resources, but my supplies have run low and I figure it's a bit safer to venture outside today. I leave my flat for the first time in several days, walk far enough to buy half an Italian sub and a cheap six pack of Knickerson (Knickers off, as we called it in school), and when I return to my building I find Saleet sitting on the front stoop. She stands as if to greet me but doesn't smile, doesn't say a word. "Hi," I say softly, then to spare her from having to return my greeting, I nod at the front door and say, "Come inside . . . "

I let her go first up the stairs. She is out of uniform, her long hair flows down her back like a waterfall of night, and she wears an indigo blue t-shirt that is very tight and has a soft sheen like velour. Her snug Kalian skirt is of metallic silver thread, and clings nicely to her full hips and bottom, though I feel guilty watching her body move under the material so I lower my eyes and notice that she is barefoot. Her strong calloused feet have been recently tattooed in lacy black web-like patterns. It's a traditional Kalian decoration—worn more in the past than today, however—revealing Saleet's attraction to her own culture, but at the same time I seem to recall that it was forbidden for anyone but a husband to see these intimate tattoos, which simultaneously reaffirms Saleet's commitment to rebellion. I follow her with lungs that ache nostalgically at the scent like sandalwood she leaves in her wake.

While I close and lock my door, she takes in the crack that splits my wall. I hold a bottle of Knickerson out to her but she shakes her head, goes and sits on my folded sofa bed. Without opening a beer either, I go and sit beside her. I sense it's what she wants me to do.

"I want to tell you a story," she says very quietly, looking across the room instead of at my face.

Timidly, I say, "All right."

"It's from my childhood. It's a folktale."

"I like your stories," I tell her very gently.

And so, in that same soft voice, as if translating a dream while asleep, she begins.

* * *

THE GHOUL AND THE GRAVE WORM

Detark was a boy of seventeen, and was glad that his father owned a farm on the very outskirts of the village, for the youths of the village often mocked him for the heavy and badly deformed foot that caused him to walk with a struggling limp. These boys joked that Detark did not need a plow to till his father's fields; he could simply walk along and drag that useless appendage of his through the soil. Young girls were not likely to mock him openly, but he thought he saw them whisper and giggle when they believed he did not see. Now that his schooling was over, he was relieved that he did not need to venture into the village center except to run errands for his father. Whether sowing or harvesting crops, Detark would gaze at that distant large village with its silhouetted rooftops and spires with a mix of anxiety and bitterness, as if the town itself leered at him in contempt. Its presence oppressed him. The open vastness of the sky above these fields was far friendlier, for being so utterly empty.

Detark's family had owned this land for generations. It had been captured from an enemy tribe by proud warrior ancestors. As a boy, Detark had pretended he was one of these heavily-armored warriors, and his mother had even made him a tunic with their sign: the profile of a bird-like Utalla demon, its long silhouetted beak open in a war cry. And Detark's father fashioned for him a sword of wood, and a wood-bladed lance which was dubbed Utalla's Beak. His father explained that their ancestor Lurrik Abdar-tuul had been a powerful warrior who had wielded a lance which he called Utalla's Beak, with which he had beheaded the chieftain of the enemy tribe. But Lurrik, two dozen arrows embedded in his black armor when he made his way back to his home, died the day following his great victory. A single arrow, its tip poisoned, had found its way through the plates of lacquered tortoise shell of which his armor was made.

There were several barrows on the farmlands of Detark's father. This was another reason why village boys mocked him. Who, they asked, would want to eat crops fertilized by the moldering bodies of buried soldiers? Look at what eating these corpse-tainted crops has done to Detark, they would laugh, pointing as always to his leg. Their favorite nickname for him was the Ghoul.

One early evening, Detark was plowing a field in the shadow of the greatest of these raised burial mounds, upon which only a sparse and wispy grass would grow. The darkening air was growing cool, and Detark knew he must return to the farm house very soon. Just this last row, he told himself, following the glebbi named Churt as it pulled the old plow. Detark glanced toward the village, hatefully outlined against the last blood-like streaks of sunlight. When he looked back to Churt, it was just in time to see her swallowed up by the earth and disappear with one frightened bleat. The plow was jerked forward, out of his hands.

Detark understood what had happened instantly; a hollow in the earth, near the base of the barrow, had opened up. The tunnels of the barrow must have extended beyond the humped mound itself. Churt had dropped down into those caverns, and now his father's best plow would be lost as well. He lunged after it, as quickly as his poor leg would allow, reaching out to grasp at the handles even though he would never be strong enough to pull the plow free, attached as it was to the body of the far heavier glebbi.

Detark saw the plow vanish utterly into that gaping maw. He lurched forward with one last desperate effort, and before he could stop himself and hurl himself backwards, he felt more earth crumbling beneath his feet as the hole began to widen.

The drop was not terribly great, and the heaped dirt that had fallen with him broke his fall, but Detark saw that poor old Churt lay dead beside him, the plow's blade having landed upon the neck of the glebbi, severing it neatly.

With tears in his eyes, agonized at the loss of the loyal beast and ashamed at having disgraced his family, thus living up to the mockery of the villagers, Detark looked up at the violet sky that had once been his vast friend, now a small circle hemmed in by the edges of the pit. That ceiling was too high to reach even if he stood upon the handle of the plow. He must try to find another way out of these ancient burial tunnels, as hopeless as that surely must be, for he had seen the entrance to this and the other barrows and they were packed solid with stones. Still, he must try to find his way upwards to that doorway, and once there attempt to heft all those heavy stones aside.

Detark detached the lantern that had been clipped to Churt's harness, lit it, and began his exploration. This tunnel, he saw, ended in a blank wall of dirt at one end, but at the other there was a circular opening. He approached this threshold and held the lantern out in front of him so as to examine it before entering. The new corridor was like the inside of a great cylinder, its walls gray and oddly glossy as if tunneled through polished stone. He ducked his head and stepped into it. And Detark had not gone far through that circular tunnel when he saw figures waiting for him ahead. Fierce-looking men in barbed and bulky tortoise armor, carrying spears and bows and swords. He nearly fled with a shriek back the way he had come. But fighting against his fear, he took several steps further toward the figures.

He nearly shrieked again. For inside those horned black helmets he saw the faces of skeletons and mummies, grinning as if in amusement at his folly. This revelation was almost more horrifying to him than if these soldiers had been alive, even though he knew now they could be of no real threat to him. And in any case, these men had been of his own blood. They were the casualties of Lurrik Abdar-tuul's battle to win these lands. This was not some army of ghouls, as his imagination had initially taunted him, but of heroes.

And indeed, when Detark grew bold enough to draw closer to these ranked suits of armor, which stood along either side of the smooth corridor, he saw that one of these suits still bristled with two dozen arrows. In its gloved fist it clutched a lance with a cruel, curving blade that still looked razor sharp these centuries later. Yes, it was the armor of Lurrik Abdar-tuul, out of which his face grinned boldly, even though his eyes were gone and his skin had become a dark leather clinging to his skull. That halberd he gripped, of course, was Utalla's

Beak.

Abruptly the earth shifted, and Detark lost his balance, had to clutch at the suit of armor to keep from falling. It must be an earthquake! That was why the earth had opened up under Churt! The very ground seemed to be shifting and rippling fluidly beneath Detark's feet.

But as he clung to Lurrik's looming armor, Detark heard a strange hissing as of steam from a geyser in the earth. He had heard that sound once before, as a much younger child. Once a great worm had come into the village on its many rustling legs, glowing white in the night. He had seen that glow across the walls of his bedroom, as the ghastly illumination came in through his open window, but his mother had seized him before he could look out the window at the monstrosity. His father had taken up his musket and made ready to defend his family and flock. But the giant worm had gone on past them toward the town, and later they heard scores of musket blasts and distant screams. They learned, come morning, that four villagers had perished at the jagged jaws of the great worm before it was killed.

And now, Detark recognized this hissing sound as the same he had heard that night.

He realized where he was at last. Not inside a barrow tunnel as he had thought . . . but inside the very belly of a worm. It had opened wide its gut to lure him in. And before it had swallowed him, it had swallowed up these stiff ranks of armored corpses as well, thinking them living men it had encountered below the earth.

The creature was burrowing upward through the soil loosened by his plow. He judged that they were moving in the direction of the village that so vexed him.

Though Detark hated that place, despised those people, he knew he must protect them. Because though they might never understand or even accept him, he was one of them, and their foe was a common one.

And also, he felt he must honor his heroic ancestors by liberating their bodies, so blasphemously removed from their revered tomb and swallowed up by this mindless demon.

Still clinging to the armor that was the coffin of Lurrik Abdar-tuul, Detark put his hand around the shaft of Utalla's Beak. He then stepped back from the corpse, and with a tug, dislodged the lance from its grip.

The lance was tall, nearly touching the curved ceiling of the worm's gut already. Detark grasped the handle firmly in both fists, and thrust upwards a mere few inches further. That crescent of blade stabbed cleanly into the roof of flesh. Detark then began loping along down the corridor, hoisting the weapon as if carrying a flag proudly into battle. He could imagine all those glorious soldiers running after him with their swords raised high.

He slit the worm's belly open as he moved, slashed it the length of the long corridor, and he heard the hissing grow louder and angrier. Before he had reached the end of its gut, the worm heaved up out of the soil, and began to writhe upon the earth in violent convulsions. Suddenly the long corridor buckled and curved, twisted and coiled around Detark. He had to let go of Utalla's Beak, and pushed his way through the great slit he had carved in the monster. He heard the suits of armor being ground together behind him like the gnashing teeth of a dying giant.

He emerged into cool open air. Yes, his friend the vast sky, now black and sown with the seeds of stars! Detark scrambled to his feet in time to see the last spasms of the giant worm, its hundreds of bone-like legs curling inward in death, its ghostly luminosity already fading away, steam rising out of its slashed back. Some of the suits of armor hung out of that wound or had been thrown clear during its final torments.

Turning toward the village, Detark saw that they had come very close to its border, and people were already converging upon him with muskets and lanterns, having been alerted by the demon's dreaded hiss.

The villagers stood in awe, absorbing the scene. The riven worm, the strewn armor, and the Ghoul with his clubbed foot. In his fist was Utalla's Beak, which he had seen lying in the grass near the monster.

Detark was never called the Ghoul again.

And when he died, many years later, having sired strong sons and grandsons who farmed his land after him, the bones of Detark the Worm Killer were interred beneath the great barrow on his property . . . to join those of Lurrik Abdar-tuul and his men.

* * *

My apartment is very still. We both sit on the sofa bed staring at the crack in the wall. At last I whisper, "I liked that story."

Saleet leans closer to me. She rests her head against my shoulder. She closes her eyes.

"Detark," she calls me.

Printed in the United States
1409200005B/88